The dead man held me somehow. He looked like the Dog in the good old days—well-fed, well-dressed, comfy, dead. He floated faceup amidst the duckweed and flotsam of a big pool. Flies crowded his bulging eyes. There was something odd about his mouth—it was stuffed with something fibrous and black, as though in drifting dead he had gouged the bottom, bitten out a weedy chunk of streambed. Or like his corpse had already been claimed by the creature world, and a muskrat or a mouse had burrowed into his mouth. The sight was strange and awful. I gagged emptily. Then I guess the Dog had a few civic instincts left. I beat trail for help.

★

THE
NAIL
KNOT

JOHN GALLIGAN

WORLDWIDE®

TORONTO • NEW YORK • LONDON
AMSTERDAM • PARIS • SYDNEY • HAMBURG
STOCKHOLM • ATHENS • TOKYO • MILAN
MADRID • WARSAW • BUDAPEST • AUCKLAND

Always, for Jinko

THE NAIL KNOT

A Worldwide Mystery/October 2006

First published by Big Earth Publishing.

ISBN-13: 978-0-373-26579-4
ISBN-10:   0-373-26579-4

Printed in U.S.A.

Acknowledgments

Like any good trout stream, this book thrives because of the many rich springs that feed it—sources that generate and sustain my fishing and writing lives. Major tributaries deserving major thanks begin with my dad, William Galligan, for taking me fishing. Thanks also to Bob Kelso, for bungling with me through the early days with the fly rod; to Madison Area Technical College for the time and faith that allowed me to start this book; to Ben LeRoy and Blake Stewart for their unwavering confidence, support, and courage; to Rachel Pastan for her many and unfailingly kind yet hard-nosed readings; and to Craig McMahon for all those miles of walking the Dog with me. And, finally, thanks to the Village of Black Earth, for its beautiful name, and for the beautiful creek that runs through it, about which I have lied like a fisherman, giving away no true secrets.

Time to get the hell out of Black Earth

All credit and blame are due to Harvey Digman, my tax guy, my cheerleader, and my liberator. But that's a long and probably schmaltzy story. So let's start with my ugly attitude.

Okay, I was telling myself. Enough with the good citizen charade. Time to get the hell out of Black Earth. I had already explained how and where I'd found the dead fisherman, and the moment the village police chief handed back my driver's license, I planned to break down my fly rod, cross the creek, throw up in some nearby stinging nettles, and hightail it on shaky legs to the road.

"Okay, Mister...uh...Og-log-livery?"

The distance between what the chief said and the name on my license suggested a fairly severe reading disability. My name is Oglivie. Ned Oglivie. Dog for short—a self-inflicted nickname, and in those days it fit.

"I'll just run this through the computer," said the chief, "and you'll be on your way."

"Damn right," I muttered. The Dog charted his course. The

county highway was just across the cow pasture, and my Cruise Master RV was parked a mile downstream in a sorry excuse for a campground called Lake Bud Park. My vision was to hit the Cruise Master at a gallop, drop the awning, hurl the wheel blocks inside, strap down the cabinet doors, and make the three hundred miles north to Big Two-Hearted River by sunup.

"So you hang on a minute," said the chief.

He was a young guy, about thirty, a shallow breather with a trainee beer gut in a tight uniform shirt, amber sunglasses up on his shaved head, toed-in cowboy boots and a worried look. About an hour earlier, he and the ambulance had screamed by on the county highway and disappeared around an upstream corner. A long minute passed, the sounds of help growing fainter. But then the patrol car had reappeared on my side of the creek, dusty up to its gold-on-cream stripe, jouncing along a tractor path ahead of the ambulance. The chief had left his lights going, as if the dozen or so Holsteins lazing under a burr oak in the pasture were going to get up and block an intersection.

He read me into his radio and waited. His junior officer squished heavily about the stream bank, bending and snapping Polaroids of the dead man. The officer was even younger than the chief. His uniform shirt had come untucked, and the pink top of his ass showed as he bent over the body. I looked away. A silver milk truck had pulled off the highway to watch. A blue van was slowing. Down the tractor lane bounced a red Chevy Suburban.

"Correct," the chief said into his radio. "Individual who found the body." Then, "Duncan! Widen out and get a shot of that deep hole behind him."

A keg-bellied man in shirtsleeves heaved out of the red Suburban. He hitched on across the mud, tugging at his jeans and puffing.

"I knew it," he said. "It's Jacobs."

The chief slung out of his patrol car. "You don't have to tell me it's Jacobs."

"O'Malley got him finally."

"We don't know who or what got him yet," said the chief. "Now stand back and keep your footprints out of there."

The keg-bellied man stiff-armed the window frame of the patrol car and propped himself against it. "Jake was out here fishing the sally," he puffed.

"He was fishing nothing," replied the chief. "He had no fly on his line."

"You better call Halverson."

"I called Halverson."

"Then where the hell is Halverson?"

"Halverson is the hell on his way."

Keg-belly slid a glance at me. I was sitting astride a box elder snag, elbows on knees, head lolling. The Dog was not doing well. A dead body…a drowned body…all the chatter… misanthropy and grief had collided inside me, mingled with the scent of rotting wood, and suddenly I was sick. The whole point of my fishing was to escape human noise, which was always so horribly amplified by the event of death. So I groped for my ugly attitude and aimed it at Keg-belly. Hell, I thought, where I came from, people were either fat or skinny—not both. The guy couldn't stand up on his own. He used his arm like a tripod against the patrol car. A pack of Camels, tucked in the pocket of a patterned yellow sport shirt, rose and fell with his ragged breathing.

"Me, I'd flip him," offered Keg-belly. "Take a look at the back side."

The chief opened his trunk. "Don't you touch him."

"I know what I'm looking for. I'd flip him."

"You would, huh?" said the chief. He lifted out a measuring tape and a roll of crime scene banner. "Well, I'd wait for Halverson. I'd let the coroner flip him."

Keg-belly lobbed me a rubbery grin. "We sent him to school, see. Now Sherlock here knows everything."

Fine, I said to myself. Good luck then. I kept my sick eye on my driver's license. The moment it was back in my hand, the Dog was done with Black Earth. The Big Two-Hearted River was seven hours north. I could be there by sunrise.

"Jacobs had to be fishing the sally," said Keg-belly to the chief. "Had to be. The sally hatch, last night, about eight o'clock. Betcha fifty."

"Let me do my job."

"I've let you do a lot of jobs," said Keg-belly. "And not one of them got done right."

The chief turned red in the face and stalked off toward the corpse. Keg-belly gave me the rubbery grin again. He swiveled stiffly—surveying pasture, cornfield, empty tractor in the hay crop, the steep wooded sides of the Black Earth coulee—but I guess he didn't see what he was looking for.

"Hell," he fumed at last, getting himself a Camel. "I'll go fetch Halverson myself."

I held on to my box elder log. I tried to push a breath down past my third rib. Pasture to highway, I reviewed, highway to campground, drop awning, chuck wheel blocks, strap cabinet doors, gas up on the highway, bust the three hundred miles to the Big Two-Hearted by sunup...

That's where I was, imaginary miles from Black Earth already, when Farmer Jane hit me with a dirt clod.

BUT LET ME SET the scene. Wisconsin, as it turns out, was not quite what the Dog had in mind. Sure, across the flat ground and the ridge tops ranged the sinuous, deep-green corn fields, broken every mile or so by a well-kept dairy operation—house and yard and cottonwood windbreak, red barn and blue silo, ceramic deer and reflecting ball in the yard—dull as hell—a neat Lutheran church in a hem of spruce trees on every third hilltop, and every ten miles a place to get gasoline, slurpies, and beef sticks. The dopey, feel-good heartland, right? A land yearning for subdivision. Home of the very best in good people.

But take a left or a right onto a county road and you find yourself plunging and twisting down into coulees where deer spook and badgers scramble, where the clock of human progress stopped sometime in the early seventies, the last time things were passably good down on the farm. In the narrow bottom lands, the terrain is rugged and the farms are small and collapsing. Life has a funky, stillborn, Appalachian look—projects half-started, fences half-mended, people half-finished, and everywhere the relentless drive of plant and animal to reclaim the land around cold spring creeks that still hold trout. A back alley of America. Decent turf, as it turned out, for the Dog to lie low and lick some wounds.

And so the shock hit me double when I came upon the body. There was no company more demanding, I'd found, than a dead body. Hell, I'd driven over ten thousand miles in the Cruise Master just to keep death behind me, and here it was anyway, rolling up like a ghost from an eddy in Nowhere, Wisconsin.

I shook myself. Jesus, Dog. He's nobody you know. Do something. Do something intelligent. Like…leave.

But the dead man held me somehow. He looked like the Dog in the good old days—well-fed, well-dressed, comfy, dead. He floated face-up amidst the duckweed and flotsam of a big pool. Flies crowded his bulging eyes. There was something odd about his mouth—it was stuffed with something fibrous and black, as though in drifting dead he had gouged the bottom, bitten out a weedy chunk of stream bed. Or like his corpse had already been claimed by the creature world, and a muskrat or a mouse had burrowed into his mouth. The sight was strange and awful. I gagged emptily. Then I guess the Dog had a few civic instincts left. I beat trail for help.

ALL DAY TO THAT POINT, I had listened to the sounds of a farmer cutting hay on the hillside above the creek, clanking and rumbling back and forth, a radio going. All along, I had assumed the farmer was a man. I assumed as much, in fact, until I got real close, and for a moment or so afterward, too. But the hay rake's pilot turned out to be a woman about thirty, thickly built and medium-tall, sunburned and sweaty and regarding me—as I staggered uphill—with a certain kind of what-the-hell-will-they-do-next expression in the set of her lips. I could tell she had observed more than a few fly fishermen from the seat of her tractor. We wore funny clothes and big hats and played in the water all day while other people worked. I could see it. Farmer Jane, she doubted the Dog. But my story changed all that in one rotation of the tractor's big treads.

"Aw, son of a buck knife!" she cursed, shutting down the engine. "You mean Jake Jacobs?"

Her eyes, wildly green, jumped at mine. Then she vaulted off the tractor and before I could catch up she was waist deep in the stream, doing what I should have done to begin with. She towed the man she called Jake Jacobs to shore and knelt over him, feeling for breath, pulse, body temperature, any sign that he might be saved.

But there was no such sign, and she sat back on her boot

heels. She pulled her bottom lip in and bit it, closed her eyes, and her brow wrinkled. She stayed that way for a long time, soaking wet, muttering fiercely, and it was impossible for me to take my eyes off her.

You expect me, I suppose, to tell you that she was a gorgeous creature, or lay out for you some other such cunning nonsense. But it wasn't like that. The last thing the Dog wanted in those days was attraction to a woman. Plus that was far from the mood, and this woman was anything but gorgeous. She was more like confusing. She had already shown me the clod-hopping agility of a teenaged boy. She was dressed like that too—dirty jeans and work boots, a t-shirt that had once been white, a dirty-green John Deere cap with a pair of cheap sunglasses up on the brim. Her thighs and arms and shoulders were thick, and her posture atop the stream mud was on the dark side of dainty. But there was a frazzled spark of red-blond ponytail sticking out the back of the cap. There were breasts strapped down by a sports bra beneath the t-shirt. There were tears in the eyes. Earth to Dog: woman.

Of course I watched her. She was not just muttering. She seemed to be praying. Then she found the rod where I had dropped it, a lovely cane rod, an eight-footer, worth about a thousand bucks, and she dragged it to her by the tip. She reeled up, pausing for a moment to inspect the fly—just as I had done in the moments before finding the body. The dead man had been fishing with a yellow sally, a large stonefly pattern, but oddly tied, upside down on the hook, with a tall, pink wingpost. Then suddenly Farmer Jane bit the fly off and flicked it into the current. She tossed the rod aside, leaned back over the dead man, and pulled the black stuffing from his mouth. She crammed the substance in the pocket of her jeans. Then from the opposite pocket she pulled out a dripping cell phone. "Oh, hog crap," she sighed. But the phone worked.

She made the call. Then she gently folded Jacobs' hands across his wader belt, returned to her tractor, and sat there. Her radio station played Captain and Tenille. Next we heard the weather report: hot, chance of a storm later. A siren screamed up the coulee. Go, I urged myself. Leave now. But the black mud held my feet, I guess. I could not take a step.

IT WAS A HALF HOUR LATER—the Dog still waiting sickly on his box elder log while the village police chief led the coroner to the body—when Farmer Jane came back down close enough to hit me with a dirt clod.

I looked at her. She made a motion—zip!—with her fingers across her lips. I wasn't supposed to get gabby with the chief—as if she had to advise the Dog on that. I made some kind of face in return, I'm not sure what. But the exchange made me re-check the mouth of Jake Jacobs. I saw again that it was empty, the normal slack hole of a dead man.

"Flop him over once," said Keg-belly. He had sidled up and planted a forearm against the trunk of a black willow that hung over the hole where the dead man lay. His gut pulled his spine to a lurid angle. He crossed his legs at the ankle.

"You want to ride my back," seethed the chief over his shoulder, "get a saddle."

"I'll get a cut bit," came the reply, "'cause you ain't broke yet."

I looked back to Farmer Jane. Zip! she went again.

Then the chief came back at me. He stood very close. His nostrils were wide, his breathing audible, his skin pale.

"Apparently that's your rig down in the park under the burr oak," he told me.

I had to wonder what difference that made right now. I was getting that rubbery smile again from Keg-belly.

"Parking limit is seventy-two hours," the chief told me. His voice jittered a little. "You been there seventy-four."

"I thought it was a campground," I said.

"It is when you pay for camping. City clerk. Ten bucks a night."

"I'll do that," I said.

He handed back my license. But he stayed on me in a menacing way. His eyes, behind sunglasses, were amber mirrors—with me reflected where his eyeballs should have been.

"You stay in the campground past noon like you did today," said the chief, "that counts as the next night. Even if you leave now. So you been there four nights."

Farmer Jane had crossed the creek and stood beside me.

"Back off, B.L."

He gave her a nervous, smirky look. "What's this?"

"What's what?" she said back.

He looked at her, at me, again at her. "Unlike you to be so friendly, that's what. You finally getting over Darrald?"

"Sit on a post, B.L.," she said, "and rotate."

The village police chief stuck his jaw at her like an angry schoolboy. Then he stalked back to the coroner and the corpse. When he was out of earshot, Farmer Jane said, "Don't worry about him. That's just B.L. He's a little bit different. Unless you're from around here. Then he's a little bit the same." She hit me with those green eyes. "That's why I hoped you just wouldn't, you know, say anything about me, and, um…this here in my pocket."

I told her I didn't plan on it.

She studied me with a certain inquisitive female energy. Then she made a gesture that would come to define her. She raised her smallish, work-worn hands and fingered a watch that hung from a loop of silver chain around her neck. It was a cheap digital watch, one of those that magnified what it had to say. It had no band. She seemed to be checking the time, or maybe the date. But according to the watch, it was 5:13 a.m., November 21. This was evening, in August.

"Well," I said, beginning to excuse myself, "I'm sorry your friend is dead."

"Oh, no, Jake was not my friend," she put in. "Not even a bit. And I don't guess anybody's going to be too disappointed that he's dead. Jake wasn't just your usual fly fisherman out here trying to look good."

She put those electric green eyes on the Dog once more, this time with a little grin. I wondered what she saw. I had strayed about as far from trying to look good as a man could go. Per my orders, Harvey Digman, my tax guy, had been cutting me twenty dollars a day—including gas, camping fees, duct tape for the waders, feathers for fly tying, everything. Two and a half years on discount vodka, Swisher Sweets, and peanut butter sandwiches will put a certain look on you.

"I'm pretty sure you know what I mean," said Farmer Jane. "The catalog type. They come through here driving fancy SUVs, having wine and crackers on the tailgate. Last week one of them asked me if I wouldn't mind cutting hay somewhere else until the caddis hatch was over."

I studied her. She had a small, sunburned nose. She had a scar on her chin. She had a sweaty curl of strawberry hair that had escaped her cap and stuck along her cheek.

"No," she said. She leaned close. "Jake wasn't around here long," she said in a low voice, "but he was a real horsefly in the potato salad. Defending the creek, getting on the farmers, the village, the developers, telling everybody what to do. There was more than a time or two—" she shot a look at B.L. "—I could have throttled him myself."

That last part made me jump. I hadn't seen that coming.

"My daddy wanted to kill him, too," she went on. "He even talked about it."

She took my arm. "That's why I need your help," she whispered. She squeezed. Her grip hurt. "Do me a little favor? Please?"

That was it. Hell-I had my driver's license back. What was I waiting for? I was out of there. Puke behind those willows, I told myself. Stumble away through those purple asters. Big Two-Hearted River by sunup.

"Hey!" Farmer Jane called after me.

Her real name was going to be Melvina.

Melvina Racheletta O'Malley.

I was going to call her Junior. And sometimes in my sleep.

"Hey!" she called after me. "Hey!"

But I leaned on my ugly attitude and kept my legs pumping. Right, I told myself. Hay. And corn. And soybeans. Look at all the lovely hog feed. Say goodbye to Black Earth. I was out of there.

In the cave of the Cruise Master

If you've ever hauled ass two miles over asphalt on a hot day in chest waders, you know how poached I felt by the time I reached the Cruise Master. If you haven't had the pleasure, imagine wrapping yourself in heavy-duty black garbage bags up to the armpits and then setting the Stairmaster on eighteen for a half hour—in the sun.

I collapsed straight into my lawn chair. Panting and blind from sweat, I tore at my wading shoes, compounding the knots. Finally I just pitched a pan of dishwater over my head, peeled everything down to the ankles, and sat there glistening like a half-shed snake. The ambient air, about eighty-five degrees, felt like refrigeration.

It was an oddly mixed-up glance I cast about the campground then. I hoped to hell no one was watching the Dog. The campground was a narrow sprawl of rough-mowed grass, and the amenities totaled a handful of warped picnic tables, a few old fire rings, his-and-her pit toilets, plus all the hazardous garbage you could step on. An iron gate stood open where the dirt lane met the county highway. Down at the dead end of the lane, about fifty yards toward the village, camped the only other occupant, a slumped and mildewed pop-up trailer that appeared deceptively abandoned. Come nighttime, there was action down there. Pickups came and went. People laughed and shouted. A radio blared. Pot smoke sweetened the air. It looked like the trailer had been there all summer, maybe longer. At least the lawnmower had been working around it for a good long time

I slowed down finally and got the shoes off. Then I removed my waders, tossed them over the bench seat inside the Cruise Master. I stowed my tackle, kicked out the wheel blocks, rolled up the awning, strapped the lawn chair over the spare tire, and went inside.

I had parked in the shade of a massive old burr oak, and it was passably cool in the galley of the Cruise Master. I rinsed the vomit taste out of my mouth and changed my sweaty pants. I poured a vodka and Tang. I lit one of my so-called cigars. Now that was better. In the cave of the Cruise Master, leaning over a map, plotting escape and getting a cheap buzz on, I felt like myself again. I felt like a proper trout hound.

THAT'S RIGHT. If you can imagine a Roger Tory Peterson Guide to Human Beings, then go a step further and picture me under Eastern Trout Hound. Order Human Drop-Outs. Species Nomadic Fly Caster. Identifying marks: permanent squint, bizarrely patterned sunburn, cigar-breath, soggy underwear, erratic movement…

You expect a life story, I guess. Well, too bad. The Dog had lived and lost. Now I was off the tether and out of the pack. With the help of my tax guy—I mean my tax guy from back in the day when I paid taxes—I had set up something that worked for me. It was about solitude and movement. It was about long stretches of new water, about stiff legs, exhaustion, vodka, and sleep. That was the way of the Dog, and I was sticking to it.

So there I was swilling a V-and-T over the road map, giving the Cruise Master another smoke bath, almost calm enough to drive away, when I heard a vehicle turn off the highway into the campground.

I was sure it was the village chief of police. He'd done such a half-assed job of questioning me, I knew he had to come back for more. I cursed myself for not leaving sooner. I had lingered over the map, spacing out in the womb of the Cruise Master and allowing the cop time to think back to whatever ten-week police-training course he had squeezed in between bowling league and rotating the tires on his monster truck.

But when I fingered back the curtain I saw it wasn't the cop. It was her, Farmer Jane, and she was clod-hopping off the running-board of a mud-spattered blue Ford pickup.

For the second time that day, I stared in something like taxonomical confusion. They did not make women like her in the tony suburbs of Boston. Women just did not cover ground like that where I came from. Their arms did not swing hands-open at their sides as if ready to shear sheep. And when a proper suburban Boston lady knocked on a door, it was a tidy little rap-rap, not the full-sized WHAM-WHAM-WHAM! that Farmer Jane laid on the Cruise Master door.

I was backing up, stumbling downstream through the galley over the detritus of a three-year road trip, planning to hide in the bunk, when she hollered.

"Hey!"

I was startled. My ugly attitude was shot. I couldn't find it.

"Hey!" hollered Farmer Jane again.

WHAM-WHAM-WHAM!

"I know you're in there! And I hope you're decent, 'cause I'm comin' in."

A woman called Junior

Like I said, Melvina Racheletta O'Malley was her proper
name, but she said I should call her Junior, like everybody else
in Black Earth. Not that she was happy about the whole Junior
thing, she wanted me to know, but that was another story.

"B.L. can't see me here," she continued, out of breath.
"He's already got ideas. Can we talk?"

What I had done is plunked down abruptly behind my little
fold-out table, faking a studious immersion in the topography
of the Middle West. My map was open to Iowa.

"Sure," I blurted. "Come on in. Nice to see you again." The
Dog groped for the proper convention. "Get you a drink?"

She raked a wrist across her sweaty forehead, exposing a
muscular underarm that had been shaved about a week ago.
She puffed and looked around the Cruise Master.

"I'll take a beer if you got one."

I popped the cooler. At my last stop, the Letort River in
Pennsylvania, the sight of a kid fishing with his dad had

triggered in me the urge to have a trout hound's party—me, my fly tying kit, and a twelve-pack of Iron City beer. But I had run out of hackle feathers and passed out in my lawn chair, and I still had four cans left. I set one on the table and reached toward the cabinet. I was intending to find a clean cup and pour my visitor a beer when a snap turned me. All I saw was the woman's freckled throat—pumping once, twice, three times. She set the can down empty.

Wow. There followed a brief and almost religious moment of quiet, where her skin flushed and her green eyes watered and I felt very close to the primal root of language. Quench, I was thinking. Slake. Christ, six feet away, I could feel that beer go down.

Then Junior squeezed the can precisely flat with her bare hands and handed it back to me. Midwestern manners, I guessed.

"So you wanted to talk about something?"

"Like I said on the stream, I think I'm going to need some help."

She tipped up her cap and glanced about the place, waiting for me to track down an excuse and wound it.

"I was just leaving town," I told her.

"Right," she said. "That's what I thought. That's why you can help me."

She lifted the curtain and checked the highway. Then she got right down to the business of horrifying me. She reached into the pocket of her jeans and pulled out the black, fibrous stuffing she had extracted from the dead man's mouth.

She laid the thing on the table. "You know what that is?"

I had no idea. The thing was wet and black—gummed together with mucous and uncurling messily on my table like the ruined nest of some hideous bird.

She said, "Had you ever met Jake?"

I said I hadn't.

Junior cracked her knuckles and cast another glance through the folds of my curtain. She didn't seem to notice the mildew spots across the sun-bleached fabric.

"Okay," she said, dropping the curtain. She gnawed her bottom lip. "Well, Jake was a bit of a special case. One look at him, you could tell that. He just moved in one summer, he and Ingrid, his wife, and right away they wanted to change the way things are run in the village. And you know how that goes usually."

I opened my own beer.

"I mean, Jake meant well," she said. "He really did. Ingrid is a different story. But Jake…well…he just didn't…"

I waited. She checked the road again.

"Dad hated Jake," she told me, her fists clenching. "The way Jake blamed farmers for messing up the creek…that made Dad real angry. He made his threat on Jake, and everybody knows it. But a lot of other people had it out for Jake, too. And this… Dad would never… I mean, I don't think…"

The fibrous mass had uncurled on my galley table, revealing a green rubber band at midpoint. "Dad wouldn't do this. I know he wouldn't."

I had kept my eyes mostly off the thing, but now my gaze lingered long enough to acknowledge the obvious: Jake Jacobs' mouth had been crammed with hair, and when I actually looked at the hair for a moment, noted its fineness and luster…it was obviously hair from the human head.

"I mean…" Junior paused and took a huge breath. "I know Dad said he would do it… I know Dad threatened Jake… but…"

She lifted and dropped the curtain.

"And see," she said, "B.L. is such a sucker. He's going to fall for it."

I raised my hands in surrender. "What is it you want from me?"

Junior O'Malley fingered the dead wristwatch that hung between her small, tight bosoms. She studied me.

"I've been watching you out there," she said. "You cover a lot of ground. You catch a lot of fish."

I shrugged. There was no need to tell her she had just covered the Dog's entire list of strong points. I could fish myself into solitary exhaustion, seven days a week, with the best of them. I had done it, all over the country, for nearly three years straight. I was going for feral—going for lone wolf— and I thought I'd nearly made it.

"So this is what happened with Jake and Daddy," she continued, deciding for some reason that I was worthy of a story. "Last month at the village board meeting, Jake stood up like he usually does and starts going on and on about mud in the creek and how it was doing something or other to the larva of the insects and how that was hurting the trout and so on, getting everybody all stirred up, like he usually does. And he was blaming the fields and the cattle and the tractor crossings—you know, blaming us farmers."

She crinkled her sunburned nose and looked at me. I was supposed to be caring about this.

"Jake blamed other people, too. Politicians, poachers, developers. That's the thing to remember." I nodded as if I meant to remember. "So I took Dad there, to the meeting. I always do—at least until this last time. Usually he just sits there whittling and staring out the window. But this time Jake went on and on about cattle in the stream. I guess Dad had just heard enough. Suddenly he reared up and he hollered—"

She was flushing, breathing through her nose and finger-ing the useless watch. She took another quick look around the Cruise Master.

"You should put some crystals in here," she told me out of nowhere. "They break up stagnant energy. And maybe a dream catcher over that bunk window. You know, because I'm sure some good ideas flow through here—some good energies—but you're just not catching them."

"Thanks," I said. "I'm fine."

"You move so fast on the stream," she said, "I kind of wonder…"

"You don't need to wonder."

She made a funny, downcast smile. She spun the crushed beer can on the table between us.

"Well, anyway," she went on, "Dad wasn't the only one on Jake's case. Everybody talked about the fancy-chicken way he looked. If you're from around here, it you're a Black Earth-ling like the rest of us, Jake was real different. I don't mean messed-up different—like B.L., our police chief. I mean like from a different planet."

While Junior struggled to gather her next thoughts, I pictured the dead man and felt my sick confusion again. Jake Jacobs, in his fly fishing garb, had looked like a Dog from a better pack—richer, younger, handsomer, more secure—and yet even more dead. There was a message there—maybe—but I wasn't sure what it was.

"So at the village board meeting," she continued, "Dad reared up, and he yelled at Jake to shut up. Of course Jake kept talking. Well, Dad's had a couple of strokes, but he's still pretty strong. And his dementia can make him a little unpredictable sometimes. He knocked a half dozen people out of the way trying to get to the front of the room. When I caught him—"

She raised her thick arm, put her hand to her ear and pinched, to show how she had caught her dad. That was the first time I noticed her tiny stud earrings—just the faintest, shiest touch of femininity, but it was quickly lost in a whiff of sweat and the startling image of her knocking chairs over, corralling an angry old farmer by the earlobe.

"—Dad had his pocket knife out, waving it around. Jake was still talking about mud in the stream and Dad hollers, 'Shut up or I'm gonna shut you up. Then I'm gonna cut that goddamn thing off and shove it in your mouth!'"

She hung her head. Both of us looked at her old leather work boots, worn to the steel in the toes.

"I didn't take Dad to the meeting this month," she told me. "That meeting was last night, seven o'clock. I left him home and went alone. Dad didn't even notice. Lately he's been back thirty years or so, talking like I'm his wife, like I'm Mom, and we're about to have me." She sighed. "Talking about me like I'm a boy already."

Junior. Now I got it. She was Melvina. Only girl-son of Melvin. The default Mel Junior. She stared down and picked at a rough spot on the back of her hand.

"But Dad's attack on Jake has been all the talk around town ever since. And now Jake is dead with this stuffed in his mouth. If B.L. finds this, he's going to blame Dad. But Dad didn't do it. So listen," she blurted. "Could you just take it away?"

I gaped at her. Take what away?

"It's his," she said. "It's Jake's."

Jake's what?

"Oh," she said. "Right. You never saw Jake."

"I never saw him."

Melvina "Junior" O'Malley looked at me. It was a look that begged the Dog to grasp things, to wake up and smell the Black Earth.

She touched the thing that had been stuffed in the dead man's mouth.

"Jake's ponytail," she told me, and waited for my answer.

The yellow sallies hatch at eight

So there sat the Dog, half-tanked inside a '70s-vintage RV, with a woman called Junior, and a dead man's ponytail on the galley table. She fingered back the curtain once more, then looked at me eagerly, ready for my answer.

"No," I said.

"Okay. Then I'll pay you to take it away."

I refused again.

"Look," she said. "Jake was a big friend of the stream. Somebody killed him, and tried to frame my dad."

"Who would do that?"

"Plenty of people."

"They hate the stream?" I asked. "Or they hate your dad?"

"Neither. They hated Jake. Practically everybody in Black Earth hated Jake. Dad's threat gave somebody the perfect opportunity."

"Or maybe your dad did what he promised."

She glowered out beneath her hat brim, scorched me with a look. "I'm telling you. He wouldn't."

I don't know why I kept talking to her. Old habits die hard, and maybe I thought I needed to solve her problem. But I told myself I was just stalling. If I used up enough time, she would just bolt. Then I would simply slip away. Big Two-Hearted by sunup.

"How about letting the cop do his job?" I suggested.

She gave that a dismissive snort. "You know why we call him B.L.? Because his daddy is Bud Bjorgstad, the village president. Bud wants to develop land on the creek. And B.L. is short for Bud Lite. He does whatever his daddy tells him."

I couldn't help myself. I said it didn't look that way. I said the son, on the stream, seemed to buck the father hard.

"He fights it," Junior said. "For show. But Bud always wins." She looked around like she needed a crystal to break up her energy. She fingered the dead watch around her neck. "Then B.L.," she said, "he takes it out on the rest of us. You don't pay that camping fee, B.L.'s gonna be on your ass like a duck on a June bug."

Jesus, I thought. Welcome to the heartland.

"But you have a county sheriff, right?" I asked her. "Why can't you just go around your local cop and give this…give the ponytail… why can't you just talk to the sheriff?"

In her exasperation at this, a patch of dewy sweat bumps sprouted across her sunburned nose.

"Because," she said. "The sheriff and President Bud bowl together."

I said nothing for a moment, during which I pictured the keg-bellied man mowing down a three-ten split and lurching back to his beer.

"They shoot skeet together, for crissake."

Now I pictured the village president beered up, with a shotgun.

"Okay," I said. "But you realize you're withholding evidence in a murder case. You're obstructing justice."

Her eyes narrowed. "What's the justice in framing Dad?" She fixed me with a sullen gaze. "Look," she said, "I own a bull that's wanted very badly by Gareth Kaltenburg. This bull has balls like grapefruits. I could give you a thousand bucks cash in about an hour."

She kept her eyes on me. I'm sure she saw my interest.

"Why don't you just take the ponytail yourself?" I asked her. "Bury it, burn it, get rid of it somehow? Why do you need me?"

Steady eyes, hot green. "Like you said, I'm withholding evidence. Not destroying it. Someday that ponytail's going to show up again and get Dad off." She nodded towards the road. "Unless B.L. catches me with it—which could happen any second."

After a long paused she added, "Besides, Ingrid, Jake's wife... I'll bet... I'll bet someday she wants it back."

Now she lowered her gaze. She put a chapped hand around the dead watch and waited for me to say something.

"You clipped off the dead guy's yellow sally."

"Because B.L. didn't need to see it."

I gave my chin a doubtful rub. I hadn't shaved since Pennsylvania, and my palm against my whiskers made the only sound for a long moment. "If the dead guy was fishing the sally," I said at last, "then he was fishing at around eight o'clock. That establishes a time of death. And seven was when you left your dad at home while you went to the village board meeting. When you pull that fly off, it looks like you're protecting your dad."

She was barely patient. "Dad didn't do it. And it didn't happen at eight. That's why I threw away Jake's fly. Everybody in town knows the yellow sallies hatch at eight. All somebody would have to do is kill Jake earlier and change his fly. Then the killer is safe at the meeting while Dad takes the blame."

I made an ugly little Dog grin as I reviewed her theory. She made some sense. Someone could have killed Jake Jacobs earlier, then tied on a yellow sally to make it look like he died while fishing at eight o'clock—since the yellow sally stone-flies only hatched just before dark, and everybody seemed to know that. Could have. But in my heart of hearts, I didn't think anybody in Black Earth—maybe nobody in the whole state of Wisconsin—could be that smart.

"You see, here's the problem," I said. "A guy like me… I can't really… I mean, I'd like to help…but there's no way to get in touch with me…so I couldn't really…"

I moved from behind the table to the door. I had made my decision.

"Time for you to go," I concluded.

She looked around the Cruise Master once more. "I'm guessing you're flat broke," she said. "I can get you a thousand bucks by nine o'clock. Then you take the ponytail with you."

"I'm long gone by nine."

"Then I'll mail you the money."

"You can't reach me. I live in this vehicle."

"I'll mail it to a friend."

"I don't have any friends. I'm a trout bum. I'm nothing to nobody."

She did an odd thing. First she rolled her eyes. Then, with the ease of someone used to redirecting stupid animals, she took me by the belt, precisely at my center of gravity, and she steered me away from the door and back where I'd come from, back against my crusty little sink, out of her way.

"You're full of manure, is what you are," she said, and she bent over my Wisconsin map with a pencil. "Everybody's something to someone," she said. "And you and I can help each other."

On the corner of my map, she wrote:

I.O.U. the price of one bull
Junior
RR 15, Box 37
Black Earth, Wisconsin 53765
608-555-9765

"Thanks for the beer," she called as she cut quickly out the door. Her mud-spattered blue pickup roared up the dirt drive, through the steel gate, and out of the campground.

"I said no!"

But she was gone. And she had left me the dead man's ponytail.

She had implicated me in her crime

It was twilight by the time I was functional enough to find a dry shirt and put a quart of oil in the Cruise Master.

I had spent the intervening hour in a dither, caught between assorted courses of action while downing the remainder of the Pennsylvania twelve-pack and nipping open and shut the curtain that faced the county highway. I thought about working for money, and I thought about working for truth, justice—you know—the goddamned human contract. I even thought about knowing a woman again. But all those roads led inward to feelings the Dog didn't do any more, and so I fell back on my standard answer: move. Just as I settled on that solution, Bud Lite's police cruiser roared down the county highway, slowed, flashed a sidelight my way, but did not turn into the campground. I knew it was my chance.

Looking back, my plan was perfectly in tune with my realities at the time. Some psycho farm woman had dumped her problem on me. That's how the Dog finally played it. She had implicated me in her crime. But I could duck the entanglement if I moved decisively. As for the fate of Jake Jacobs…how was that my problem?

So about ten, with the Cruise Master all prepped for travel, I dug out my cell phone and tried to call my tax guy, Harvey Digman. But the old coot was out somewhere, probably practicing Tai Chi on Boston Commons with a new girlfriend from one of his book clubs—or maybe at his gourmet cooking club in Back Bay, shredding shallots with a Wusthof knife. I left him a message—the Dog was moving—and I asked him to send my next hundred to a bank about five hours north. Then I drained the last beer and used a pencil to shove Jake Jacobs' ponytail into a Ziploc bag. I tore the map corner off, the piece with Junior's address, balled and stuffed it, and then I dropped the pencil in as well. Outside the Cruise Master, I added a handful of gravel and sealed the bag. Then, flashlight in hand, I made a careful inspection of my surroundings.

Along the highway, the campground was bordered by a brushy line of sumac that harbored nothing more threatening than coons, skunks, and possums. I checked the pop-up trailer at the south end of the campground. No vehicles, no lights, no action. It was early. The usual round of partying kicked in around bar time. I walked to the campground's other border, the disappointing body of water that the locals called Lake Bud.

It was a breezy evening. As I shone my flashlight over the water, a Styrofoam cup kited across the rippled surface. The same breeze brought up a murky, fetid smell, and I was reminded of what I had learned from an exploratory ramble the day before. Lake Bud was in fact a defunct mill pond. It was Black Earth Creek backed up and spread out muddily for a mile behind an old millhouse and a treacherous slab of hundred-year-old concrete. Standing on the foundation of the old mill and looking downstream toward the village about a half mile distant, I had spent a minute or two wondering why the hell the dam hadn't been taken out a long time ago, wondering why the so-called lake was even there—serving no purpose that I could see, except to ruin one whole stretch of a perfectly lovely trout stream. But Black Earthlings had their ways, I decided. So never mind.

Just then, a pair of headlights swung into the campground. I froze behind the cover of some cattails. To my relief, the lights were not followed by the profile of a cop car—nor by the returning shape of Junior's pickup. This vehicle had a higher, thicker profile. I crouched and watched the dark shape crawl past the Cruise Master and continue down to the pop-up camper. There it circled, went halfway back toward the Cruise Master, and stopped. The headlights went out. The interior lights went on. A figure moved about inside. Okay, I told myself. Another camper. Big deal.

So I made a simple change to my plan. I would do my deed from the far shore of Lake Bud. I knew I could hike up to the thin end of the mill pond, where the stream flowed in. I could cross the current on an old two-plank bridge. From there I could skirt the edge of the woody hillside where I had seen LOTS FOR SALE signs through my binoculars. Back in there somewhere, opposite my position in the campground, I planned to wind up and hurl the bag of ponytail-and-gravel and let it sink deep into Lake Bud. I could make the Big Two-Hearted River by morning. I could have miles and miles of solo water.

I made it up to the end of Lake Bud, my trail broadcast in the night by the expanding stillness of frogs. I located the little plank bridge, which was slippery with dew and springier than I remembered. I smelled the cold trout water against the warm black mud, and I teetered twice, but I got across. From there I led a legion of mosquitoes through the dark woods along the far side of the lake, aiming my flashlight at the For Sale signs and orange tree tags. Across Lake Bud, I could still make out the new vehicle in the campground, a figure moving inside. But he couldn't see me, I decided. Itchy and out of breath, unwilling to go further, I put out my flashlight and approached the water.

That's when I saw the ghost. No. Not true. I *heard* it first. I was pushing through a stand of black willow shoots at the water's edge when I heard what I figured first was a muskrat splashing around its den. In the dark, of course, there is always a separation between what the mind thinks and the body feels, and the sound froze me for a moment, while my pulse galloped. *Down boy,* I commanded. *No more ghosts. Think muskrat.*

But it was as I waited for physical calm, for the reconnection of mind and body, that the whole muskrat illusion began to break down. The sound was too regular—a slow *swish-splash-swish* through the water—and then against my will I saw them: human feet, haloed in light, moving slowly out across the surface of the lake.

Doubt the Dog. Go ahead. I was skittish as hell in those days, always seeing things at night, before the vodka took hold. But I am telling you that I saw human feet that night on Lake Bud. Bare feet. White ankles. All else was in black shadow behind the beam of a small and precise flashlight.

And I am telling you that those feet were walking on the water.

On the water. On top of it. Out twenty, thirty, fifty feet away from my position and then turning northwest toward a little back bay in the millpond. Then the feet paused. I heard a rattle, a pause, and then a sound like faint rainfall. The sound stopped. The light turned, and then the feet turned—headed back toward me. I gave it one *swish-splash-swish.*

I suppose the Dog in flight might have passed for a buck deer, blind and running sideways, with a hockey stick caught in his antlers—but otherwise I'm pretty sure I was detected. The flashlight beam chased me a hundred yards through brush, nipping at my heels. When I reached the campground, I stayed outside the Cruise Master for a good long time, gasping, flayed and itching, afraid to open any doors for the telltale dome lights that would spark across the lake and give me away.

But give me away to whom, I wondered. Or what? My ghosts, to that point, had never carried flashlights.

With my hand on the Cruise Master door handle, afraid to open it, I was a sitting duck for the guy in the other vehicle. *His* dome light went on. He spilled out the driver's side of a large red Suburban.

He was a keg-bellied guy with a brisk, unbalanced stride, angling across the thick black grass.

"Oh, there you are," said Bud Bjorgstad, Village President.

Be sure now, fella

He was right. There I was. Could I argue?

The village president came at me in a top-heavy canter, keys in one hand, can of beer in the other—massive, work-scarred hands.

"Hey, fella, seriously," he said, giving me the rubbery smile, "so sorry you had to be the one. Gosh, you come here to fish and look what you get in the middle of. A dang murder of all things. You gotta be shaking your head, I'll bet. Too bad."

High beams flashed over our heads and caught in the burr oak. A patrol car had turned through the steel gate into the campground. Its beams blasted the dusty flank of the Cruise Master, the faded aqua stripe and the deep, rusty wound where I had backed drunk into a fire grill at a campground in Idaho. Slowly, I pushed the bag of hair into my hip pocket.

"You know," said Bud Bjorgstad, "we just want to thank you and let you know we appreciate the service you done for our community. Dirty work, you know. Heh-heh. Seriously." He thrust an out-sized, beer-cooled paw and introduced himself. "Village president since I sold my farm in '89," he said. "That's my kid, coming in here in the soup-and-nuts car. Kinda learning on the job."

Bud Lite got out alongside us and left his engine running, headlights blazing, radio squawking, the pointless occupation of kinetic space and the wanton consumption of fuel being parts of the cop thing he had gotten down just right.

"Here's our fisherman," said the village president to his son. "I had to come out and find him myself. And like I says to him, we appreciate his service to the community. Real sorry he had to get into this and all. Not a pretty thing. So no camping fees." He gave his son a chin-first look. "You got that?"

The police chief responded stiffly. "When did that get decided?"

"About ten seconds ago," said the president. He tucked at his shirttail and puffed. He turned to me. "See now, the thing is, fella, we got some oddities going on here. One thing, I'll tell you, strikes me funny, our friend Jake Jacobs was out there fly fishing only he had no fly on. You fellas do that often?"

I answered that we didn't.

The president tucked and hitched and moved in closer. Time to lean. He put his big mitt against the prow of the Cruise Master, right in the dried bug spat, and canted his weight against it. "So how might that happen? A fella with no fly on." Bud Lite began to speak, but Bud Heavy shut him up with a terse, "You just listen."

I said, "Fly fishermen change flies all the time. Sometimes, during a hatch, every couple of minutes. Or else we break flies off—on fish, rocks, trees, brush, or snap them off in the air, with a bad cast."

"See?" said the president, turning to B.L. "I knew if we asked a real fisherman, we'd get ourselves an answer that made some sense. So in other words, fella, our friend Jake had a fly on, but somehow it came off…"

I said that could have happened.

"As in, say, somebody took it off."

I said that could have happened, too. Bud Lite snorted. He rapped out a pinch of Copenhagen and tucked it under his bottom lip. I was only half-conscious of my hand, pushing the ponytail deeper into my pocket. Not that I was agreeing to help out Junior O'Malley. Not yet. But watching those two catch up with the facts of the case was like watching a couple of mean dogs figure out they could go ahead and walk on the linoleum. I wasn't about to help them either.

"Now that farm gal," said the president, "Junior, she came down around the body, I gather. 'Cause when she called the boy here, she said it was Jake Jacobs that was dead in the creek. In other words, she came down and saw who it was. Am I right? She got off her tractor and she came down? Fella?"

I said he was right.

"She touch Jake's tackle at all? Maybe take his fly off?"

Now you might imagine that here the Dog was faced with a moral dilemma. But the fact is that I was nothing more than determined to leave.

"No," I said. "As far as I know, she didn't touch his tackle."

Bud Lite spat and said, "See? That's what I'm saying. Junior ain't touched nobody's tackle in a long time. That's what worries me."

The president, Bud Heavy, turned to his son with a dismayed look. B.L. said quickly, "I mean it's been three, four years. She could be getting over Darrald."

"What's that got to do with it?"

The chief nodded toward me. "She and him seemed pretty friendly by the time I got there. So I figure—"

President Bud stopped him with a seething interruption. "What in the hell has that got to do with the price of beef, Dwighty? Goddamn it!"

I guess he was Dwighty. I guess he didn't know he was called Bud Lite. He spat and put a scowl on me, like I had tricked him into trouble. President Bud said, "See fella, we're still working out the kinks in this village police force situation. Had none for the longest time. Then all these big houses go up around the edges of town, fancy folks driving around all over, suddenly we need a little traffic work, you know? Little radar here and there. Little bit of education on the proper way to park. So that's where we're at, see?"

"I see," I said. "But you're also in a county." God help me, for some reason I was talking back to the guy. "And if you're in a county, you've got a sheriff."

Bud Bjorgstad let go of the Cruise Master long enough to dismiss my idea with a two-handed wave. "Oh, hell no," he said. "We don't need to bother the sheriff about this."

"I can handle it," said Bud Lite.

His father re-set his stiff-arm against the Cruise Master. "Darn right you can, Dwighty."

We stood there in the dark for a moment. I looked over Lake Bud. It was black and smooth and smelly. It was a tragedy, a diminishment, a slowly seeping poison. Trout water had to move. It had to flow. It had to push against you.

"Funny thing, though," said the president, "and I'm glad we caught you, fella, because the boy here finally got himself braved up to flopping over the body—"

"I waited for Halverson," huffed the chief defensively. "That's what you're supposed to do. Wait for the coroner."

"So we had our little exercise in book learning," the president went on, "and finally we got poor Jake flipped over.

Come to find out, he was missing something. Used to have him one of those cindy-handles on the back."

"Ponytail," said B.L.

"All gone," said the president. "And now his wife, she's upset as all get out, I can tell you, but she was sure Jake didn't get a haircut. I mean, not on purpose, anyway." He had a rubbery wince, too, besides the smile, and he gave me that. "Goddamned awful thing to find out," the president informed me.

"And Halverson," said B.L., jetting tobacco juice into the dark grass, "he found some hairs in Jake's mouth."

I waited for the question. The police chief puffed and squirmed around a little, waiting for his father to ask it. The president had sagged too far against the Cruise Master, and he adjusted his feet. I thought about my hip pocket. It felt hot, tight, bulging. Bud sent his other hand out through the dark and found my shoulder.

"Be sure now, fella," he said. "'Cause I'm going to ask you a question."

I waited.

"You saw her, right? That farm gal, Junior, she took that ponytail out of Jake's mouth, didn't she?"

"No," I lied. "She didn't."

He repeated himself. "Be sure now, fella."

"I'm sure."

I swear I wasn't helping her. I was helping myself. The Dog was five minutes from gone. The village president shook his head and regarded me sorrowfully for a long moment. His son the chief spat and breathed aloud. "Well, then, come on, boy," said Bud. "The fella says he's sure. So let's carry on. Lead the way."

I watched them drive up the dirt lane and out onto the county highway, where they both stopped and climbed out of their vehicles. Then, side by side, Bud and Bud Lite walked back and swung the iron gate closed on the campground with a loud *clang*. I could be sure if I wanted, I guess. I could play games.

But so could they.

I heard the ring of a chain and the snap of a lock as they shut me in. The Dog, they were saying, was going to be part of this, property of the Village of Black Earth until this thing was solved.

This man is here to help us

Like hell I was. I tossed that bag of hair. I did a piss poor job of it, too, but at least I put an end to my part in whatever crime was taking place. I crossed the black grass to the soupy shore of Lake Bud and prepared to fling the bag as hard as I could. While my arm was rushing back, though, the weight of the ponytail caused the bag to flop back and under my wrist, so that when I fired forward, the geometries were all mixed up. The energy went more up and sideways than out, and the bag flew a mere fifteen feet before rattling in among some cattails. A real shitty toss. But anyway, I was rid of it.

My next step was to take out that iron gate. For a dizzy while, I was actually convinced I could do it with the Cruise Master at about thirty miles per hour. I would drive down around the pop-up camper, floor that big old eight-cylinder engine, and pound my way through—or die trying.

But some deeper instinct made me walk up and look the situation over first. The gate poles were forged steel pipe, about eight inches in diameter, set in concrete footings. The chain wasn't much, but the gate was back-blocked against the poles from the inside, and the piping was heavy-gauge and narrowly spaced. It was difficult to imagine that gate sprawled out on the highway in front of me. It was much easier to imagine myself stamped like a waffle through the steering wheel of the Cruise Master. And though the truth is that a big part of me still wanted to die, I guess I didn't quite want it that bad.

So I kept walking, across the highway and down the black chute of a driveway leading to the farm opposite the campground. *Sundvig,* said the mailbox. The place was dark, and I thought I knew enough about farms to imagine some serious tools in the barn—blowtorches, sledgehammers, maybe even dynamite. I could steal something. I could take down the gate. I could be gone in an hour.

I was about three steps up the long, pitted drive when a pair of mutts tore from beneath a manure spreader and cancelled my plans. In cartoons you'll see now and then the kind of dogs who run so fast that their back legs get ahead of their front legs, as if their passion to tear out an asshole was a greater force than any known to physics. These were those dogs, and I was that asshole. I got back across the road before they caught me, and they skidded to a stop on the shoulder, whining with savage disappointment. A light went on at the farmhouse porch, and I moved on up the road.

The next farm was more than a mile upstream, about halfway to where I'd found the body. This time I avoided the driveway. Two hundred yards from the mailbox, I rolled under barbed wire and followed the last row of corn to the back of the field. From there, I skirted inward, illuminating the ground with my tiny flashlight, pushing quietly through the coarse leaves. Creatures scuttled ahead of me, darks shapes with glowing eyes—coons, possums, gargoyles, I don't know. I was rashy and bathed in sweat by the time I emerged behind the barn, fists full of dirt clods, ready for more dogs.

But the farm was quiet. I could hear cows inside the barn, shifting, sighing, their joints cracking, their manure slopping on the barn floor. The house was smallish and set beside a stand of ragged cottonwoods that stretched into the deep, starry sky. I could see the light of a television flickering in the front room. At the side of the house, another window let out light and the sound of running water. The air smelled sweet and lush above the aromas of dirt, manure, and hay.

I killed my light and snuck around to the barn's big, slumping gape of a door. Inside, the moment my light shone again, I saw that the ceiling was low, scarcely above my head, and the beams were clotted with bird nests, little igloos of swallow mud, and what seemed like a century of spider webs and dust. The floor was a hay-strewn path between gutters clogged with a foul black compost of cow piss and anything else that could fall off or out of an animal. A few startled cattle struggled awkwardly to their feet. A scrawny tabby cat sidled toward me, mewing hoarsely, her swollen teats nearly dragging. Barn swallows, beady-eyed, followed my progress.

At the back of the barn one cow caught my eye. She sprawled in a corner. Foam clogged her nostrils and she breathed heavily. Her gut was distended, her tail was peeled back, and from her vagina protruded a tiny, bloody hoof. Startled by my flashlight, she bawled mournfully, and several sisters in the barn answered. I killed the beam, but she kept on bawling, looking moon-eyed in my direction. "Sorry," I muttered. "I'm not a vet."

In the tool room, only ten steps away, all manner of powerful-looking implements hung on a rough-hewn wall. At the tool room door, on a fifty-gallon drum top, sat a box of dynamite. *Stump-Blaster,* the box read. Its top was torn open, but it hadn't been moved in decades—or however long a solid half-inch of black dust indicated. But it looked dry, and I meant to grab it.

And that's when the barn light snapped on. A rough voice said, "Whoosere?" Scuffling footsteps proceeded down the central alley of the barn. I ducked past the suffering cow and beneath the pipes of a milking stall. Down low, through the shifting legs of the cattle, I glimpsed plaid house slippers plowing through dirty straw. Above that, clean coveralls, and two gnarled old hands closed around something I took to be the stock of a shotgun.

"Come on outta there," growled the voice. "'Fore I pop ya."

I thought I had a plan. The farmer would search his way to the end of the barn and see the cow in trouble. Meanwhile I would work my way around him into the tool room. He would see me then, but he wouldn't fire into his animals, I figured, so I was safe. And then I would escape into the cornfield.

I crouched at the back of a milking stall, my heart like a bubble in my throat, and a cow's tail slapping me across the top of the head. A city boy like me, I never saw the hoof coming. It caught me in the hip and sent me clattering over a stack of plastic buckets, bellowing in pain. When I looked up, he was over me.

I'm not sure what I hoped for. First aid, maybe. Or sympathy. Hell, how about a hearty guffaw and some salty advice from an old stump of a gentleman who looked like Robert Frost and had an extra blowtorch he was looking to get rid of. Anything but the massive old warrior who towered over me in a trembling rage. Anything but a red-eyed, bent-nosed, hump-backed, messy-haired old giant, wielding a shovel blade as wide as a tractor seat and fully ready to knock me dead and scoop me out of his barn like so much cow flop.

I scrambled as the shovel crashed down. Cows scattered as best they could in the narrow spaces and the old man limped after me. "Git," he muttered. "Step out." And the cows seemed to know what he wanted. They made way for his slow, dragging step. But they kept me in confusion, stamping and shying erratically around me, eyes rolling, hooves ready to strike.

Near the front of the barn, his huge head plowing through spiders' webs, the farmer lunged in and caught me with a blow to the mid-back. I sprawled against a feed bin and slumped down, gasping, my wind knocked out, my arms wrapped desperately around my head. I felt the wind of the shovel as he just missed me. I rolled and the next blow thundered off the feed bin.

Then *"Daddy!"* shrieked a voice. Everything became still. I peered out between my forearms. She had him—Melvina "Junior" O'Malley, wet-haired, in a bathrobe and barn boots—had her old man, Mel Senior, by the ear.

"Daddy," she said more calmly. "This man is here to help us."

Everything is going to work out

"No," I panted. "No, I'm not. I'm not here to help you."

She didn't seem to hear that. She made her wrinkle-nose grin at me. She smelled like shampoo—a wet-haired, sunburned, sweet-smelling female linebacker in shit-crusted boots and a white terry cloth robe, grinning like she was glad to see me.

"This is him, Daddy. This is the guy."

"He shoulda been back a long time ago," seethed the old man, his pale blue, bloodshot eyes darting around the barn.

"He's not Darrald, Daddy. Look." With a tug on his giant ear, Junior brought his focus back to me. She took the shovel away and tossed it along the floor toward the dark maw of the barn. "See? He's the man from the campground. The fisherman who found Jake. I gave him the ponytail. He's helping us."

She let go of the ear. The old man felt his pinched spot like a child, his attention drifting.

"I'm not helping you," I repeated. "I got locked in down at the campground. I was leaving and they shut that gate on me."

"Who shut the gate on you?"

"The village president," I told her. "And his son, the cop."

"Figures," said Junior. She tipped her head, squeezed her wet hair. "Anyway, I was going to come down to the campground after my shower. I got your money already. Hang on a sec."

Just like that, still acting on her premonition that I was full of manure, that I wasn't really leaving, she galumphed briskly away toward the house in her big boots, leaving me alone with the old man who less than five minutes before had tried to smack my brains out with a shovel. I tensed. I plotted my escape from his next homicidal lunge. But Mel O'Malley Senior stared vaguely at a spot somewhere on my mid-chest and said, "Dance."

"I'm sorry?"

"What I like," he said, his voice a high-pitched rasp. "I like the dancing."

I nodded carefully. "Me, too."

The old man nodded back. "Ice cream," he added eventually.

"Sure," I said. "Ice cream is good stuff."

He pulled at his saggy ear. The pregnant cow released a snuffling sigh from the back of the barn.

"What kind of ice cream do you like?"

As though this were the wrong thing to say, the old man glared at me beneath his great, shrub-like eyebrows. His mouth hung open.

"I see you two had a chat," said Junior, galumphing back into the barn, carrying a fistful of cash and a pair of long-handled bolt cutters. She put a finger under her father's chin and closed his mouth. "Is he making any sense? Kind of a rummage sale up there sometimes."

Then she counted out twenty fifty-dollar bills into my hand. "I told you Gareth Kaltenburg wanted that bull," she said cheerfully. She handed me the bolt cutters. "There you go. Just nip that chain and swing the gate open to the inside. Daddy," she said, "move aside and let him out of there."

She gave the old man a shove. He moved over stubbornly. I got as far as the barn door and Junior said, "You call me in a week, all right? Everything should be all straightened out by then, and I expect Jake's poor wife is going to want his hair back. He did have beautiful hair."

I hesitated, thinking about that Ziploc bag somewhere on the muddy bottom of Lake Bud. I wasn't going to call Junior. The dead man's wife would never see his hair again. Those decisions had already been made.

"Thanks again," Junior urged me. "Go on. Don't worry. Everything is going to work out just fine."

I still couldn't move. She looked at me curiously. Her reddish-blond hair had started to dry to its odd, stiff length. Even after washing, it was slightly bent above the ear from being under a cap all day. That dead wristwatch still hung from her neck, but it was inside against her skin, tucked under the thick collar of the bathrobe. I guess she never took it off. I guess I was noticing things about her.

"Is something wrong?" she asked me.

"Uh…you might want to look in the back of the barn. There's a cow back there—I think she's in trouble."

Junior's eyes widened and she roused her old man with a stiff nudge. "Daddy. Darl's in breach again." Her eyes came back to me. "See? You did come here to help us. Hey—what's your name?"

"Dog."

"Your real name."

"That's as real as it gets."

She gave me the grin again. She didn't buy that, I could

tell. More manure. But she was playing along. Then she turned and trooped off with her dad in tow to help the cow.

"Thanks, Dog!" she hollered over her shoulder. "We'll talk in a week."

THAT WAS MY CHANCE. I had a pair of bolt cutters. I had a thousand bucks cash, which meant another fifty days on the road. The Dog was free again. But I stood there. I just stood there under the beady eyes of the barn swallows, a damaged Dog, mid-stream in a reckless, asinine, beautifully mixed up attempt to re-dissolve myself in waters. Upstream, I urged myself. Upstream.

And then I did move—only I moved deeper into the barn, my mind and my feet in trancelike disconnection, following Junior and her dad. The why is clear to me only now. The Dog was drawn to them, father and child, and to the idea of getting to the truth behind a drowning that could be the ruin of their little family. The Dog had his needs, his buried bones.

I found them in the rear of the barn. They had mustered to save the cow and her calf. The old man was uncoiling a dusty rope. Junior was running water into a five-gallon plastic bucket and dumping in what looked like iodine. Then she rolled up the sleeve of her robe and dipped her right arm in to the shoulder. The curled robe sleeve came out wet and stained. She saw me as she raised up, and she grinned.

"More help?" she said. "Don't tell me. Let me guess. Now my house is on fire."

She shook her arm dry and squeezed iodine water out of the sleeve. Her dead watch was hanging out now, flopping around. She cinched her robe sash into a square knot. "No? Then…my goats are in the road?"

I cleared my throat. "Why?" I asked. "Why did they lock me in the campground?"

"Oh," she shrugged, and she lifted the cow's tail. "That would be classic Bud." Casually, she inserted her arm into the cow's birth canal, working her way all the way in to the shoulder as she talked and I stared in city-boy horror. Sure, I had gutted fish. But Junior was wiggling her fingers halfway across the insides of a thousand-pound live animal.

"See," she said, "Jake Jacobs moved out here three years ago from Madison. He bought the old Krauthammer mansion on Depot Street. Fixed it up. Painted it, hell, I don't know, celery, mauve, and goose-shit, something like that. His wife, Ingrid, poor thing, she really suffered here at first. She couldn't get any decent coffee in town." Mel Senior broke into hacking laugh. "This other leg is folded," Junior grunted to him, changing her angle.

Blood had begun to seep from the cow's vagina and soak into the white robe, but Junior didn't seem concerned. The old man stepped forward and pushed a toe into the cow's abdomen, working it around until Junior said, "Got it. Anyway," she went on, pulling a second small hoof into view, "the coffee's been just fine with us Black Earthlings all these years—but what do we know, right? So Ingrid opens up a coffee shop right across from the Lunch Bucket, which has only been there about two hundred years. And Jake decides the creek needs protection. And we're all wondering...*protection from what?* You know what it turns out? Protection from us! The creek needs protection from us!"

Junior pulled her arm out. She stuck it back in the bucket. The water turned pink from blood.

"Funny thing is," she said, dropping about six feet of the rope into the bucket, "Ingrid and Jake, they were newcomers and all, but they were both right in what they brought to Black Earth. I mean, don't tell anybody, but those espressos Ingrid makes are great. They're worth about ten cups of that Lunch Bucket junk. When I take Dad in to the clinic on Wednesdays, I grab one of those every time."

She grinned at me, stirring the rope around. Now the water was mauve—dust and blood—afloat with animal hair. Mel Senior had gone to the nose of the cow to stroke her.

"And the truth is," Junior told me, "Jake was right, too. Between all the poaching that goes on around here, and the pollution, and the development, we're on a course to ruin the creek in no time. Daddy doesn't know it, but Jake sold me on that. He really did. About two years ago he formed this group, Friends of Black Earth Creek, and…"

She paused to instruct herself in whispers on the tying of a slip knot at the end of the wet rope. She seemed happy to get it on the first try.

"Anyway, my point was that Jake managed to hack a lot of us off in a very short period of time, most of all President Bud. Jake wanted the Lake Bud dam out. He said it was a hazard, and it was slowly destroying the stream. He filed an open-records request, and that's how we all found Jake was right about the safety hazard. We found out what we had been paying all these years to keep the dam maintained and insured."

She looped the knot around the cow's hooves and drove it back inside the cow until she caught hold of something. Then she tugged on the rope. "Okay, Daddy," she said. The old farmer took the rope end back around a post and pulled it tight. "Go slow," his daughter instructed him.

She watched her dad pull, walking around the post, until she seemed satisfied with the tension. "Okay, now, Darlene, sweetie, you push." She turned to me. She spoke as she rinsed her arm again. "Turns out Bud had been spending a hundred grand a year on insurance premiums alone, tucking it into the general liability budget. Because that's his land across there, opposite the campground. And he's trying to develop it as lakefront property. Pull Daddy. More. And Darl, honey, I know it hurts, but you gotta get busy."

The cow rolled her big brown eyes and shook.

"So Jake got White Milkerson, the retired DNR guy, to do a study on the effect of Lake Bud on the creek, and it was bad news. Then Jake filed a lawsuit—"

I was staring horrified at the cow, her bulging, bleeding organ, her sweat-foamed pelt and bulging eyes.

"Don't worry," Junior told me. "Darl always does this. She lies down so much on the hillside her calves always get turned around. Anyway, for a while we all wondered why President Bud wouldn't want the dam out. His land would only get larger. But Jake was one step ahead of him. With the dam gone, the water flows. That whole part of the valley would be creek again, and Jake had already gotten a setback written into county zoning laws. We're the only county in the state with a law like it: no new construction within fifteen hundred feet of the creek. So if it's creek again, all Bud's got himself is a bunch of muskrats, herons, and trout. And B.L.... I'll tell you right now, B.L.'s not going to—"

She stopped to check the tension on the rope. The calf's hind end appeared, its little tail twitching, its pink anus spilling black sludge. Junior didn't need to finish her explanation. Obviously, Bud Lite wouldn't be inclined to look beyond a frame-up in the case of Jacobs' death. But I asked Junior why the village president would want to set up her dad.

"Around here," she said, "land values have gone up three hundred percent in the last decade. Land around the stream has gone up five times. Last year Bud got all this land up here annexed into the village—over Daddy's dead body, practically. He and Bud used to be friends, but now they hate each other. And if Daddy goes bye-bye, that leaves only me on top of all this streamside real estate up in the coulee here. Then maybe Bud figures he can press me into selling."

With a grunt, she reinserted her arm. This time she fished around hard, forgetting me completely while I stood there in a sweat, aware that I was believing her. What was I thinking? Hadn't Melvin O'Malley threatened to cut off Jacobs' ponytail and stuff it in his mouth? Hadn't the old man been at home while Jacobs was on the stream and the rest of the village was at a meeting? Hadn't Junior nipped his fly off and swiped the ponytail? What the hell was I doing, standing there listening to her?

"Okay, Daddy," Junior said. "Heave ho." In my distress, I managed to notice she now had the second pair of hooves pointing out. "If you can stand to look," she told me, "this is pretty cool."

Then before I could turn away, the O'Malleys, Junior and Senior, hauled on that rope, threw their backs and haunches into it and reefed and yanked until the cow bawled mournfully and out on a slippery gout of blood and tissue rafted a baby boy calf, encased in mucous and struggling dumbly on the dirty barn floor.

We were all silent a long moment. The air smelled oddly, bloodily sweet, and Junior puffed it in and out. Her dad gasped raggedly. Then the old man kicked the iodine bucket over into the barn gutter and sat on it. The cow, Darlene, moaned and twitched and ran her long purple tongue in and out.

"Cheer up, sweetheart," Junior told her. "You got family."

Finally Mel Senior rose. He straddled the calf and hoisted it into his chest. He gave a grunt and one hard squeeze. A plug of greenish phlegm popped from the calf's mouth onto the floor. Immediately, the wet, awkward creature began to stagger around. A minute more and Darlene the cow struggled to her feet. The calf began to nurse.

I don't know how long I stood there before the old man backhanded me hard in the shoulder. I looked at him. He wore a loopy smile. He opened a grimy, round-shouldered refrigerator by the tool room door and got us all Pepsis. When we raised our cans together, the old farmer winked at me and said, "Here's to screwing in the pasture."

Junior slugged his arm. *"Daddy."*

"'Bout time you came back," the old man told me.

"Daddy! He is *not* Darrald."

Junior looked at me, flushed, her squinchy-nose grin a little forced. She was coated in blood, straw, mucous, and sweat. Her hand encircled the dead wristwatch that hung around her neck.

"Thank you," she told me then. "Now please go on. You wanted to leave and we're holding you up. After you've done so much for us."

Still I hesitated.

"Really," she said. "Don't worry. You've been a tremendous help. Everything is going to work out just fine. Right, Daddy? Everything is going to work out. It always does."

I took a couple of steps toward the barn door and stopped. She took another shot at the grin and got it right this time.

"Thanks. And you can keep those cutters. Maybe you'll need them again."

There followed a long and awkward pause. Then she dropped the watch, turned from me, and spread her arms. "Daddy, look at me," she laughed. "I'm going to have to take my shower all over again."

The way of the Dog

I didn't leave. I sat in my lawn chair, staring out at Lake Bud with the bolt cutters across my lap, and then I got drunk.

And by morning, I had decided.

Stay.

For a while. See how things turn out.

I snagged Jake Jacobs' ponytail out of the cattails in Lake Bud and locked it in my little safe box with my Glock pistol and Junior's money. I put the safe box under the sink. Then, apropos of further introspection, the Dog went fishing.

IT WAS STILL HALF-DARK and chilly when I slipped into my waders, tied on a big deer-hair cricket, and stepped into the creek at the first County K bridge, just up from the campground. Here the stream swung in a wide meander through the upper Sundvig pasture, then back beneath a second bridge into Junior's turf. I took a long look at it and felt myself relax a little. The big western rivers tended to frazzle me with their noise and thrust, and the eastern brook trout water tended to

give up its tiny fish too easily. But the stretch of Midwestern
spring creek ahead of me—sparkling runs and deep pools,
tight corners under box elders, meadow runs flanked in purple
asters and green hillside pastures—I took a long, slow breath
of it. Then I bore down and fished hard, one cast in fifty
picking a good-sized brown off the cut-back bank. I released
each fish, dried my cricket, and went after the next. I got in a
rhythm. Cast, step, cast…fish…look up…look around…and
plunge back in. I fired up one of my so-called cigars and
hard-wired that rhythm into every muscle I had. I took that
stream apart.

There it was: the way of the Dog. In two-plus years I had
done this to a hundred streams. I rolled in and set up camp in
the Cruise Master, then fished a stream stem to stern and to the
brink of exhaustion, day after day, until the place became
familiar, until I could tell myself I had cracked it like a nut.
Then the trick was to leave fast, because I knew next I would
begin to drift back into myself, talk to myself, or I would meet
someone, begin to talk to them—and I knew the noise of human
interaction as the noise of death. But there I was, *staying*.

Backsliding, I worried. Caretaking. I knew it all derived
from being a good boy too long. I was nearly forty-three
years old. For forty of those years, I had tried to please.
Loyalty, hard work, sacrifice…the Dog was not to be outdone.
I got good grades, went to tech college in small business man-
agement, and built a modest career in corporate security, in
the protection of things. I married a modest wife. I remodeled
a home and grew a lawn. When I became a father, I pulled the
sled, I growled at the bad guys, I peed at the corners of my
turf, and I walked around the house, three times, every night,
before falling into my shallow, one-eyed sleep. When my son
was only two, I was dutifully looking ahead. I was already

challenging for pack position in the PTA, the Boy Scouts, and the neighborhood soccer club. I woofed and groveled and snarled and nipped and thought I was happy. Everything— *everything*—mattered.

Then everything came apart. One day, suddenly, *nothing* mattered. Nothing was ever together in the first place, except in my own mind. And after that day, in the short space of three years, I lost family, house, savings, friendships, job. I howled at the moon for a couple years. I roamed around. I tried to join new packs. But hell, at my nadir (I took a security position at a paint factory), I was still trying to protect things. I was trying to protect paint.

That's when the Dog went feral. Or so I told myself. If I cashed in my meager insurance holdings, I had sixteen thousand bucks left to my name. I picked up the Cruise Master for four grand. It needed a ring job and tires. I bought a pistol, a fly rod, and a cell phone. Then I saw my old tax guy, Harvey Digman, and I gave him the ten grand I had left. I told him I couldn't trust myself to carry it. I told him I wanted three years at a hundred bucks a week. I told him I'd call and tell him where to send the money. I told him when it was over, it was over.

Harvey wagged his spotted old head. "Okay, Dog. What is it? You're going out to soak some worms?"

"I'm going fly fishing."

"What fishing?"

"Fly fishing. You float imitations of insects on the water. You catch trout."

"Dog—you can get trout at the market."

"Harvey, please. Can you set it up for me?"

He sighed. "Where are you going?"

"Wherever. Until the money runs out."

"I'm worried about you," he said.

"Thank you," I answered.

Harvey set his black plastic half-glasses atop his nose and looked again at the sum I'd handed him, at the title to the Cruise Master, at the scrap of paper with my cell phone number. But I don't imagine he had ever seen a more desperate set of numbers.

But good old Harvey, he smiled and cleared his mossy throat. I had seen that smile and heard that sound a thousand times. He had coached my father into solvency through the fifties and kept him afloat in the seventies. He had steered me through funeral expenses, divorce, bankruptcy. Now, boldly, hopelessly, I was asking him to be my lifeline.

Harvey shrugged. He stacked some papers.

"I'll take care of it, Dog," he said, rising to shake my hand. "Good luck."

AND IF LUCK MEANT catching fish, I guess I'd had some. I'd been back and forth between the coasts twice, fished every one of the Hundred Best Trout Streams in a book I had bought in Boston. I was headed back on a third zig-zag, fishing favorites, trying "second tier" streams that hadn't made the book but in truth were a good deal more satisfying than most that had. I had weathered a bit in the process. I didn't know it really, as I hadn't looked in mirrors much, but my face was lined and tan, my hair was a brown thicket held down by a scrap of bandana and a bent straw hat, and I had burned forty pounds of suburban tallow off my six-foot frame. Somewhere in my haze I knew I was running out of time and streams. My three years was nearly over. I would have to do something, get into something, soon. But if I could keep my feet moving, my fly on the water, and vodka in my old tin cup, I didn't have to think about *it* much.

That morning, though, felt different. I was staying. Death. *Drowning* death. But I was staying, and my mind kept wandering, back to the scene with Junior and her Dad in the barn. What was Junior going to do if and when they came for her dad?

THAT'S WHERE I WAS when I saw something moving in the creek about a hundred yards up. I kept a small pair of field glasses in my vest, and I raised them to my face. I struggled for a long moment before I centered on something large and whitish, bobbing up and down in the center of a big pool.

My heart snagged. The object was pale and round and twitching…just the size of a human head…bobbing through an eddy and out of view behind a dark knot of nettles and woodland sunflowers.

By the time I found the object it had moved up into the next hole, and my first look at it took away what breath I had left. It was exactly the size of a human head, and it twitched and thrashed just below the surface in a bend of the stream, bashing with a hollow rattle against the limestone boulders that bulwarked the corner. Reluctantly, I came closer. When I made out the object to be nothing more than a plastic milk jug, I relaxed—but only slightly. It was still a creepy and disarming sight. I couldn't make sense of it. Why was it moving as if alive?

I put my rod in my teeth. I waded in and grabbed the jug, tugged on the line tied to its handle. The jug tugged back mightily. I heaved. Up—rolling and tail-whipping—came a giant brown trout. I mean shockingly big. I mean a fish that was close to thirty inches long—all out of the proportion to the setting—a record-type trout like you see coming out of a tailwater in Arkansas, or cruising around with the muskellunge in an aquarium. Too *big*.

I stared in astonishment. The fish was hooked deep behind the tongue by a large bait hook. To prevent the trout from sawing its way to freedom, the poacher had used a leader of at least 50-pound test. But somehow the trout had snapped a different line—the line connecting the jug to its anchor line—and the jug trailed about ten yards of what looked like deep-sea braided nylon.

No sooner had I put all this together than the brown put on a burst, tore the line from my hand, and took off powerfully downstream, dragging the jug.

I waded sloppily after, out of breath, staggering over the stream bottom and feeling strangely frantic. Maybe every fisherman understands this. Maybe it's just me. But forget Jake Jacobs for a minute. Forget who killed him. Forget Bud and Bud Lite, and Junior and her dad. I *had* to catch that fish.

I chased the jug. The fish felt me coming and streaked away. I stumbled through a limestone riffle, caught the jug again, but the fish tugged me off balance and I had to let go or fill my waders in the next big hole. So I circled, came upstream at it—but the trout streaked past, dragging the jug just beyond my reach into a wide, flat, sticky-bottomed stretch that sucked my boots and slowed me to a Frankenstein stagger. On and on we went, downstream, upstream, then downstream again and nearly back to the campground before the fish conceded and held in a deep hole beneath the first County K bridge. I got hold of the jug again, waded to the muddy bank, and sat down among the coon prints, gasping for air.

It was just dawn. The mud smelled cold. Swallows dipped in and out of the dark hole beneath the bridge. Slowly, I drew the giant trout toward me. She rolled up sideways, a blunt-nosed female, gulping water through her gills. I cut her free. But she was exhausted, unable to stay righted in the shallows between my boots. She was breathing mud, so I pushed her back out, but she floated up sideways and began to drift with the current. I waded in to the rim of my waders and grabbed her tail. I put my other hand under her belly to steady her and began to work her back and forth, forcing water through her gills. She was coming around, I thought. I gasped as the stream slopped in over my wader tops. I was in too deep. But maybe she was coming around. Maybe I could save her.

Then the bridge rumbled above my head. Brakes hissed. A door slammed. I kept working the fish, at the same time trying to back out of the hole. But the mud was slick and I couldn't find the incline I had come in on. Somehow every baby-step seemed to take me another millimeter deeper, until I could feel that my boots had filled up to the ankles. Now my feet felt heavy, and just as totally as I had once pursued the giant fish, I now strained desperately for just a finger's height more elevation. When the fish tugged me back toward the hole, I let her go. I heard boots crunch on gravel above. People die like this, I realized suddenly. *People die like this.*

Something touched me on the head—landed roughly and scratched across my skull. Skidding and slipping, I looked up. It was a tree branch, dry and flaky with old bark, jerking about just above my face, and at its other end, over the bridge rail, extended a hairy wrist. My panic doubled. One more little jab and I was under. Whoever he was, he could finish me.

People die like this!

"Well, go on," said a twangy voice. "Grab it."

I raised an arm and felt my opposite shoulder dip to let in about twenty more pounds of cold water. I flailed my hand above my head and I swear the guy up there was playing with me. Everywhere I reached for the branch it was gone. Finally it clubbed me in the side of the head.

"Shit," I cursed.

"Don't you shit me," twanged the voice. "I'm trying to haul your ass out of there."

I grabbed the branch. My feet left the bottom and I spun into the hole.

"Both hands," he said impatiently, like I was some kind of fool. Leaning over the bridge now, exerting himself, my savior towed me until I could stand in hip-deep water. I staggered water-stuffed to the bank and collapsed like a leaky, shivering sausage.

A moment later the man with the stick appeared under the bridge. He was a feisty-looking character, no more than five-six, wearing tight denim jeans, a Harley-Davidson T-shirt, and a clean yellow cap that said Black Earth Dairy. He had a neat black beard with no moustache, Abe Lincoln-style.

I sputtered, "Thanks."

No answer. He didn't even look at me. He stepped around me, reached out with the branch and hooked in the giant trout. The fish wallowed helplessly into his grasp.

"I think…" I puffed, "I think she'll make it. She needs help breathing. Pump her gills a little, she'll make it."

Again no answer. But now with the trout by the gills he was looking at me. A miniature Abe Lincoln with a very ugly smirk. He reached into his back pocket and snapped out a long Bowie knife. The blade flashed in the shaft of sunrise that had pried its way under the bridge.

"You can't do that," I told him. "This part of the stream is no-kill."

But the knife was already through slick green skin behind the trout's eyes. Mini-Abe drove the blade deep and with a faint crunch the fish flapped hard twice, quivered, and was still. With astonishing speed he spilled her voluminous, eggy guts out across the mud. He flushed out the body cavity with stream water, thumbed clear the mud line, rinsed the knife, and stood.

"Say what?" he asked me then.

"You can't kill fish here. It's against the regulations."

Very deliberately, he dried the knife on the thigh of his tight jeans. He was chewing tobacco, and he worked his quid, then spit tidily onto the mud. His mouth dry now, he blew moisture from the crevices of the knife, and I imagined the long blade slicing through Jake Jacobs' ponytail. Clean. Easy. Fast.

He snicked the knife shut and slid it into his back pocket. He squinted at me, up and down.

"No-kill, my ass." He spat again. "You're probably going to go home and have a goddamn steak."

"I—"

"I live here," he said. "Save the sermon. I grew up here. My daddy and my granddaddy grew up here. We been fishing this creek a hundred years."

"If you call that fishing," I said.

He looked me over. I was rigged to be out all day: waders, vest, water bottle, a dozen fly boxes, hemostats, nippers, leaders and tippet spools, fly gink, net, the whole deal.

"Hell yes, I call this fishing," he retorted.

The man's tight and twangy voice made me think of a settler—some half-starved homesteader confronting a stranger from his porch, rock salt jammed down into his musket. But this man seemed as much like a mall shopper and an internet surfer, neat to a fault, cocksure and preening. He had just poached a trout, and his T-shirt was still tucked in. With a hooked finger he cleared the snuff from his lower lip. He reloaded from a tin of Copenhagen. "Fella just like you, name of Jacobs, got dunked in here just the other day," he told me around the fresh bump in his lip. "Out fishing the sally." He grabbed the big trout under the gills. It was half as long as he was.

"This Jacobs fella had a problem with the way things work around here. Kinda stepped in too deep, if you know what I mean."

I didn't say anything.

"Farmer up the road here, O'Malley, is getting all the credit in the bars," he said. He gave a little smile. "Folks are drinking shots to the man. Gives you a sense, don't it?"

"A sense of what?" I said.

"A sense of what you can do with your rules."

He looked me over real good then: once more, up and down the necessary accoutrements of a fly fisherman. "Where you carry fish?" he wanted to know.

"I don't."

"That's what I thought," he said with a smirk. Then: "So you're helping Junior, like I heard?" He spat brown juice into the mud. "Elmer Sundvig seen you up at Junior's barn last night, coming out of there with bolt cutters. Then you didn't leave."

I didn't respond. But he thought he had his answer. "Well then I'll tell you what," he said, spitting again. "Mel O'Malley is going to prison. Junior, too, if she don't stop fiddlin. No pansy-ass fly fisherman is going to help that."

With that, he disappeared up through the riprap to the road. I stepped back far enough to see a long silver milk truck pull away across the bridge.

Something caught my eye then. The trout's guts gleamed among the coon prints, and through the white viscera of the stomach something bulged oddly. I thought it was a large snail. That was the shape of it. But it distended the stomach tissue in a strange way, and through the translucent flesh I made out a metallic sheen.

Mosquitoes pestered my hands as I pulled the stomach free from the eggs and other tissues. I felt the object—hard, round, with a smooth, raised center.

With my hemostats, I chewed open the wet, pearly stomach tissue. I rinsed insect shucks and half-digested crayfish parts from the object and held it squarely in the sun.

No pansy-ass fly fisherman is going to help that, the poacher had said.

What I had found, in big trout's stomach, was a large and gaudy woman's earring.

Things might not work out

I leaned my rod outside the doorway of O'Malley's ancient rock barn. The radio was on. Junior was inside. She was milking.

I watched her a while before she saw me. I had not understood correctly how a person milked these days. Like a good city Dog, reading bedtime books to my little boy, I had cultivated a Rockwellian scene that included a three-legged stool and a pail, complete with a brawny, teat-squeezing farmer and a circle of mewling kittens.

But this was different. Somewhere a pump hissed and clanked and shuddered its pneumatic suction along a network of pipes that bungled through the web-clogged ceiling beams. The cows were stalled-up and stamping, restless. Junior moved through this with a darting, efficient energy, knowing just where to duck and step through the cluttered space. She worked an alternating pair of udder clamps that fastened mad-scientist-style to the teats and sucked powerfully. Over all this racket and motion the radio blared—not the weather report, not hog prices, but heavy metal. Zeppelin. And Junior sang along badly.

Been a long time since I rock and rolled...

"Oh. Hi."

You couldn't startle her, apparently. Or embarrass her. She raised up and gave me the squinchy-nosed grin. She was dressed exactly the same as she had been the day before: boots, jeans, T-shirt with the sports bra showing through, John Deere cap with her stiff strawberry hair stuck out the back. The dead watch hung around her neck.

"See?" she said to the cow beside her. "I told you he wasn't done here. Didn't I tell you?" She nudged the cow with her knee. "Didn't I tell you? Huh? Huh?" She gave it a playful swat on the nose. "Everything happens for a reason. But you're a pessimist, Frieda. That's what you are. Always mooning around, thinking the worst. Poor Frieda."

Junior stepped through a stanchion toward me. She turned down the radio.

"Frieda's smart, but she's got this hang-dog attitude." She looked me over. I was wet and a little shaky.

"You okay?"

I said I was.

"Good," she said, "because last night, when Daddy and I were saying bedtime prayers, I saw you doing something even better than taking that ponytail away from here. I saw you coming back one more time. For your own sake," she said, "more than me and Daddy's." She dug a chapped hand into her jeans pocket. She held out a pinkish stone. "I'm giving this to you. It's a rose crystal. Wherever you park that RV next, put the rose crystal in the window to the east. It'll break up the sunlight into streams of energy. It'll kind of loosen things up for you a little."

I just stared at her. The milk pump chugged away. "And the next time you stop at a drugstore," she added, "get some multi-vitamins. Big as your finger if you can find them. Screw the directions and take three a day."

I cleared my throat. I was feeling something shift inside. Words came up like sharp bones.

"Thanks," I managed. "But listen. I thought I'd tell you. Last night, when you said things were going to work out fine for you and your dad?"

She waited eagerly. "Yeah?"

"Well...they might not."

"But they might," she countered.

"I guess I wouldn't count on it."

She tipped her head a bit. "You know," she said, "I've been meaning to ask a fly fisherman. Does it just feel good? You know, to touch the flies? To tie the knots? To hold the rod? To walk in the water? It seems like it would just feel good."

"I like it pretty good," I said. "But listen. I just met a guy on the stream. Milk truck driver. From what I gathered, he thinks your dad killed Jake Jacobs. From what I gathered, it seems like everybody thinks that."

"Well, there you go," responded Junior. "That's just too perfect, isn't it? Whoever set up Daddy had it worked out just right."

She stepped past me, uncapped a liter of Pepsi she had set on the dirty floor, and took a big, thirsty swig. She moved one milking appendage to the next cow. The pipes hissed and sucked. She came back to me.

"You gave me a thousand bucks," I said, "to tamper with evidence. That doesn't look right."

"I've been told a hundred times that nothing about me looks right." She grinned at me. "So I gave up trying to look right a while ago."

"You oughta just—"

"What? Tell B.L.? Or the sheriff? I told you. Those boys are nothing but a bunch of suck-asses. I can't trust them."

"But you trust me."

Junior shrugged. "Last night, I couldn't really sleep. So I took a little walk. I went up that hill there." She pointed toward the cobwebby window to the east, hung across with hanks of old rope and tack and so clogged with dust and straw and cow hair that even the sunrise could hardly penetrate. But I knew the hill she meant. There was a mowed hayfield, interrupted by rock outcrops, then steepening into sumac and shrubby evergreens before finishing with a crown of hickories.

"And you know what I saw?"

I did not.

"Stars," she said. I chewed my lip and waited uneasily for the significance. "I saw every star in the whole dang sky," she said. "And do you know what I thought?" She blew at a fly that was pestering her lips. "I thought, you know, anything is possible. *Anything!* And yet here we are. I happen to be near the stream when you find Jake. You happen to be a guy with some guts. Gareth Kaltenburg happens to be not full of shit for a change and actually does give me a thousand bucks for my bull. All these things happen despite all the possibilities, the supposedly random whatever that puts the odds against them, and so I figure, why can't things keep going my way?"

I looked at my feet and said, "Yeah, well, I tossed that ponytail in the lake."

She was silent a while. She leapfrogged the second milker to the next cow.

"And then I fished it back out," I said.

I felt the earring again. I had studied it on the walk up to Junior's. It was the kind women didn't wear anymore—a petaled cup of faux-gold with a button of pearly white plastic in the middle and a painful-looking clamp on the back. It was badly tarnished. It was a lot older than the fish itself. But it couldn't have been inside the trout for long without killing it. It didn't make sense. And anyway, how had a fish eaten an earring? I plunged forward.

"And then…I wondered… maybe I could stick around a day or two," I said, "look around a little bit."

When I glanced up, she was beaming. "That'd be great."

"I mean… I'm not a cop or anything. I've got a few skills, I guess, but I…well, I'm basically just a fisherman, who…"

"Who believes me," Junior finished. "Hot damn."

Jesus—what the hell was I doing? Why, Dog, why?

"I don't know," I told her. "Don't expect… I mean, probably…your dad may have actually done…and this guy I met…so…things might not work out…"

Junior stepped through a stanchion and popped me with a flat hand, hard in the chest, like we were a couple of football players celebrating a touchdown. "Don't you see?" Her grin looked a little wild. "Like heck things might not work out," she said. "Don't you see?"

The Dog did not see. Junior popped me again. "Don't you see?" She grabbed my shoulders.

"Everything happens for a reason," she said. "Which means things work out! They always do!"

All possibilities remained open

I was a hundred yards up the road when she put her fingers in her teeth and whistled like a drill sergeant.

"Hey!"

I turned. I had a view of the whole O'Malley farm in dawn light. The house appeared to be sinking like an old ship into waves of shaggy lawn. Out front was a statue of the Virgin Mary, enshrined beneath the top of a bathtub buried in the grass. A couple of giant woodpiles flanked the run-around porch. A tool shed between the house and old stone barn was decorated with the dried tails of a dozen unfortunate beavers, nailed to the siding.

"Hey, Trout Guy!" Junior hollered at me. "Breakfast's at seven! Bacon and eggs!"

I waved uneasily and walked on. Trout Guy. What the hell was I doing?

I lurched up the road—waders, vest, hat, rod, lighting one of my so-called cigars—groping for a version of my ugly attitude. Understand that when you grow up in a large and famous city on the East Coast you are trained to dismiss the entire rest of the country as secondary, and the Midwest as particularly retarded, both socially and geographically. So for a few strides I tried out the idea that the Dog was simply doing business. I knew a little about investigation. Twenty years' worth of employee theft, plus the odd assault in a warehouse and a little corporate espionage—my career had to be worth something. How hard could it be? I would clear up the death of Jake Jacobs, earn my thousand bucks, and blow little Black Earth, Wisconsin—all by nightfall.

So picture the Dog, chugging along in wet waders, talking shop to himself, waving cheap tobacco. I can tell you now that the air smelled of mowed hay, and meadowlarks trilled from the fenceposts. Oak, hickory, birch, sumac—all these were in full mid-summer leaf. Chicory starred the roadside, and the road humped and cracked every two hundred feet where a culvert let under a chuckling rivulet of spring water. But the Dog didn't catch a bit of it. Not then. The Dog was seeing an earring in a trout's guts. The Dog was seeing a dead man's severed ponytail, a dead man's yellow sally floating off downstream. The Dog was seeing a campground gate swing shut. The Dog was hearing Junior: everything happened for a reason.

I stopped. *Everything happened for a reason…so therefore things always worked out?* That's what I was doing business with—I realized—that idea. Junior's idea. I realized I wanted to believe her. I realized I needed to believe her. But I had to wonder: *how?*

IN A FEW MINUTES MORE I was under the second bridge, breathing the cold and earthy air, looking for stoneflies in the spider webs. I was forming theories. Start with the basics.

So if Junior was right—taking that theory first—then the

killer had set things up to look like Jake Jacobs was fishing a hatch of the yellow sally stonefly—a big stonefly, easily identified, easily caught by streamside spiders. But hatches were unpredictable. I'd been downstream on Black Earth Creek for two days and hadn't hit the hatch. I hadn't seen a single yellow sally stonefly. Who knew exactly why? Insects hatched on spring creeks according to a complex alignment of factors that fly fishermen only pretended to understand. What if there had been no sally hatch on the stretch of the creek where Jacobs died? What if the substrate, the light, the water temperature—what if conditions weren't quite lined up? What if the yellow sally nymphs were still in the mud at the bottom of the creek, waiting? Then just like that, Junior would be right. The yellow sally on Jacobs' line would have been a fraud. The plot—someone's plot—would be exposed. The spider webs would tell me.

I crawled through the mud and coon prints, looking for an intact web in the undergirding of the bridge. The swallows had tattered most of them. When I found one at last, I shined my little flashlight through the silky spans. Yellow sallies. Dozens of them. Dried, fresh, more than an army of spiders could eat. The web was heavy, twisted up with yellow sallies.

I crawled back out and stood in the sun. So there had been a hatch up this far on the creek. A big hatch. Last night, the night before, and maybe the night beyond.

Then all possibilities remained open. Junior's dad could have dunked Jacobs during an actual sally hatch. Or a killer could have nailed him earlier and set the scene. As I walked upstream toward the corner where I had found the body, I began to wonder: how could someone drown a healthy grown man in three feet of water? What kind of man was Jacobs? Was he easy?

I felt the firmness of my own legs in the limestone rubble of the creek bottom. What would it take to drown the Dog?

That question stopped me. I didn't know why. But it moved me.

What would it take to drown the Dog?

I put on a searching fly—a cricket again—so I could keep my head up and fish the banks, and I began to move slowly upstream toward the place where Jacobs had died. What would he have walked through? Black mud, limestone rubble, coontail reefs, asters and sunflowers and nettles on the banks. What would he have seen, I asked myself. The view was clear here. Beyond the flowered banks, there was pasture on either side. Corn on the distant east, a half-cut hayfield on the distant west. Hardly enough cover for a man to hide in—certainly not a man of the magnitude of a Melvin O'Malley or a Bud Bjorgstad. These were both huge and awkward men who, if they had dunked Jacobs, had not used stealth to do it.

Fishing absently, I hooked a nice brown, about fourteen inches and fat, and I wondered if Jacobs could have been taken by surprise while fighting a fish. After tens of thousands of trout, each one still stopped time for me, as if the creature's dancing weight unrooted my whole consciousness and washed it in the stream. Was Jacobs the same? Maybe—yet it still seemed unlikely he could have been ambushed. But what about in the heat of a major stonefly hatch? Didn't all but the fishing senses shut down? It could get wild. Some nights the insects came up thick as a snowstorm. The birds went crazy. The bats came out early. The trout got real choosy, and a fisherman could go through a thrilling kind of hell. All over the country, I'd seen guys staggering back toward their cars after a heavy hatch, looking dazed and beat up, as if they weren't quite sure what had just happened to them.

Then suddenly, by projection, I had an image of Jake Jacobs out on the stream the night before last. What if he had *planned* to be at the Village Board meeting? But then the sally hatch had come on early, and strong. He would have been able to feel it coming on. The nymphs would have begun to move in the water, and Jacobs would have seen trout tails as the fish backed up to snatch the nymphs on their way to the surface. Birds— towhees, red-winged blackbirds, thrushes—would have lined up in the trees, waiting. So there was Jacobs, I imagined, telling himself, *I'll just catch one trout. Then I'll quit and go to the meeting. Just one.* Meanwhile—he couldn't quite get that one fish—and before he knew it, the sallies had popped and swarmed. Birds and bats knifed through the air. The water boiled with trout, but not one of them would so much as swirl at his fly. *Just one damn fish! Come on!* And he became stuck. He entered a mental quicksand where time stopped and focus narrowed and the casts piled up by the dozens, by the hundreds, by the thousands…awareness of the outside world shrank to a primal race with darkness, and nothing, not even the approach of his own killer, could heave Jake Jacobs up from the mud of his obsession. *Just one fish!* And meanwhile the Village Board meeting was gaveled into order…

Feeling cold, I hauled myself onto the bank and into the new sun. I walked a while, smoking another little Swisher and taking in the bigger picture. Yes—striding along above quiet water, you could hear a car on the highway at least a mile down the coulee. You could even hear Junior's cows, across the road, jockeying for trail space as they ambled from the barn toward the pasture. Jacobs would have known if anyone had parked at the road and approached him. If he was any kind of fisherman, few sounds would have caught his attention like the slam of a car door, like the approach of another fisherman.

I ducked the yellow tape and walked in a circle around the crime scene. Yesterday, I had watched B.L. order his officer to do the same thing, but the kid had proceeded with one hand on his pants, keeping the cuffs out of the mud, and the other hand above his brow because it was early evening and the sun was gunning right up the coulee. I thought I might do a better job.

But I couldn't find much. I covered the immediate pasture. Then I rooted around in suckholes and marshy spots where springs bubbled up to join the creek. Nothing but the usual oddities—a thirty-year-old Schlitz beer can, five hundred feet from the road; the muddy lid of a washing machine, sheltering crayfish and sculpins in at the mouth of a feeder creek. Jacobs' killer had left nothing behind.

I was about to move on upstream when I saw a snapping turtle the size of a steering wheel. He had lifted his leathery snout out of a slip of coontail weed and he was eying me. Then he sank back down and I watched him burrow into the weed, mud puffing behind him. I thought nothing of this until a second, smaller snapper emerged ahead of him, driven out. Then the first turtle came back up with a bloated trout in his jaws. The trout was a small brown, pale and puffed in death, its tail gone and half its guts chewed out. When I stepped toward the creek, a third snapper startled me, slipping into the water ahead of my foot with a surly backward stare. At my feet, lodged in the mud, was a second little trout, nearly chewed up to the head.

I stepped in, shoved my net around the coontail. A third little trout rose belly first and drifted along in a puff of mud. The smaller, vanquished snapper paddled cross-current and took it down.

A meaningless distraction, I told myself. I walked upstream a quarter mile until I hit barbed wire fences on either side. Grasping, I studied the barbs, a hundred yards east and west, finding nothing but cow hair. On a post at the fisherman's ladder, a sign reading RESPECT LANDOWNER'S RIGHTS hung upside down, its top nail missing. That was it. Dead trout. Hungry turtles. Cow hair. A broken sign.

Nothing, I thought—and in my dissatisfaction, the Dog did a most unusual thing. The Dog sat down to think.

The guy who got him killed

I eased myself down on a bank of head-high nettles and asters and waited for despair to sweep in.

By necessity and habit, I never stopped moving in daylight. I never sat down and let my mind off the tether of movement until after dusk, when I collapsed into my lawn chair under the night sky with a sandwich in one hand, a vodka-Tang in the other, my feet sore, my ears still full with stream sounds, my bunk only steps away.

In thirty-three months on the road, I had reached this point close to a thousand times. Half the time I slept in the lawn chair itself, waking up in the small hours to stumble dew-soaked and mosquito bitten into the warmth of the Cruise Master. I never just sat down and let the thoughts come. Never.

But my last few hours in Black Earth had nudged things way off-base. It was just after six in the morning, and I was in streamside repose. Not comfortable, mind you—but nevertheless I was not hitching and thrashing along upstream, *covering a lot of ground,* as Junior had put it. Here, in Black

Earth, a man had drowned, and there was a reason. Someone had drowned him. Someone was at fault. I could solve it. I felt oddly relaxed. I felt weirdly and momentarily content. The Dog was still—but the Dog was moving.

I stretched back and worked a hand down inside my waders into my hip pocket. That earring was a puzzle. I tried to remember the last time I had seen one like it. My own mother, perhaps. Thirty years ago. Sometime around when I was in high school outside Boston, girls had started piercing their ear lobes, and about that time it seemed to me that older women, clearly outdone, had dropped the whole idea of clipping gewgaws the size of tea saucers to their ears. But maybe I was wrong. I didn't notice things like that too well—or so I'd been told, back when I had a wife around to point out the things I failed to see.

But the bigger puzzle was how, and when, and why the trout had swallowed the earring. Try as I did, I could make no headway on that, other than to suppose that the earring had somehow been in motion and therefore had looked and felt like food, long enough to get past the sphincter in the back of the huge trout's mouth. But when had this happened? And where? And so what?

I was mulling this over unsuccessfully, fighting the urge to sweep it away by *covering some ground,* when I heard the liquid trill of a meadowlark. I couldn't find the bird. But I sat up, wanting to see it, and gradually the bird came closer, singing with startling volume. Then abruptly the song changed. Out of the same direction came the unmistakable gurgle of an Eastern bluebird. That kept up for a few minutes. Then the bird called again in the voice of an oriole—then I heard a curse and a heavy splash—a two-hundred-pound oriole?—followed by, "Well suck my nuts…"

A flask went floating by—a battered silver thing, hinged open—sinking.

"Say, grab that, will you? And have a snort if you like."

I lurched up in the asters and got my net under the flask, which was spewing amber fluid into the coontail weed. I righted the flask and capped it, smelling whiskey.

"Appreciate it," called a voice.

Down the center of the current about ten yards upstream waded a stocky old fellow who looked more creek than man, like a piece of the bank that had broken free and was moving to a new location.

"Handy with a net, I see. Good man."

He sloshed over. He was decked out in scabby hip waders and several layers of frayed, multi-pocketed shirts that were soiled to a crusty, burr-stuck brown. He wore a sweat-stained blue bandana around his neck and a floppy leather hat tipped back on his head. As for his face—that was a squint inside a sunburn around a cigarette, with a long and sloppy moustache draped over.

Now *here*, I told myself, was a trout hound.

But he had no rod. He had no vest full of gear. Instead he was draped with a clanking array of thermometers, dip nets, waterproof tubes, a pen on a string. On his back was a kind of hard-plastic backpack, muddy yellow, with knobs and dials, a pull cord like a lawn mower, and a long, wand-like instrument clipped to the side.

"Tagging fish," he grunted as an explanation. "Doing a study. Go ahead. Knock yourself out."

I pulled whisky thinned by stream water and tossed the flask back. He caught it—"Gotcha!"—and partook himself.

"Goddamn fumbled," he explained, tucking the flask back into a shirt pocket. He eyed me through his squint. "You're the guy who found Jake."

I nodded.

"Well," he said, "I'm the guy who got him killed."

He waded over beside me. "Yeahhh," he sighed, and he didn't look first as he sat down heavily on the bank. He just sort of slopped back on one elbow against mud and stinging nettles as if the whole bank were an old porch sofa. His legs stayed in the water. The current lapped at his knees. "Yeah," he sighed again. "Poor Jake. I might as well have painted a target on his back."

He put his hand out. "Manfred Milkerson, retired Regional Fish Biologist, Department of Natural Resources. I just go by White. Jake used my studies to piss a lot of people off."

I nodded. White Milkerson was a trail-worn, chain-smoking, hard-drinking sixty-five or so. The Dog, I guessed, in another twenty years.

"Yeah," he went on, "we've seen the trout numbers go down on this creek over the last decade. Native brookies are just about gone. Jake, well, if you knew the kind of guy he was, he thought he could stop it. He thought he could make people change. Young guy, you know. Full of hope."

He shifted in the nettles and uncapped his flask again. The sun had just cleared the bluff behind Junior's farm and shone down strongly on us. The hard-plastic pack on White Milkerson's back propped him up just right. He stuck the flask under his dirty moustache and tilted his head.

"So he took your studies?" I prompted clumsily. "And fish counts are down…"

He wiped his mouth. "Poachers."

I nodded. "I met the guy who drives the milk truck."

"Bostock," Milkerson said. "Lumen Bostock. A real red-ass, that one. Catching him in the act was like nailing Jell-O to a tree, but Jake finally did it."

He paused to see if I was interested. I gave him a nod.

"Jake caught Bostock raising a jug line about a month ago. Got him busted by the DNR for a five hundred dollar fine. I don't expect Lumen ever paid it, though."

I pretended to think over my next question. It was question built on what stuck with me: *what did it take to drown in shallow water?* "Would Lumen Bostock kill somebody?"

Milkerson fluffed his moustache with a snort. "Hell, yes, Lumen would kill somebody. His own dad killed his own mom. Burnt the house down on her. One of his brothers is up at Oxford for shooting a game warden out in Green County. The whole brood of those Bostocks is mean as weasels."

"You think he killed Jake Jacobs?"

White Milkerson shook his floppy hat as he passed me the flask. "Who knows? Jake got himself hated by everybody. The poachers, the president of the village, the farmers, the developers. Jake loved this creek. He went after everybody he thought was hurting it. Hell, though, if I'd known he would die over it, I'd have queered the data. I'd have made the stream look better, helped Jake relax a little."

He shifted on the bank, twisting the tank-like pack on his back so he could face me with his sunburned squint. For a moment I imagined his eyes were searching me, making a cold analysis of my response to queered data. But I couldn't really see his eyes. And after a moment he chuckled uneasily.

"Data doesn't matter anyway," he told me finally. "My studies don't matter in the big picture." He was gazing up into the rapidly thinning blue sky. "Every acre of new asphalt takes a million gallons out of the aquifer. Every pretty green yard adds in a thousand pounds of poison. The construction of one road shifts fifty thousand tons of sediment into the watershed. Meanwhile, global warming is going to heat the groundwater eventually. But all that's moot anyway. Another decade or two, this valley is gonna be in condominiums. This stream will hold carp. Jake wasn't going to stop it. Not with a few puny facts and figures from an old nut like me."

He blew out his moustache and whistled expertly back at a towhee in the box elder across the stream. *Drink-your-tea...drink-your-tea!* He took another nip. After a minute he sighed and said, "But Jake didn't buy that..."

Reflexively, I made a floundering attempt to agree with Jacobs. Humankind wasn't hopeless, I maintained—which of course was a bizarre position for the Dog to assume. And White Milkerson just puffed his moustache and shook his head. His old leather hat flopped. He laughed at me, but not unkindly.

"You belong to one of those groups, I'll bet. Trout Unlimited. They do some good work. But they're pissing into the wind. Limits are what nature is all about. Nature is one big and ever-shifting mess of boundaries. We humans are going to push ourselves right to the edge of collapse. See this?"

He held his flask out on its side. He dripped stream water on it and flicked off all but one drop. The boundaries of the drop held, but I saw them shrink as he turned the flask to the sun, which was low but already hot. The shrinkage was inexorable. In a minute the drop was gone.

"Trout water," he said.

Then as unceremoniously as he had joined me on the bank, he stood, shedding mud and crushed nettle leaves. He hitched his pack off his shoulders to the bank.

"I heard they locked you in down at the park," he said. He squinted at me, shaking a Winston from a rumpled pack. "So Bud and B.L. must think you're helping Junior." He lit the cigarette. "That true?"

"Helping Junior do what?" was my answer.

He guffawed smoke and ended up coughing. "She's got

you," he managed through his mirth. "She's got you. Must be she's getting over Darrald."

Darrald again. B.L. had mentioned Darrald—yesterday, on the stream, when Junior had backed him off me. Who the hell was Darrald?

White Milkerson recovered a little. "So you're working for Junior?"

"Helping Junior do what?" I insisted.

"Listen," he said, and he put a sun-fried hand on my shoulder. "The Milkersons and the O'Malleys go way back. Melvin Senior and I have been friends for decades. Hunting buddies, drinking buddies, you name it. I love that nutty old bastard. And Junior's my goddaughter. I hate to see them in a mess like this."

By mess, I gathered White Milkerson thought Mel Senior had killed Jake Jacobs. He seemed like a guy who shot straight, so I asked him that directly.

Milkerson looked at me sadly. "He said he would. And Mel's one of those guys, once he says something, he does it. And Junior, too, she's about as stubborn as a tick. She believes what she wants to believe, and that's that." He let his hand drop. His eyes had become rheumy and troubled. "Folks are saying Junior probably took the ponytail out of Jacobs' mouth and did something with it. She shouldn't have done that, I guess. Not even for her own dad. I just hate to see her go down with him."

"Junior thinks the village president might have done it."

Milkerson shook his head. "Might have. But didn't. Hell, Bud was chairing the village board meeting at the time."

"At which time? You mean the coroner has a time of death?"

He shrugged. "What I heard at the coffee shop this morning, they're putting the time of death any time from three to nine p.m. day before yesterday, which includes the sally."

"But why would a guy like Jacobs skip a village board meeting?"

"You ever fished the sally hatch?" White Milkerson asked me. I said I hadn't hit it yet.

"Thing like a sally hatch has a tendency to change your plans," Milkerson said. He took a long draw on his Winston and exhaled over the creek. "There's a guy or two around here who planned to stay married," he said wistfully. "Until he met sally."

"But what about the poacher?" I said. "Lumen Bostock?"

"Lumen was at the village board meeting."

"The developers?"

"Board meeting."

"What about Jacobs' other enemies?"

Bending to make some adjustment to his yellow plastic pack, he said it again: "Board meeting."

Sensing he was about to move on, I dug down past my wader belt and pulled up the earring. I told him how I had found it. White Milkerson looked it over without a lot of curiosity. "Now how," I asked, "could that end up in a trout's gut? And anyway, what's a fish that size doing in Black Earth Creek? The thing could hardly turn around."

"Bluegills," said the fishery scientist. "And snowmobile races."

He gave me back the earring. I waited for an explanation.

"About twenty years ago," he said, grunting over his rig, "about the time Bud took over as village president, he had some buddy of his dump a truckload of bluegill in behind the dam. Now the trout eat big all winter. Some of the browns get like you saw." He flipped a switch and pumped a black rubber nipple. The thing was a generator, I realized. "As for the earring, hell, you get a few barrels of beer and some snow-mobiles out on the lake in winter, Bud calls it a jamboree or some damn thing. Everybody gets good and ripped, plenty of stuff gets lost in the snow. Wallets, keys, change, earring or two. Come spring, I guess it falls through the water column and now and then a trout strikes."

He looked up at me and shook my hand.

"Be too noisy to talk in a minute," he said. "So you take care."

He pulled a starter cord, causing me to jump. The pack was a little generator, maybe five horsepower. He slung it snarling and sputtering onto his back. He turned toward me.

"You're thinking about helping out Junior," he hollered over his rig, "you might oughta talk to Jake's wife. Runs that new coffee shop in town. The *Pêche Tôt*. Ingrid's her name. Ask Ingrid about the time old Melvin O'Malley came in the *Pêche Tôt* with a shovel. Put it through the pastry case. Walked back out."

He gave me a nod and moved along then, unsnapping the aluminum prong. As he waded toward the deep corner, sweeping back and forth, the prong's faint electrical field conjured up a steady stream of small brown trout, stunned and swimming oddly, sailing off-kilter and dreamlike toward the probe. White Milkerson let the little fish pass. Downstream, around my legs, they flipped and darted, recovered and disappeared. Then a larger trout sailed up and Milkerson snared it in his net. He bent over it, attaching a tag to the dorsal fin, his probe trailing in the current.

I thought I should feel the charge, too. Stepping into his wake, hot sun on my face, the smooth, cold pressure of water against my legs, I imagined I would feel a tingle of electricity seeping through my waders, but I didn't.

Jake's yellow sallies

I was hiking downstream along County K toward Junior's farm when a familiar blue panel van tooted softly and pulled up beside me.

"Gonna be a hot one," the driver remarked.

I mumbled something and kept walking. The guy had said the same thing yesterday. Besides, the Dog didn't do weather. It's gonna whatever. That was my position. But the blue van idled along beside me.

"Gonna get hotter than a tail pipe out here. Wind'll kick up in a couple hours. Hopper weather." He turned his radio down. "You set for hoppers?"

I looked over at him. Yesterday was cloudy and he had tried to sell me crickets. He was a young guy, maybe thirty, burly in the shoulders, with longish dirty-blond hair and photo-sensitive wire-rimmed glasses that even the Dog could see were a lap or two behind the fashion curve. His skin was pale, his shaving was spotty, and his eyes were intense. He was smoking a cigarette no-handed because his hands were busy—one on the wheel, the other opening a fly box against his chest.

"Need hoppers?"

He drove along beside me, spilling smoke and ashes, holding the open box out the window. Inside were tidy rows of hair-and-feather grasshopper imitations. I didn't have to be that close to tell they were exquisitely tied. They were large, stylish and neat.

"Buck fifty," he said. "Fifteen bucks a dozen. Can't beat the price."

He was a pest, but he was right. You couldn't beat the price. Still, I wasn't carrying money.

"Common problem," he said, undaunted. "Here's my card. You get home, you mail me a check. You don't like my flies, then screw it. Throw the damn things away and fish what you like. That's what it's all about, right? That's why we're out here."

I crunched along. He stayed with me.

"Long hot day ahead," he said. He set the hopper box down and held another out the window. "Sallies should come up tonight. You're going to want to be set up for it. Some big browns up here sucking sallies this time of year."

He held the box out. They were pretty sallies—parachute ties, long yellow bodies, tall white wing posts.

So I relented. I stopped walking and took a dozen sallies. I received a business card. Dickie P. Johnsrud was his name. *Mobile Fly Shop—"Meet Me on the Road, Thank Me on the Stream."* He thrust a powerful hand out the window.

"These days the bastards around here call me Dickie Pee in a Bag. Nothing I can do about it. Gotta be a good sport, you know. You got enough hoppers?"

I took a dozen hoppers, too.

"You're down at the campground," he told me. "I'll

swing by later, you can pay me. Maybe we'll have a beer."
I grimaced. "Say," he said, "I guess you're the guy who
found Jake."

I said I was and started walking again. Dickie Pee in a Bag
crept his van alongside me. There was something odd about
the way he moved, the busy motions of his driving, the way
his neck and shoulders moved in a stiffly muscled block.

"Big goddamn shame," he said. "That old teat-puller Mel
O'Malley dunking Jake like that. Jake was going to save this
stream. Jake was going to get that dam out." He paused awkwardly, gazing in the direction of Lake Bud. "Say—you know
about Friends of Black Earth Creek?"

I said I did. Junior had mentioned it. The stream conser-
vation group.

"Right. Jake and me's group." He surged the van a little ways
ahead of me and braked with a jolt. "You mind holding on a bit?"

He didn't wait for an answer. With an odd clattering
motion, he disappeared from the driver's window. At the same
time, the van's side door clicked and heaved open as if by
magic. Inside were tiers of hand-made shelves, drawers, and
display racks, crammed with lines and tippet spools, fly
display cases, hand-built rods, hats, sunglasses, insect repellent—everything a fly fisherman could need or want. As I
stared at these, a ramp hummed down, and Dickie Pee in a
Bag, seated in a wheelchair, yanked through and centered
himself. The ramp lowered him to the road.

He faced me, puffing around his cigarette. His legs dangled
off-kilter, undersized and pale, from voluminous cargo shorts.
Some kind of broad, black, plastic bracelet encircled his thin
left ankle. One of his powerful fists clenched a brochure.

"Fifty bucks," he told me. "Annual membership. Money
goes to stream work, education, programs, legal fees, that kind

of stuff. You get to help keep a place like this from going to shit any faster than it already is."

His cigarette was down to a nub. It looked painful between his fingertips, but he wasn't letting it go. With a flick of his head, he tossed hair from his eyes.

"Plus you get a weekly stream report by e-mail."

He passed me the brochure. It was slick. Color pictures of the stream. Bulleted agenda items. Membership application.

"It says here membership is thirty-five dollars a year," I said. "Not fifty."

"Yeah." He pinched the butt and sucked it. "Well, Jake was going to raise the price."

"You work for Jake?"

"I got over two hundred memberships for Jake."

I was still looking over the brochure. A picture of the Lake Bud dam was on the final fold, X-ed out over a heading that said DAM IT, NO!

"My idea there," said Dickie Pee, jabbing his hot cigarette stub at the picture. "I gave it to Jake. I said, go ahead and use it. Whatever helps the stream. I don't gotta have credit for everything."

He coughed and suddenly said, "Fuck. You know what it's like, not being able to step on a goddamn cigarette when you're done with it?"

He looked at me almost defiantly, flicking hair from his outmoded glasses again. He was a potentially handsome guy who hadn't looked in the mirror in a good while. I guess that made two of us.

"Go ahead," I said.

He tossed the butt to the road. He watched me crush it. Then he sat back in his wheelchair and let some of the air out of his shoulders.

"Gonna be a hot one," he said finally. "Hot as a whore. Hey—you mind grabbing my coffee. It's in the cup holder."

I opened the driver's door and reached into the van. There were clamps for the wheelchair. He accelerated and braked with a joy stick. The wheel had a knob for one-handed steering. The coffee was in a tall paper take-out cup that said *Pêche Tôt*. I accessed my high school French and got a lucky hit. *Fish Soon*. This was the "fancy coffee shop" White Milkerson had told me about, run by the dead man's wife. Inked on the side of the cup were the words *triple latte*.

"I guess Ingrid Jacobs' place is open today," I remarked.

"If Inkie's place wasn't open," Dickie Pee said, "I'd have to kill somebody." He chucked the hair out of his glasses and fit his lips around the hole in the cup lid. He took a slug. "I need this shit."

"No period of mourning for the dead man's wife?"

He took another slug.

"Major shit like this," he said, "it takes a few days to realize what the hell just happened to you. You don't have a clue for a couple days. Take it from me."

I thought this over a while, watching a pair of yellow goldfinches chase among the pink-tipped thistles beyond the fence. I, too, had gone to work after my disaster. But not *the day after*. Still, Dickie Pee had a point.

"Let me guess," I said finally. "You used to fish."

He stared at me—bloodshot blue eyes behind the big wire frames. His glasses were *glasses*—I mean, like slabs from a beer schooner, the frames rectified with what appeared to be fly-tying wire. "I used to fish *every fucking day,*" said Dickie Pee. He stared at me as if to say, *Next question.* I didn't have one.

"I could fish this stream left-handed with my eyes closed," he told me. "When Jake came to town and started talking about taking care of the stream before we lost it, I said, 'No shit. Here's what we gotta do. We gotta blow that fucking dam out of there.' But Jake was all mellow about it, you know, work within the process, one step at a time kind of stuff." He shook out a new cigarette and lit it. He squinted through smoke at me. He nodded at the FOBEC brochure. "Jake was going to change that membership fee to fifty bucks a year," he said. "I promise. Couldn't talk him into blowing up the dam, but I finally talked him into raising the membership. So what do you say?"

"I'm on a pretty fixed budget," I told him.

"Must be rough," he responded flatly.

"Listen," I said. "You really think Melvin O'Malley killed Jacobs?"

"He said he would."

"But Jacobs had a lot of enemies. If you were working for him, you must have known something about that."

"When'd I say I was working for him?"

"You just—"

"I was working *with* Jake. Goddamn it. See, once a guy's in a chair, he can't be in charge of anything anymore. But we can be nice and let him *help out*. Well, fuck that. I built FOBEC just as much as Jake did. I talked up about a thousand people out here these last few years. And now, look what I'm doing. Jake is dead and I'm still out here, raising money. Does that look to you like I was working *for* him?"

Abruptly he lurched his chair back toward the van. He finished his *Pêche Tôt* triple espresso and tossed the empty cup inside. His movements were jerky and violent. "Hey," he said vehemently, "okay, so Jake's a hero now. A martyr for the movement. Fine. Jake was a good guy. He was a warrior for this creek you're fishing. I ain't saying anything against him. So I just got an idea. See these sallies?"

He thrust out a new box of yellow sallies. These were different than the ones he had just sold to me. They were tied upside down, with fancy forked tails and pink hi-vis wing posts.

"These are Jake's sallies. I tied these special order for Jake just the other day. How about I sell these as memorials to Jake? Sell these for fifty bucks apiece, then maybe build some kind of tribute out here, a sign, a bench, something like that. Sell about a hundred of these things. Five grand oughta do something."

I picked a fly from the box and looked at it more closely. It was the yellow sally I had seen on the end of Jacobs' line, the one Junior had snapped off and tossed into the stream.

"Maybe…" mused Dickie Pee, and I looked up to see that his face had changed. He was looking downstream, a hardness in his eye. "Maybe, hey, guy, listen—maybe, you know how they name dams after people. You know, like Hoover Dam? How about naming a non-dam after somebody? I mean—get this—a non-dam, the absence of a dam, the Jake Jacobs Used-To-Be-A-Fucking-Dam. Big sign. Ha. I like that. You like that, guy?"

He was rather desperately shaking out a fresh cigarette as if to toast himself. He had a crooked grin aimed at me.

"You tied these for Jake when?"

"About a week ago. Not even that. But Jake and me'd been talking about it before then. And you want to know my guess?" He lit up, held up the fly. "This sucker was working. Jake was cleaning up. That's why he didn't make it in to the village board meeting. Me and Jake had finally cracked the sally."

I turned the odd-looking fly upside down in my hand. Now it looked right side up.

"Hell, that's right," said Dickie Pee to himself, blowing smoke straight up. "I'll sell those things for fifty."

I knew why Jacobs and Dickie Pee had designed the fly like that. The yellow sally was a spindly insect and too big to be a good flier. Typically—from what I had seen—the wing sets would separate on lift-off, one pair still stuck in the surface film while the tail strained upward and the second wing pair beat the air a quarter inch above the water. It was these emerging insects, trapped but tantalizingly active, that the trout keyed on. Maybe one in fifty bugs got stuck like that, but a feeding trout would get picky and wait for it, and find it every time. The upside-down tie looked like stuck wings, body lifting, yellow sally in distress. It was clever.

"I heard they can't pin down Jake's time of death," said Dickie Pee beside me. "Three to nine p.m., like hell," he scoffed. "B.L. gave Jake's gear to Ingrid. So check his tippet. There's gonna be one of my sallies on there. Should be simple as that. Jake was out fishing the sally. Eight o'clock. And Mel O'Malley got him."

He sucked hard and stared off toward the stream, holding the smoke in for a long time. He had the right idea. So far everybody in Black Earth seemed to have the right idea. And either Junior was dead right—someone killed Jacobs earlier and had framed her dad—or she was dead wrong—Jacobs *was* fishing the sally, and her dad had done the deed himself. There wasn't any middle ground, and the fly Junior had snapped off was gone forever.

"I'll take one of these Jake's Sallies," I told the man in the wheelchair. "And a membership."

"Comes to one-thirty," Dickie Pee said, handing me the fly. "A hundred thirty bucks even."

I hesitated. I couldn't figure the price.

"Membership is fifty," he reminded me. "As of today."

A little more faith would be appreciated

Junior's face was tight. No grin. "I saw who dropped you off," she told me as she set down a cup of coffee. "What did Loser have to say?"

I guess Dickie Pee in a Bag wasn't a strong enough epithet for her. Her whole posture had changed. She looked older. She bit her sunburned bottom lip as she put a plate down for me.

"Loser thinks your dad killed Jacobs."

"He's entitled to his opinion," she said stiffly. "And what did White Milkerson think?"

I stared at my plate a moment. A trio of fried eggs over easy, a half dozen thick strips of bacon, a gooey store-bought cinnamon bun, and a huge multi-vitamin. It was beautiful. "How do you know I talked to Milkerson?"

Junior set a plate down for Dad. "You smell like whiskey."

"Maybe I'm just a bum."

She sat in front of her own plate. She had the same amount of food I had, plus a protein shake. She had told me she was going to spend the day stacking hay in the barn loft. "You're not a bum," she informed me. "Half the guys in Black Earth are bums. But you're not."

"You don't even know my name."

"You haven't told me."

"Dog," I said.

"I don't believe you."

I shrugged. "You probably will, eventually."

"I'll try not to," she said.

She reached over and stopped her father from overflowing his coffee cup with cream. "So what did White tell you?"

The same, I told her. He suspected her dad had killed Jake Jacobs, just like he said he would. I watched her redden. "But he was upset about it," I added. "He said he was an old friend."

"Daddy," Junior said loudly, "how long have you known White?"

"Eh?" the old man jerked his head up, dripping egg yolk down his chin.

"Manfred Milkerson. Your friend. My godfather." She nearly yelled at him. It occurred to me that Dad had good and bad days. "How long have we known White?"

The old man rumbled for a moment. He slurped coffee. I saw he was pleased to be engaged, thinking of a friend and working back to the day. But by the time he located the answer, he seemed to have forgotten the question. He glowered at me. I looked down and forked an egg into quarters.

"Well, that ticks me off just a little bit," Junior said quietly. I could tell she was understating her feelings. "A little more faith would be appreciated."

She said her own grace, slowly and somberly, and we ate a while. I chewed eggs more alive with flavor than any I could remember, meanwhile sneaking looks around the kitchen. The sink was a deep, glazed-iron tub set into buckling gray countertops that had been wiped of their original color. The cabinets were a soiled and buttery white, worn to the wood around the pulls. The curtains and floor had once picked up the forget-me-not blue in the Dutch girl wallpaper, but that effort had been made long ago, no doubt by Junior's mother in better days. It was easy to see that Junior herself was in a survival mode. Her sole decorating touches amounted to a crystal in one window, a God's eye in the other, and a giant vitamin bottle on the counter. Nothing was a speck cleaner than it had to be. Every non-essential bit of counter and floor space spilled over with newspapers and mail and tools and heaps of clothes, folded and otherwise. On the table near my elbow rested a box of spark plugs. The television chattered from the living room behind me. A Madison station reported the weather. Hot. Humid. Chance of thunderstorms later.

But it was still cool in Junior's kitchen. I put down a pair of over-easies in a hurry and slowed down to savor the last one, dumping on Lawry's seasoning salt from the shaker in the middle of the table. I was crunching through my bacon when Junior sighed and said, "Okay, so come on, Dog. What did White tell you?"

I met her anxious green eyes. "That Jake probably got caught up fishing the sally hatch. And everyone else was at the village board meeting. He told me that, and…"

I glanced at the old man. Was he listening? It was hard to say. He was mopping egg yolk from his plate with a fistful of cinnamon bun.

"I know," Junior sighed. "Daddy threatened Jake. In front of everybody. And then exactly one week later, Jake shows up dead with his ponytail stuffed in his mouth, just like Daddy said." She leaned in. The dead watch swung away from her chest and hit the table. "So don't you see? It's too neat. Daddy doesn't remember things from one minute to the next, let alone over a period of days. Lately it's not like Daddy to follow through." Then she startled me. "Daddy!" she hollered. "Do you remember Jake Jacobs?"

The old man's eyes slid beneath his great white eyebrows. Those eyes were rheumy and weak, milky with cataracts, but they found mine.

"The man with the ponytail?" Junior hollered. "You cussed him out at the village board meeting a couple weeks ago?"

The old man looked down and his daughter looked at me. "See? He doesn't even know what I'm talking about. Jake was blaming farmers for mud in the creek, and Daddy was mad as a hornet, but now he's thinking about what's on TV."

On cue, the huge old man rose and limped across the dog-eared floor tiles to the off-orange shag carpet of the living room. He sank into a brown vinyl recliner and picked up a remote. The volume zoomed.

When I looked back, Junior was grinning hopefully at me. "Isn't he cute?" she said. "He loves that remote. We only get three channels, and two of them are fuzzy, but he loves to surf anyway. More coffee?"

She re-filled me. "Let's go on the porch," she said.

"HERE YOU GO," she said, sitting down beside me. The steps were narrow and we were close enough to bang knees. Her knee was round and solid beneath faded denim. Mine was bony—damned near gaunt as it poked through my threadbare wading pants. Junior passed me a few sheets of paper.

"These are the minutes from the last two village board meetings," she told me. "I got them for you. My mom's old friend Mary Malarkey is the clerk. Mary dropped them off this morning."

I hesitated. In my hand I held about five pages in ten-point, single-spaced type, detailing the minutiae of the Village of Black Earth, Wisconsin. Driveway permits. Contested parking tickets. Plans for the Jet Ski Jamboree on Lake Bud. I wasn't exactly sure what the point was.

"What you do," Junior said, "is you find who was there two meetings ago to hear Daddy threaten Jake—"

"But everybody heard the rumor."

"If you were there," Junior explained, "it was pretty convincing. You'd more think to take it seriously. Daddy had his nuts twisted up real good and everybody there believed him except me. Then—" she paged deeper for me "—you see who came back the next week and got read into the record to set themselves up an alibi. That shows you who to focus on."

"But doesn't everybody go to the meetings? The whole village?"

"Not in summer," she said. "Between haying and softball, not many people have the time. So those that do go, they really have an interest."

She looked at me over her coffee cup, as if to say, See? *Simple.*

"Think about it," she went on when I hesitated again. "Whoever killed Jake, they purposely made it look like he was out fishing during the meeting. Therefore, the killer went to the meeting. For an alibi. Right? I mean, otherwise, why go to the trouble to tie on a yellow sally? To set yourself up as unavailable, at the meeting when Jake died, while he fished the sally, supposedly. There's no other point."

Her certainty made me squirm. It still seemed a lot more likely that Jacobs *was* fishing the sally—and that her dad had dunked him. I decided to change directions. "Who's Loser?" I asked her.

She frowned. "Dickie P. Johnsrud. He sells stuff to fishermen."

"I know. But who is he? What's his story?"

Her hand went to the watch she wore as a necklace. She took a deep breath and looked out over the coulee, where her cows grazed among tall, blooming thistles. "Well," she said, "we all used to call him Ditchard. You know—his given name is Richard…so, because of his drunk driving, all the accidents, Ditchard…

"Now he's Dickie Pee. As in Dickie Pee in a Bag, which is what he does."

That was cruel, I thought. But Junior seemed utterly without her usual sympathy.

"He finally hit a tree or something?"

She answered me flatly, "No," and looked away, fingering the watch.

My vest hung on the porch newel. I plucked the upside-down yellow sally off my drying patch.

"You snapped one of these off Jake's tippet and threw it in the water. Right?"

She looked at the fly. "I guess."

"How did you know it was a yellow sally?"

"It's yellow."

"It's an unusual way to tie the fly."

She sighed and got up. A minute later she returned with a book on trout flies. It was beat up, water stained, and opened to a page on yellow sallies. There was something on there like it. Not as stylish as Dickie Pee's fly—but inverted, with the tall pink wing post. For night fishing, the text said.

"Darrald was always talking about getting into fly fishing," she said. She sat down beside me. She lifted her cup to drink before she noticed it was empty. "But Darrald was the kind of guy who always tried to know every fact about a new thing before he started it, so he wouldn't make mistakes. As a result, Darrald never started anything. Nothing in his whole life. He just had to know everything before he jumped in. And Daddy was always teasing him, telling him just get some dynamite out of the barn if he wanted to catch some trout."

She had her fingers around the defunct wristwatch again.

"Okay," I said after a minute of silence. "So who's Darrald then? What's his story?"

"His story," she said, "is he's gone."

She was picking at her boots. The leather on the toes had dried and scuffed up into little curls, and she plucked at those, flicked them out into the yard. A kitten wandered out from under the porch to sniff at my wading socks.

"We were engaged for about two years," she finally said. "Darrald, for once, just wanted to jump in and do it. But it was me holding out, saying let's wait, thinking maybe one day I'd end up someplace besides Black Earth, this farm. You know. So Darrald went out bow hunting for deer one day in October. Darrald and Ditchard. They were old buddies. Drinking buddies. Toking buddies. They hadn't seen each other much since me and Darrald got together. They went back up there."

Junior pointed a thumb over her shoulder at the house. Behind it was about a hundred acres of corn, and then a thickly wooded hillside.

"Darrald wouldn't get messed up and hunt generally. He never did by himself. But with Dickie, of course, he did. Drunk, stoned, the works. And Darrald fell out of his tree stand. I mean his tree stand fell out of the tree. I mean—" She stopped and cleared her throat. Then she got up, went through the screen door again, and came back with the coffee pot.

"I get so mad," she said, sitting back down, "I can hardly say what really happened."

I waited. A blunt silver milk truck roared down the coulee, engine noise beating off the hillsides, a wake of air and gravel spewing blackbirds from the ditches. A quarter mile down the coulee, the truck jake-braked to a stop and matched windows with Bud Lite's police car coming up the other direction.

Junior was back to picking at her boots.

"You shouldn't hunt shit-faced," she said. "And that's Darrald's own fault. Nobody made him do anything. But he was minding his business up in his tree stand. I know that. Then Dickie Pee in a Bag gets the idea they need to smoke another bowl. So he climbs out of his stand and comes over to Darrald's. He climbs up there with Darrald, starts packing a bowl, two big, two-hundred-pound guys in one tree stand rated for three hundred pounds, and the whole thing comes down." She straightened up. She blew out a breath and shook her hands in the air like she was sick of herself picking at her boots. "I'm glad you're here right now," she told me. "Every time I tell someone the story, I feel a little tiny bit less pissed."

I nodded. The conversation down the road—Lumen Bostock and B.L.—continued.

"Dickie fell on Darrald," she said. "Dickie came down on top of him. Neither one of them could move. It was real cold. They were out there until the next morning, until I went looking. And Darrald just didn't make it."

She swiped at her face in tomboy discomfort. She gripped the dead watch.

"I'm sorry."

"Yeah? Well, no shit. Me, too. Sorry, and mad. That loser. I can't forgive him."

A while passed. Finally she tapped the Black Earth village

board meeting minutes on my lap. "Anyway, thanks. I looked through it, and I've got my ideas. But let me know what you find out. I've got twenty-five acres of hay to get in and get stacked before it rains."

As she stood, I stared blankly at the official record of a re-pavement request and the ensuing debate. Maybe the thrill of my breakfast was wearing off. Or maybe I'd had too much real coffee. I rose to a rare moment of verbal courage. I felt I had to. For my sake, I guess, as much as hers.

"Listen," I said to Junior. "Is there the slightest possibility that your dad did do this?" Her pink cheeks ballooned in an angry puff, but I kept going. "Is there a chance that your idea about somebody retying Jacobs' fly is just too much of a long shot? And that because you love your dad so much you're just not seeing it?"

She had stiffened. She set her cup down hard.

"You don't trust me."

"I didn't say that. I guess I'm asking if you trust yourself."

"I'm not losing Daddy," she said. "I trust myself on that."

"But…"

"Look," she said. "If you don't believe me, that's fine. You choose. If you don't think I'm right, just drive away with the money and have a nice life. I'll work this out myself."

I didn't move. I felt stunned by Junior's stubborn faith. She needed to believe, so therefore she did. I didn't understand, and it stopped me cold. Meanwhile, the conversation down the road had broken up. The police car rolled toward us up the coulee. "Go on," she said, taking a step toward the barn. "I got to stack hay while Daddy's quiet." She made an unconvincing grin. "It's all going to work out anyway."

I watched B.L. crawl his car upstream on County K. He drove deliberately, like he was looking for something.

"Listen," I said, "your police chief's coming up the road. It'd be best if he didn't find me here."

Junior looked up. B.L. was making progress, but slowly. He rolled his patrol car over the road-hump of a little feeder creek, then between the green pasture flanks groomed by Junior's dairy cattle. That moment, as I looked at her face, I saw past the burnt-cheeked, square-jawed, can-do tomboy. I saw a woman. And at that same moment, I heard an engine surge.

"You know what?" Junior said, leaping up the steps beside me. "You know what—Dog? Right now, if you're not going to trust me, I don't really give a fat goddamn where he finds you."

With that, she strode across the porch and pulled open the squeaky screen door. *"Daddy,"* she said sharply. Then the screen door closed and the big door closed after it. The lock snapped. The television went off. The old man bawled a protest and Junior cussed him fiercely. Curtains rattled shut.

"Hey Massachusetts," called B.L. I turned back to the driveway. He was stepping from the car. "Are we having fun yet?"

It was the two of them. The village president, Bud Heavy, was winching himself out of the passenger seat. They both wore amber mirrored sunglasses.

"Fancy meeting you here," said the president. "How's fishing?"

"Nobody's home," I answered.

"Heh, heh," said the president. "Funny answer. Funny kind of fishing report."

"Nobody's home," I repeated.

"Well then," said B.L., rocking a little in his cowboy boots. "Okay… Well…then…"

The village president hitched over and stiff-armed the

corner of Junior's house. He leaned hard. "Well then, what?" he asked his son. He gave me the rubber smile.

"Well then we'll just have a look around."

"Atta boy."

I stepped in front of the chief as he moved toward the steps.

"You'd better have a warrant then."

I had surprised myself as much as them. A stranger in bare feet, holding a coffee cup, his waders hung like spent rubbers on the porch rail, defending the lady inside. I knew how it looked. The dogs were on the linoleum now.

"You hear what I just heard?" the president asked the cop.

"I did."

"You heard it? The guy protecting Junior?"

"I heard it."

"Same guy who said he didn't see Junior do nothing yesterday."

B.L. sounded peeved. "I heard it."

"Kind of a hard guy to believe then, huh Dwighty?"

B.L. stared at the driveway.

"Well then...?" Bud Bjorgstad twisted, cricked the sway in his back. He shifted his feet and leered at his son. He looked like a man about to carnalize a goat. His son had begun to sweat.

"He's thinking," President Bud told me with a wink. "He'll get it."

"What I was gonna do all along," said the Black Earth village police chief finally, sullenly, "was ask for two warrants. One for this place. One for that RV of his down in the campground."

He glared at his father. His father slapped his back.

"Atta boy," said the president.

The Pêche Tôt

In my thirty-three months on the road, the Cruise Master had
been violated twice, once outside Philadelphia, and once at a
turn-out on an Appalachian brook trout stream near Shady
Valley, Tennessee. Both times I'd lost a week's worth of vodka
and all my tools. The Tennessee folks took my Red Wing
boots, too. But my safe box was never touched. I wasn't afraid
of a warrant. I had a strategy.

I checked inside the box. I had a Glock .40 caliber pistol
and Junior's thousand bucks in cash. I peeled off four fifties
and stuffed them in my pocket. I put the earring in the box. I
double-bagged the box in bread sacks, in case of rain, and set
it on top of the Cruise Master, out of view to anything but a
bird. Then I walked to town.

THE DEAD MAN'S WIFE stood behind the counter at the *Pêche
Tôt*. Ingrid Jacobs. There could be no doubt about that.

Just as they did not make women like Junior in the suburbs
of Boston, they did not make women like Ingrid Jacobs in

Black Earth. She was tall and lean and elegantly bohemian. The closed-lip smile she gave me was a very polished affair— an expression not of welcome or even grief, but of flawless technique, like a guy casting a fly perfectly into the far corner of an empty swimming pool. She was absolutely air-tight pretty, and she knew it.

She tipped her head—vaguely impatient. So what would I have? I stared so long at the densely lettered chalkboard menu that she turned her backside to me and began wiping down some kind of multi-nozzled machine. Maybe Junior had got my sap running, I don't know. But it occurred to me that Jake Jacobs, at some point, had been a very happy man.

"So, do you need some help choosing?"

Her back still to me. Wiping. The wife of a dead man, I reminded myself. Just order any damn thing.

"Our special coffee today," she told me, "is a Brazilian shade-grown."

"Okay, that," I said. I looked at the food. I remembered White Milkerson's story. I pictured Melvin O'Malley putting a shovel through the pastry case. "And an elderberry scone."

She turned. Her smile, still all lips, had shifted very subtly to a different corner of the swimming pool. I noticed her clothes—studiously tattered jeans, a tight T-shirt with the face of Malcom X glowering out past the buttons of a long-tailed mechanic's work shirt that said, drolly over the pocket, *Chucky*. She was about thirty. Her hair was a luxuriant nest of black curls.

"I'll bring that right out."

I sat down at a table near the window and spread the Village Board notes out before me. The coffee shop appeared to be an old general store that had been aggressively stripped to its elements—brick and pipe, oak floorboards and pressed tin ceiling—and then painted in bulky earth tones. Everywhere, unusual plants hung nakedly in tall antique bottles. The fishing theme emerged subtly in the prints and photographs that traveled gallery-style around the room above the wainscoting. The napkin holder on my table was an empty classic fly reel, cleverly mounted. And the reading rack held Isaac Walton, Hemingway, fishing magazines and brochures for Friends of Black Earth Creek. A table in the rear was set up for fly tying. A large orange cat slept beneath the vise among the feathers.

Ingrid Jacobs set down my order.

"I'm sorry," I told her before she could glide back to the counter.

She stopped. *What did you do?* said her puzzled expression.

"I heard about your husband. I'm sorry."

"Oh." She looked away. When her gaze came back to me, she had laid another perfect lip-smile over empty water. "Thank you."

"It's a good idea," I persisted. "Keeping busy here in the shop. You must be devastated."

"Yes. Thank you so much. Should I know you?"

I shook my head.

"Just a trout bum. Passing through."

"Oh. Well, thank you so much."

She escaped behind the counter. I sipped my coffee and picked at my scone. It was too rich for me, this stuff, after two-plus years on instant Maxim, Tang, and peanut butter sandwiches. These were Jake Jacobs' rations, though—the beautiful woman included—the rations of a guy who knew exactly how to have it all. That didn't go down easily in a place like Black Earth, I imagined, where people knew how to have exactly what they had.

I focused on the notes. The Black Earth Village Board meeting had been called to order at 7:03 p.m., around the time the first few yellow sallies had begun to stir in the creek. But Junior had me thinking. Had Jacobs really lingered on the stream as the meeting started? Nearly every agenda item intersected his issues somehow. Zoning, jet ski races on Lake Bud, a village-commissioned stream study... Had the pull of the sally hatch been that strong? What kind of man was Jacobs, anyway?

I sipped my coffee and watched Jacobs' widow grind beans. She was almost catatonically graceful. I supposed the rhythms of grief into her movements, but her face showed nothing.

I looked back to the village board minutes. Ingrid herself had been the first to speak at the meeting, petitioning for permission to serve *Pêche Tôt* fare at tables on the sidewalk. President Bud Bjorgstad wondered why Ingrid Jacobs had not previously presented the idea to the Downtown Planning Committee. Bud Lite (the minutes called him *Police Chief Dwight Bjorgstad*) then spoke against the petition, citing public safety. A lengthy wrangle followed, and the petition had been tabled for review. I looked back at the agenda. Ingrid Jacobs, first up.

I remembered what Junior had said. *See who got read into the record...to set themselves up an alibi. That shows you who to focus on.* I nibbled my scone, wondering.

Manfred Milkerson, the retired fisheries scientist, had spoken next. He had answered questions about funding for his study on Lake Bud. Yes, he reported, the study had been paid for by Friends of Black Earth Creek, Jake Jacobs' organization. Didn't that discredit the study's findings? asked the president. To which Milkerson had replied, Why? Because Jacobs wanted the dam out, answered the president. He paid for the study, replied Milkerson, not the results. But then couldn't the village pay for its own study and report its own results? Be my guest, replied Milkerson. The idea was referred to committee for consideration. Milkerson was thanked by the president for volunteering to speak to the board. I made a note to myself: *see the study*.

Lumen Bostock, the trout-poaching milk truck driver, had appeared next to contest the fine he received for using his jake brakes inside village limits. The president noted that traffic tickets could not be contested before the village board. Bostock then revised his challenge to the anti-jake brake ordinance itself. Another lengthy discussion ensued, with Bostock trying to challenge the concept of noise pollution as the sort of "politically correct" nonsense Jake Jacobs had brought to Black Earth. He proposed a "no ponytails on men" ordinance. At this point someone named Shelly Milkerson had been forcibly removed by Bud Lite from the meeting room. Further discussion was re-directed to the public comment period.

None other than Junior made herself memorable next. Fourth on the agenda. She wanted a DEAF CHILD sign put up on County K, a quarter-mile north and south of her farm—to protect her Daddy. And she wanted the speed limits enforced. This drew an irate response from the president, who pointed out that Junior had made exactly these same demands at the last meeting, then reiterated that the village had been so busy responding to lawsuits filed by Jake Jacobs over the dam that it hardly had time to process the water and sewer requests for the new subdivision homes, let alone worry about "people wandering in the road."

I imagined Junior sitting down, stony-faced, steaming—but *read into the record*. I sipped coffee and watched Ingrid Jacobs take a phone call. She replied to something rather tersely and hung up. I wondered about Jake Jacobs' funeral.

Drownings…accidental or otherwise… the cops did autopsies, toxicology tests, I knew that all too well. The results came slowly, a week or more. But the body somehow wasn't part of it. The body came back almost too soon—tissues sampled, fluids drained, bones scanned, a life and a death reduced to measurable quantities in a lab, waiting in line. Ingrid looked at me. She lip-smiled. I went back to the meeting minutes.

Next, a visitor, County Supervisor Ronald Hellenbrand, spoke to the economic potential, tax-base-and-recreation-wise, of keeping the water in Lake Bud—and as just one example, he reminded people of the upcoming Jet Ski Jamboree, which would draw a hundred or so people the following weekend. Thanks for coming, said the president.

Ronald Hellenbrand. There was a new name.

Then came the President's Report. Bud Bjorgstad announced the chartering of a new tax-exempt organization to be called the Friends of Black Earth *People*—pointedly replacing the Creek in Jacobs' Friends of Black Earth Creek. "It's about *people,* not water and fish," spoke the President into the record. He displayed membership papers, including one set with Jacobs' name already filled in. The membership fees would be waived for Jacobs, Supervisor Hellenbrand put in. If Jacobs wanted to join the *people*. At 9:27 p.m., the president entertained a motion to adjourn. Dickie Pee in a Bag *(Richard P. Johnsrud, Treasurer)* appeared suddenly in the record to second the motion.

I TOOK ANOTHER SIP and sat back to ponder. If Jacobs had indeed fished the yellow sally hatch and died during the meeting, then what I was looking at was a list of potentially motivated people who nevertheless could not possibly have dunked him in the creek, then hacked off his ponytail and stuffed it in his mouth. And that made it simple. Dad did it. Just like he said he would. And Junior was lying. Or kidding herself. And paying me to help.

But that just wouldn't stick. Junior may have been working me in some way—the Dog clung stubbornly to as much ugliness as he could—but it still didn't make sense that Jacobs would have been on the stream instead of at the meeting. His wife had needed him. The stream had needed him.

So, on the other hand, what if Jacobs' killer *had* been clever enough to dunk him at, say, five o'clock and re-rig him with a yellow sally? Someone that clever could then pull the ponytail trick to implicate old Melvin O'Malley and follow that with a bit of grandstanding at the village board meeting. If that were the scenario, then what I was looking at was a list of suspects, Lumen Bostock and President Bud at the top, with a surprise showing by "Richard P. Johnsrud, Treasurer." Two elements of the death scene—the yellow sally, the ponytail in the mouth— made the alibi complete, but Junior had scotched that. And so the killer was uneasy now, unprotected, on the move.

Maybe.

The crux was to know whether or not Jacobs' fly had been re-tied after his death. But how? Since Junior had snatched it off, there was nothing to go on. Dickie Pee told me Ingrid Jacobs had her husband's gear. Would she let me see it? If so, what would I be looking for? How could I tell whether or not Jacobs had tied on his own final fly?

Over-caffeinated and anxious, I rose and poked about the margins of the room. Ingrid watched me. Self-consciously, I inspected the display of small artworks and photos around the walls, soon discovering from the photographs something I hadn't noticed when I had seen Jake Jacobs as a dead man.

As a live human being, Jacobs was a strong-looking character. He wasn't big or burly. But he was about six feet tall and wiry, with a lightness in his carriage that suggested a background in athletics and probably some mid-life martial arts. And while the Dog was ignorant on the question of whether women dig men with ponytails, I was pretty certain that the rest of Jake Jacobs was okay by women. He was handsome, dark-skinned and well-featured, with playful green eyes. When he held up a trout to the camera, the trout looked lucky.

I went to the counter and paid the lovely widow seven dollars from a fifty. Then, gambling, I said, "I was the one who found your husband."

If her smile had been a blandly perfect cast over nothing, her expression now snapped to and came down on live water. I nearly glimpsed her teeth.

"You what?"

"I found Jake."

"You—?"

Her eyes widened. They were a deep, exotic brown, and slowly they seemed to let in light and take on depth, *seeing* me. She was suddenly eager to talk.

"Then you must have noticed Jake's ponytail in his mouth. Didn't you?"

"No," I lied. "I didn't look that closely."

"I heard Junior was there."

I admitted that.

"When I saw the body at the morgue, I knew it," said Ingrid Jacobs, gripping a rag in her elegant hand and staring across Main Street toward the Lunch Bucket Café. There was something about her mouth when she spoke—a funny crinkle—and I fixated on it. "I was at the meeting before last," she said. "I heard Mel O'Malley say he would kill Jake. He threatened to do it, and he did. I'll bet Junior took the ponytail out of Jake's mouth to protect her dad. And B.L.'s too much of a dumb-ass to figure it out."

Her eyes returned to me. I have a blank Boston stare, which I gave back to her. Actually, things were moving a little fast for the Dog. I hadn't planned on more than getting a first feel for who she was. But we had crossed some line, and I said, "From what I've heard, there were a few other people with a reason to kill your husband."

"Like who?" she demanded, and quickly rolled her lips inward.

I suggested poachers, but she dismissed that with a slightly inelegant huff. Nor did she go for Junior's theory that Bud Bjorgstad wanted Jake out of the way badly enough to kill him—and that setting up Mel O'Malley gave the president access to Junior's farm, now that he had forced through its annexation into the village. That idea made her turn away from me and stare once more toward the window.

"Jake's killer could have been anybody," I said, "anybody with an interest in keeping Black Earth the way it is. Your husband wanted to change things, and—"

"Look," she stopped me. She tossed her perfectly messy black hair. "You don't understand. Jake died about eight o'clock. Everybody in town who hated Jake was at the village board meeting—except for Melvin O'Malley—"

It was my turn to stop her. "I thought the coroner could only place Jake's death within a six-hour range. I imagine that's because of the cold water, which makes the body—"

I saw her careful, closed-lip smile reappear and head back over blank water. Calmly, crinkle-mouthed, she said, "B.L. gave me Jake's stuff. Jake had a yellow sally on. So he was fishing at eight o'clock. That's when Mel O'Malley drowned my husband. And Junior took the ponytail to cover for him."

I stared at her a minute, wanting to be sure I heard right.

"You've got your husband's rod?" I said. "And there's a yellow sally on it?"

She nodded.

Slowly and carefully, watching her mouth, I tucked forty-three dollars change back into my billfold. Tying another sally on Jacobs' line was a cheap trick that nevertheless had a certain shrewdness to it. Only Junior or I could expose this fraud. But in doing so, Junior herself was exposed—her tampering with the crime scene was forced into the open—and thus the finger would point straight at Junior's dad.

Somebody *was* clever in Black Earth. I had to admit that. I felt another chunk fall out of my ugly attitude. Then I moved straight ahead. "But Jake would have been at the meeting, too—not out fishing. I'm sure he planned on being there. And given that everyone in town seems to know that the yellow sally hatches at eight o'clock, couldn't someone have killed him at four and then just retied his fly?"

That cracked it—her smile. It came open. Her lips split apart—slowly, reluctantly, with a lot of friction—into an open-mouthed grimace until I could see what was inside them.

Braces.

The lovely Ingrid Jacobs wore braces. Straps and bands and full-out SOO LINE tracks from one corner of her pretty mouth to the other.

She gaped at me, flushed and fierce-looking. Her lips strained to close over the braces and finally made it. She spoke from the back of her throat.

"Who *are* you?"

There followed a weird exchange of energies. The Dog had

worked hard to be no one. And before me was a woman who I gathered had worked just as hard to be *someone*. We stood there stalemated, intersecting in some no-man's land of personal identity. It was no accident, I guess, that Junior jumped to mind right then—so absolutely sure of herself. So absolutely sure the world had order. So absolutely sure the killer was not her Dad. Now that Jacobs' fly line had a yellow sally on it again, she had to be right.

Didn't she?

"Just a trout bum," I repeated to Ingrid Jacobs. "Just passing through."

Her skin flushed and her lips strained and she looked like an angry child.

"You're working for Junior," she accused me.

When I didn't answer, she began to wipe a milk steamer. Her cheeks appeared red-hot.

"Look, Ingrid, can you show me the fly on Jake's line? Maybe I can help you."

I felt stupid as I said it. The old, gullible, Dog—everything to everybody. But Ingrid took my offer and flounced away with a huff. Startled, the big orange cat bolted from the fly-tying bench. In the cat's wake, a few duck feathers swirled and settled.

Ingrid went upstairs. I heard her walking above me. In a minute she returned with her husband's pricey bamboo rod. Sure enough, the fly on Jake's line was the upside-down tie, the Jake's Yellow Sally, by Dickie Pee, the same type of fly Junior had snapped off and tossed in the creek. But this had to be a second, different Jake's Sally. The knot was crude. It looked like a few hasty, chubby-fingered half-hitches.

"See?" said Ingrid.

"I see."

Reaching out, her hands shook. I gave back the rod.

"Melvin O'Malley killed Jake," she said. "Just like he promised."

"Junior's just as sure that somebody set up her dad. Somebody who had it out for Jake *and* Mel Senior."

She rolled her lips in.

"What if somebody did set this whole thing up?" I asked. I watched her. She scowled. "Who might do that?"

She tossed her hair and turned away from me. "I don't know."

"Tell me about Dickie P. Johnsrud."

"What about him?"

"He have anything against Junior and her dad?"

"They sued him," she answered. She looked at her husband's rod as if she couldn't remember how it had come to be in her hands. "Over the hunting accident. They lost. But I guess Junior stayed after him. She got that house-arrest cuff put on him. For drunk driving. He can't go out after dark. He has to be home for the computer to call him."

"What about Dickie and Jake? Didn't they work together?"

She held the rod and looked away toward the window, where B.L.'s cream and gold patrol car cruised by. "Jake and Dickie had a big fight. Dickie got all these memberships for FOBEC, and he wanted to be paid for it, but Jake said FOBEC was a volunteer organization. Dickie raised membership prices on his own and started taking a cut. Jake told Dickie FOBEC didn't want his help anymore."

I chewed on that a minute. As I did so, Lumen Bostock's silver milk truck hissed to a stop and the mini-Abe Lincoln sprang out and strutted toward the *Pêche Tôt*. Ingrid Jacobs leaned the rod on the counter, tapped coffee into a tall paper cup and capped it. She met Bostock at the door. They exchanged neither money nor words. I could only guess that they knew each other pretty well. As Bostock stalked off with his triple espresso, Ingrid drifted back to the counter.

"When did B.L. give you Jake's rod?"

"About ten last night. When he came to tell me about Jake."

"He say anything?

"He said Jake was killed and he was sorry."

"Funny," I said. "That he'd give the rod to you. With a sally on it. You'd think he'd have the sense to hang on to it." She didn't say anything. "In a fishing town like this," I said, "where everybody knows the hatches, it seems obvious he'd keep that rod to help him with the time of death."

Ingrid shrugged lamely. "I just noticed the sally this morning and I called him. I thought it might help. But B.L. was real quiet. He sounded kind of dumbfounded. I don't think he saw it before. He called back about five minutes before you got here and said he had to go to the county courthouse to get some warrants, then he'd be by to pick up the rod."

I nodded. Tying on a second yellow sally—that was a cheap trick. But who was playing it? We both stared out at Main Street for a while. It looked hot. For the time being, I decided to let Ingrid Jacobs think the yellow sally on her husband's line was authentic. Or to let her think that I thought it was authentic. I wondered where the rod had been before ten o'clock last night, when B.L. dropped it off. On the stream bank—but after that, where? And who, aside from Jake and Ingrid Jacobs, had access to the second floor of the *Pêche Tôt?*

"One problem with the Dickie Pee idea," I said after a minute, talking mostly to myself, "is that the man's in a wheelchair."

Ingrid didn't respond. She had become still, her face divided by the angle of the fly rod.

I asked her, "Did you sleep here last night?"

"We… I have a house…on Depot Street."

She seemed astonished at the sound of her own words. We had become *I*. She seemed about to slip into wholly convincing tears at the realization, but just then the phone rang. She jumped to it. *"Pêche Tôt,"* she said tightly and gave the caller what I figured was about half a sentence.

"No," she said. Her voice was hot. "I don't need you today. I didn't ever need you. Give me back the apron and anything else you borrowed and pick up your stuff."

She set the phone on the counter. "I'm sorry," she told me. "I'm closing. You'll have to leave."

Ingrid Jacobs turned her back to me. She wiped at a coffee grinder for a moment or two. Then her shoulders shriveled. She fought the shakes. But she kept wiping.

"I'm at the campground," I said. "In the RV."

She turned. The wash cloth snagged across her forearm. A wet slug of coffee grounds dropped from its folds. "Yeah?" She made a big gasp. "Well, you're next."

"I'm next what?"

No answer. She turned her back. Many things needed wiping suddenly. Too many for words. She was weeping now. "I'm at the RV in the campground," I said again, "in case you want to tell me anything."

I pushed through the heavy door. Outside, in Black Earth proper, in the heavy heat of an August morning, I turned to look back.

The wife of the dead man was locking up behind me.

Dickie Pee

The address on Dickie Pee's business card read 26 Cynthia Street. I walked west on First and found Ann Street, then Bernice Street, and then Cynthia Street. Twenty-six, Dickie's place, was in the middle of the second block. Ahead were another two blocks of small, square houses—Dorothy and Eve streets—and then a very thirsty cornfield.

But Dickie Pee's place brought my gaze back. In Boston, in another life, I had followed the New England Patriots, and few sights raised more hair on the Dog's neck than the green and gold of the Green Bay Packers. For one thing, no fan seemed more insane than a Cheesehead. But I had never imagined a house painted in Packers colors—cheese-gold siding with green doors, a giant cheese-gold G on the green garage door, all of it fading and peeling and the full effect blocked by a raw-looking wheelchair ramp that took three switchbacks to reach the front door. The lawn was scorched and rocky with dog turds. Dickie's blue panel van was in the driveway.

A haggard woman in a sweat suit answered the door. As

she yelled for "Richard," I rolled my wrist and checked the time. It was eleven o'clock.

"I bought some flies this morning," I explained, trying to assuage the woman's irritation. Was she Dickie's wife? His mother? She was more used-up than old. "I thought I'd drop off the money."

"Richard!" she screamed again. Then she disappeared down a dim hallway and shut a door behind her. The house, dismally small and plain and neat to the point of exhaustion, smelled of ashtrays and air freshener. A large-screen TV dominated the living room. Then a second door in the hallway clicked open. Chatter from a different TV leaked out. "Easier if you come in here," called Dickie Pee.

"My sister works nights," he said as I came through the door. "Packing boxes out at Lands' End. Works her ass off. She ain't up yet."

The proprietor of Mobile Fly Shop half-turned from a fly-tying desk that was heaped shoulder-deep with necks and pelts and spools of thread and little plastic boxes. The mess continued off the side of the desk and onto the floor, where I noted an open box of Friends of Black Earth Creek brochures. His bed was a nest of tangled sheets and pillows. A large box fan sat right on the bed, whirring away across the scalp of an ancient bull terrier. Above the bed was an apparatus for strong-arming your way in and out of it, like a piece of gymnastic equipment. Bart Starr and Brett Favre posters covered the walls, except for the spot claimed by the Matco Tool girl. The TV was playing a war movie. I held out two fifties. Dickie Pee took them. "Hang on," he murmured at me, his eyes sliding to the TV. "You gotta catch this. This is awesome."

We watched a World War II bomber drone over dense jungle. Seconds later a bridge blew up and collapsed into the river below.

"Yeah!" celebrated Dickie Pee. He turned to me. My two fifties were in his shirt pocket already. "Sorry man, I don't have change right now."

"Then I'll take it out in tackle. I need some tippet spools."

"Well shit," he said. "Then we gotta go out to the van."

"Then never mind," I said. "I'll take it in a fly-tying lesson," I told him. "Show me how you tie that upside-down Jake's Sally."

He shook out a cigarette and lit it. He flicked his hair out of his glasses. "That's proprietary, man. I'm trying to make a living here." He caught me glancing around—checking out the living. "Hey, man. I'm serious. I support myself. I got a place," he said. "My own place. I got eleven acres up the coulee and I'm gonna build a house on it when I get the money together. I can't help it if a piece of defective merchandise gave out and I broke my fucking C-8."

It took me a second. Okay. So Darrald's tree stand was defective. That was his story. And the C-8 was a vertebra. I moved on.

"How many sallies did you sell to Jake?"

"Sell to Jake? Shit, I gave to Jake. Man, I supported that dude."

"A dozen?" I said. "Two dozen?"

"Six."

"Six dozen?"

"One-two-three-four-five-six flies. Total. He wanted any more, he was going to have to buy them. I'm already giving my time." He nodded at the box of FOBEC brochures on the floor.

I did a quick calculation. If Jacobs had been killed earlier in the day, when he *wasn't* fishing the sally, then his killer had taken off, say, an elk hair caddis, and tied on the sally that Junior tossed. That would leave five Jake's Sallies in his box. Now another had been tied on his tippet. If the killer had access to Jake's fly box—Bud Heavy, for example, along the stream—there should be four sallies left. If there were five left, or six, then Jacobs' killer had supplied his own yellow sallies—and that killer could be sitting right here in front of me.

"Does anyone else know how to tie a Jake's Sally?"

Dickie tossed hair from his eyes and squinted at me through smoke.

"Man, you got a lot of questions."

I managed a little Dog smile. I thought I'd figured out how to work with him. "You owe me twenty bucks. How many can I afford?"

He tossed his hair again. Maybe he was thinking of his property up the coulee when he glanced at the video. On cue, a tank exploded. "Five bucks a question," said Dickie Pee. "No guarantee I'll answer."

I did the smile again. "Deal. So what was it that you liked so much about fly fishing?"

I had surprised him. Myself, too. But back in the corporate security days, a guy in assembly steals, say, a crate of product, sells it to a fence to pay for his kid's hockey equipment—that's your hypothesis—you don't start out with "Mister Schultz, did you steal the product?" No. You start with, "Hey, Schultzy—you see McMurphy's hat trick last night? I missed it. Hadda be at PTA." Make him want to talk to you. Then when suddenly he doesn't want to talk to you anymore, you know something.

The movement, Dickie Pee told me. He liked the movement. The water coming down against you, and you working up against it. Plus the beauty of a live trout in your hands.

I nodded. "Yeah, I hear you." I pointed at the cuff around his ankle. "So speaking of movement, what happens if you're not at home when the computer calls?"

He snorted. His cigarette was done. He pushed the butt through the lid into a *Pêche Tôt* cup. *Hiss*. "I fuck up my probation. They can call me in for re-sentencing."

"Hey," I said, "I was just over there, at the *Pêche Tôt*. Great coffee." He was looking at me oddly through his big smudged glasses. My tone was off. I was rusty.

"I saw a tying bench in there. Does anyone besides you know how to tie a Jake's Sally?"

"Nope. And that's three questions. Fifteen bucks."

I pointed back to the cuff around his bone-thin ankle. "The phone rings after dark and you're not here, you could end up in jail. So you were taking a pretty big risk, going to the village board meeting the other night when there was no treasurer's report on the agenda—all just to second a motion to adjourn."

He scowled at me, patting his shirt pocket for smokes. "That's four questions," he said. "I'm done."

"That wasn't a question," I said back evenly, and watched him pause a cigarette just beyond his lips.

"So what did Ingrid Jacobs mean," I asked him, "when she said I'm next at the campground?"

What Ingrid Jacobs meant

I banged on the *Pêche Tôt* door but got no answer. I stepped back and looked up. There were two windows above, framed in brick and straddling a mortared inset that read 1921. In the right-hand window, I saw blinds sway. I banged again.

The orange cat sat upright on the fly-tying bench, swished its tail back and forth.

A small sign taped in the corner of the door said DELIVERIES IN THE REAR. When I looked back up, the cat had disappeared.

I walked to the end of the block and then up the alley. The surface was sparse gravel over hard dirt. Dumpsters lined one side, picket fences and back yards the other. At the rear of the *Pêche Tôt* sat a homely pile of belongings, toppled into the outer wheel ruts of the alley: a Scooby Doo sleeping bag, a pair of scuffed black pumps, a cardboard box, a clock radio, a soiled blue goose-down parka. I looked to the door. It was a replacement for the 1921 original, and the job was poorly done. Rear entry to the *Pêche Tôt* was guarded by a hollow-core door, unfinished veneer peeling, hung with long, opposite-matched isosceles triangles of space on top and bottom. Behind it, the cat mewed.

I turned at the rumble of an engine in the alley. An El Camino approached at reckless speed and stopped in a swirl of dust and gravel beside the pile of belongings. The vehicle was probably thirty years old, and it was in bad shape. In the back rode White Milkerson's yellow electrofishing generator, along with nets, jugs, gear boxes, boots and gloves, and assorted trash.

"Hello, Shelly," I said, as the driver stepped out.

The girl used both hands to tug her cut-off jeans out from where the car seat had pushed them, at the same time stepping forward in dirty flip-flops—one pink, one blue— two steps, *snap-snap*.

"Do I know you?"

"Dickie Pee just told me about you. We're neighbors down at the campground."

"Yeah?"

"Yeah."

She sized up the Dog. As always, my inner mirror showed me the pasty skin and the gut, the cheap uniform, the wallet fat with kid pictures, the dutiful gold band, the good Dog. Dog the factotum. The Fetch King. As for her, Shelly Milkerson had her Dad's funny round face and too-blue eyes, but otherwise Manfred Milkerson had dipped his wick into a deeper gene pool. The daughter was a little blonder, a little taller, a little bit better looking. She was tanned to an odd butterscotch color, tattooed around the navel, pierced in the ears and left eyebrow. She was skinny and muscular—everything but her breasts, which were too big and slung about beneath a blue bikini top in a made-you-look kind of way. Dickie Pee had told me she was eighteen. He said she looked like her mother.

He said she was a good time. He said that's what Ingrid Jacobs meant, *you're next*.

"You're a fisherman?"

"The guy in the RV."

"Cool," she said, offhand. "You gotta give me a ride sometime."

She stepped past me. As she heaved up the cardboard box, I smelled a gust of unmetabolized alcohol. She dropped the box in the back of the El Camino. It tilted off the side of her dad's yellow electrofishing pack and spilled a small avalanche of framed pictures and loose bits of jewelry.

"Shit."

She vaulted into the El Camino's bed. Curling the toes of her right foot inside its pink flip-flop, she shoved her dad's stuff aside. Her left flip-flop, I noticed again, was blue.

"Okay," she said. "You want to hand that to me?"

I gave her the Scooby Doo sleeping bag, the blue parka, the clock radio. Her hands were rough, dirty around the nails.

"You were staying here?"

"Off and on."

"Looks like you're moving out."

"Yeah?" She looked up at the rear windows above the *Pêche Tôt*. "Well, whatever."

"Back to the campground?"

She jumped down.

"Whatever," she repeated. "Listen, you got a few bucks?"

"Not on me."

"Yeah, right." She looked at me like she had never met an out-of-town fly fisherman without more than a few bucks to spare on a girl like her. I imagined she hadn't. She watched me long enough to figure out I wasn't biting. Then she rolled her eyes away. She stared at the back door of the *Pêche Tôt* for a long time. When she looked back at me, her eyes were bloodshot and teary.

"Whatever," she said vehemently. "I mean, really."

"Really, what?"

"I'm not in the mood anyway. So what's your name?"

"Dog."

"Dog?"

"Dog."

"You heard about Jake?"

"I found Jake."

She looked away at the coffee shop again.

"Whatever. I mean, I'm sorry for her, but Ingrid's such a bitch. She thinks I did something with Jake. She treated me like shit."

"But she let you stay here? She let you work here?"

"Jake did. Jake let me. I was in that little camper last winter and Jake got me out. I was freezing my ass off. But he and Ingrid always fought about it."

"But you weren't at the *Pêche Tôt* last night?"

Her eyes narrowed on me. They were rheumy now like her father's. It was amazing how much he and she looked alike. Shelly Milkerson wore her impossible breasts the way her father wore his impossible moustache—like a part of each of them that was beyond their control.

"I was in the shop this morning," I told her, "when you called Ingrid about working today."

She glanced toward an upstairs window. "I…I have some other places…where I sleep. Sometimes."

"Like your dad's?"

No reply.

"Sorry. I guess I'm being nosy."

"So welcome to Black Earth," she said. "Everybody's nosy."

"Dickie said the same thing. He also said you two go way back."

"I'm eighteen. How far back could we go?"

I didn't have a chance to answer that. From above us, the old sash window dragged open and around the blind thrust a hand holding a large black tool box. The hand let go. The tool box fell fast and square. Plastic shattered and tools flew and spun around our ankles.

"Fuck," said Shelly.

The hand reappeared and flung a battered silver t-square. The thing nose-dived like a wingless airplane into a gravel chuck-hole behind the El Camino. A brace of drywall tools followed.

"Fuck," said Shelly as the window closed.

She bent to pick up tools. "What a bitch," she fumed. I smelled alcohol again. "I was fixing Jake's office. But she's got a one-track mind. Everybody's after Jake. The whole world exists to take Jake away from her."

"Somebody did take Jake away from her," I pointed out.

Shelly's eyes had teared up. She stooped around in a bizarre display of tits and ass and tools. Here, in the flesh, was Dickie Pee's MATCO tool girl, though a little young, a little tipsy, a little smudged. "Jake was *leaving* Ingrid," she said. "She didn't appreciate Jake when he was alive. She drove him completely nuts. People wouldn't have hated Jake half as much without Ingrid."

As she straightened with a fistful of fitted wrenches, the surge of an engine made us both look down the alley. Here came B.L. in his police cruiser.

His amber mirrored lenses didn't tell whether his eyes slid over us as he got out—didn't let on if he was checking out Shelly's poster girl pose or if he had been successful in getting a warrant to search the Cruise Master.

He banged on the flimsy back door of the *Pêche Tôt*. I knew what he was there for. Jake's rod. The rod with the bogus yellow sally on it. Maybe last night's empty tippet could be forgotten about. Maybe the killer was getting his set-up back. A faked death, followed by a faked investigation. Who was going to protest? Me? Junior?

He banged again. The cat mewed. But the police chief got no other answer. He stood back a step, put his hands atop the fat rolls on his hips, rocked a little in his cowboy boots, and muttered.

"Said she'd be here. Goddamned crazy daisy."

Behind him, Shelly flip-flopped up, slinging a dirty-white macramé purse. She reached inside and brought out a set of keys. She found the one she wanted easily and fit it into the lock.

"You got crazy right," she said to B.L., and she let him in.

I was watching B.L. stumble over the orange cat when I felt her hand slip into mine. "Come on," she said. "Let's go."

Good work by Jacobs

"Your shithole," said Shelly back at the campground, "or mine?"

She had to leave the El Camino at the gate. After ferrying her belongings to the pop-up camper, she had hauled a twelve-pack of Miller Lite from the passenger seat. She put a can in my hand. The can was air temperature, about eighty-five degrees.

"Uh," I said, "noplace. Thanks."

I handed the beer back. She seemed disappointed more than angry. She wore a variation of her father's look of wounded amusement.

"Look, I want to take a closer look at this dam Jake was so upset about. I'm going to walk over there. Wanna come along?"

Shelly Milkerson sat down on the step of her pop-up, in the shade of its moldy little awning, and snapped open a beer can. She put her elbows on her knees and leaned into the warm foam, suckling at the can. "I'll wait," she said.

Beyond the pop-up, a pair of crows contended noisily over something in the grass. They timed my arrival, then flew cawing off to a cottonwood down by the dam, leaving behind a small brown trout, pecked apart and stiff. I glanced back at Shelly. I saw the bottom of her beer can.

I retreated into the heavy summer afternoon. Cicadas reamed from the cottonwoods, and grasshoppers snapped into flight at my feet. The air smelled of black dirt, hay, heat, and rain. Gray clouds had massed in the western sky, over the far shore of Lake Bud. On President Bud's land, strips of orange tape circled trees to be cut down. I could also see the white squares of the LOTS FOR SALE signs. If the dam went out, I remembered Junior telling me, then this was a stream again, and a setback law went into effect. No development within a quarter mile of the stream. That was good work by Jacobs. Bud must have felt trapped.

But the dam surprised me. I hadn't expected the Grand Coulee, but the Black Earth mill pond dam was little more than a long heap of earth cornered on the far bank by a cracked and pitted concrete slab that twisted toward the downstream side. A two-inch sheet of water slipped over its mossy rim. Stacked up against the dam were several decades of flotsam—tree branches and fence posts and hunks of Styrofoam, woven with fishing line and bobbers and bound up in a grimy, sudsy, sun-encrusted sludge. The graffiti-splotched foundation of the old mill lay crumbled on the bank beyond the slab. Downstream of this, the creek ran wide, shallow, and straight through a quarter-mile wasteland of overgrazed Sundvig pasture before it slipped into a concrete jacket behind the lumber yard that marked the far edge of the Village of Black Earth.

It was a sad end to a beautiful trout stream. And without an actual mill to use the pond, it was pointless, too, unless you meant to develop "lakefront property."

Before me, a disused dirt road emerged from a tangle of dogwood saplings and ended atop the concrete slab. The shoreline was soupy and brush-snarled, thick with mosquitoes, but I slogged my way over. The road hadn't seen traffic in years, and the shore around the slab was littered with the usual detritus left by bait fisherman—including one carp, long dead. But the high weeds and dogwoods were freshly hacked back, as if with a machete, to widen the road toward its original single lane. Thin tire tracks had rutted it and dried in the mud, as though someone had ridden a bicycle back and forth to the dam.

I stepped onto the slab. The splash pool was about fifteen feet down, wide and frothy. A pair of blue-winged teal poked for food at the margins. Then the stream sheeted out over pasture, ankle deep and clogged with milfoil. A hundred yards down, cattle stood in the water.

I wondered if a person could walk across the mossy rim to the dirt mound on the other side. The water was no more than a few inches deep as it poured out of Lake Bud and into the pasture below, and the concrete spout of the dam was no more than twenty feet across. From there, and easily it seemed, one could descend the earthen mound through a manageable tangle of grass and sumac. One could get at the base of the dam—or easily into President Bud's lakefront lots on the other side.

As I considered the possibility of crossing, I saw something lodged in the foam crust around the pool below. The object was pinkish and pulpy, bobbing as the foam worked its way around the muddy edge.

A guy like me—a hundred rivers waded—should have known better, but I tried to walk across the dam spout. I got halfway over when the push of the lake became too strong and suddenly I feared to lift a foot. I stood there cussing, both boots planted in six inches of water atop slick algae, a thousand tons of water bearing down on my ankles. Too late, I realized that the slightest crack between my boot sole and the dam spout would let a lever of water under my feet that would flip me. I actually gave up a derisive snort—the Dog, back on the leash again—stuck in another well-intentioned, idiotic pose—trapped with his feet on the slipperiest possible ground, unable to move, unable to do anything but await disaster. Classic, classic Dog.

But something felt different this time. Hell—I was going down anyway. We were all going down eventually, right? I jumped.

The teal blew upward as I hit the splash pool—one duck right through my air space. In the instant before I went under, I felt the dry rasp of a wing across my face—then the shock of cold spring water. The pool was deep enough not to kill me, but shallow enough to jar my spine and collapse my legs and pitch me forward in a painful skid over limestone rubble.

When I washed up in the outer foam, I saw what I had jumped for: Shelly's lost pink flip-flop.

I WONDERED HOW she had lost it. Walking on water? But she was gone from the step of her camper. Her beer can and mine, too, were tossed on the grass. The El Camino was gone from the gate. When I pushed open the camper door, a musty, canvas-scented heat came pouring out. She had set up housekeeping inside. The Scooby Doo sleeping bag was unrolled on the narrow bunk. The down jacket was folded up like a pillow. On the foldout table she had arranged the contents of the cardboard box. In the center of the table, she had propped a group of small framed photographs. In the center stood a professional portrait of a blond-haired young woman, wearing dark lipstick, a tight-fitting black sweater, a necklace with a crucifix, and large, showy earrings. A half dozen other old snapshots showed the same woman with a child—in a stroller, on a beach somewhere, at a highchair with a spoonful of food, the usual stuff. Arranged around these pictures were several objects, oddly disconnected. A slotted enamel serving spoon, blue, well-used. A faded aqua shower puff. A pair of sunglasses. A pumice stone.

Who was she? I wondered for a moment. But of course: Shelly's mother. Shelly had to have a mother. White Milkerson, at some point, had to have a wife. So…the question was…*where* was she?

THE SOUND OF A CAR on County K made me drop the salvaged pink flip-flop for Shelly and back out.

But the car passed. The road was empty. The heat was heavy, the sky pulsing with dark clouds. I felt exhausted. Out of nowhere, I felt bereft, confused—hungry, maybe, but most of all tired. I retreated to the Cruise Master. I stripped off my wet clothes and lay on my bunk, listening to the cicadas and the drone and clank of a tractor.

I needed sleep, but as usual my veins seemed to widen and hum with a kind of gnawing, hollow energy—like tracks with trains approaching from the near distance of the day my family ended. If I fished enough, and drank enough, the trains went slow, usually, and most times I could drift off before they collided inside and I found myself in the dream-scrambled train wreck of the past. But I hadn't properly fished at all that day. I thought of vodka but didn't have the energy. The Dog just lay there inside the tin can of the Cruise Master, listening to a storm build outside, waiting for the vein-trains to start.

Hey, trout guy

"Hey...hey, trout guy."

Someone was in the Cruise Master, wiggling my leg. I sat up groggily.

"Nice skivvies," said Junior. "You missed supper." She held up a take-out bag. "Today's A&W Day. Every Thursday. Dad's a bit regular."

I swung my legs off the bunk. Funny thing—bizarre and unfamiliar thing—I'd slept hard—deeply, fishless and alcohol-free. I could tell by the strong light in the Cruise Master that a storm had passed. The sun was full and low.

"You know," said Junior, "tightie-whities went out of style about twenty years ago."

I didn't know what she was talking about until I saw where she was looking. My underwear—thereabouts. She stood a little jauntily, grinning at me just inside the Cruise Master door, dressed in her usual boots and blue jeans, sweat-smudged white T-shirt with the sports bra under, a John Deere cap with her stiff little ponytail sticking out the back. She'd had her sunburn touched up by the long, hot day, and her lips were parched, with white crusts in the corners. She played with the dead watch around her neck.

"But you don't care, do you? Darrald didn't care either. That old boy was J.C. Penney all the way, bless his heart." She rattled an A&W bag. "So. You hungry? You wanna come up and eat with us?"

She drove her blue pickup fast into the first curve. "Whoa," she said as Lumen Bostock's milk truck came barreling down the coulee. He blew his horn. She blew hers back. A hail of gravel lashed the pickup. "Little prick," she muttered, leveling onto a flat stretch where the stream ran alongside in a sleeve of purple asters. After a quarter mile she said, "So—Mister Dog— I guess my hunch was on about you. You haven't left yet."

I looked at her.

"You must be having fun, right?"

I didn't answer that. But I told her somebody had gotten to the fly rod she had altered and altered it back. Now the rod had a yellow sally on it again—a Jake's Yellow Sally, just like the one she had pulled off.

She seemed excited. "No shit? Someone tied a sally back on there? That narrows it, right?"

"Could be. Could have been Bud Bjorgstad," I said, "except Bud Lite didn't seem to know about it. He seemed surprised as hell, Ingrid said."

She slung the pickup into another corner. This time it was a hay wagon coming the other way. "That's my hay," she said. "I sell to Elmer Sundvig, who doesn't have enough acreage of his own now because he sold good farm land to Bud—who will mess with anyone, by the way. Especially B.L. So how did this rod thing happen?"

"B.L. gave the rod back to Ingrid last night. This morning,

she called him to point out there was a sally on it. As in, Jake died around eight o'clock."

Junior straightened the pickup and the road climbed through a hump of sugar maples and hickories, leaving the stream behind.

"Somebody's working hard to make that point," she said.

"Or to see," I said, "if you'll argue it."

That slowed her. She drove thoughtfully through the last turn and up her driveway. "B.L.," she concluded at last, "is not that smart." She turned the engine off and seemed to ponder a bit more. Her dad was on the porch, flipping a bobber into the grass with a bait rod, reeling it up, flipping it again, glaring at us with his lips offset.

"But Bud is," she said.

ON HER WAY ACROSS the yard, Junior called, "Let it soak, Daddy! Burgers are here!"

Melvin O'Malley propped his rod against the porch rail and gathered a bacon cheeseburger into his huge hands. Junior set a soda on the porch beside his chair. He ate like a man who had crops rotting on the vine. In a matter of seconds, he was done with the burger. He began snorkeling into his soda. "Oh, Daddy," Junior sighed, sitting down on the step beside me.

"Ice cream," he replied.

"In a minute. Let your belly rest." She handed me a burger. "So what do you eat usually?" she said. "Dog food?"

Pretty much, I told her.

"Vegetables ever?"

"I eat cress from the streams."

She nodded, chewing. I changed the subject, told her Shelly Milkerson had a key to the *Pêche Tôt*. So, probably, did Dickie Pee. And of course there was Ingrid. As for the second yellow sally on Jake Jacobs' line, that knot, I said, was amateur, the work of a non-fisherman. Which, I declared, along with the wheelchair, left out Dickie.

"You'd be surprised about Dickie," she replied. "He still plays softball. Left field." I tried to picture this—and succeeded. I saw him tossing hair from his eyes, backing up under a fly ball. "But you're right," Junior said. "Dickie does know knots. He used to fish the creek a lot. As for me, I don't have a clue. So show me," she said, "the knot you mean."

She took Dad's rod and reeled it up. "Shush," she said over his protests. "They're not biting anyway."

She swung the bobber up and I caught it. I showed her the hook.

"Like that," I said.

She bit off a French fry and bent in closer. The monofilament was piled in six neat wraps above the hook eye, a small tag end sticking out. Dad tied a decent knot. Or someone did.

"Does that knot have a name?"

"A clinch knot. A textbook clinch knot."

"And what's on Jake's rod now?"

"A mess. A granny. Somebody just trying to fasten a fly on there as fast as possible."

She mused, "Too bad I didn't see the knot I broke."

I agreed. She flipped the bobber back into the grass. Her dad began to grunt and mumble. Junior reeled up and cast farther, to the edge of a toppled woodpile. The old man went quiet.

"Daddy's real precise," she told me. "He likes things a certain way. He sat here all day," she said, indicating that very spot on the porch, now occupied by the hulking old man in his scallop-backed metal lawn chair. "He was watching that hayfield, making sure I cut it in the right pattern."

I looked across the highway, across the pasture and the

stream, to the field on the hill. The hay rows were horizontal, nicely ruled against the tree line. Junior stretched her back as she looked with me. "I've been sitting crooked on that hill all day," she said, and she scooted across the step and put her back against her dad's right foot. "Go on, Daddy," she said, "you owe me now," and he began to dig his huge, sock-clad toes into her spine. She writhed against him, sighing a little, getting back to our previous conversation. "Well, as for someone getting into the *Pêche Tôt,* Shelly slept in there, I heard. She was living in that camper down by you in the park, but Jake and Ingrid took her in."

"*Jake* took her in," I corrected. "That's what Shelly said. Jake and Ingrid fought about her. Now Ingrid's kicked her out. She thought Jake and Shelly were sleeping together."

Junior sighed. "Poor Shelly. She's got a bit of a reputation with men."

"Deserved," I guessed.

"Yup." Junior shifted on her dad's foot. She leaned back and slid higher into his weight. "If you mean she makes it with a lot of guys, including married guys, old guys, you name it. But can you blame her? Really?"

Lumen Bostock thundered back the other way. Gravel strafed Junior's mailbox. It was that time of day, I figured, in the milk business.

I said, "Where's Shelly's mother?"

"She and White had a hard time," Junior said. "White—" She pulled away from her dad's foot. She lifted the dead watch sideways and drew the chain unconsciously through her teeth. "Well, you probably noticed White was half-plowed the other day. He had a pretty rough time with his family, oh, what was it, about ten years ago, more like fifteen I guess. He…"

She increased her volume. "Manfred, Daddy. I'm telling him about Manfred and Nanette and Shelly."

Melvin Senior gazed out at his bobber in the yard. Just as I was about to wonder how, two weeks ago, he could have been coherent enough to threaten Jake Jacobs, and then remember the threat, he cleared his baggy old throat and said, "White's a good man. You don't do that to a good man. She ruined him."

He gave me the eye.

"It's sad what happened," Junior went on, "and it doesn't matter now. I mean, we have to get over stuff. Right? But he married Nanette Margolis, this girl who— Well, everybody but him knew it was a bad idea. She was a lot younger. I mean, a lot. Really pretty. Really wild. And they had a kid and all. Shelly. Then one day Nanette and this guy from the Harvestore company, the guy that sold Daddy that tractor out there, he and Nanette just took off, left White with their daughter to raise on his own. And White—"

She glanced at her dad, who had both hands clenched, trembling, around his rod butt.

"Poor White, he botched it, obviously. Shelly hates his guts, acts out, makes trouble. They both drink. Shelly won't live with him, but she takes whatever she needs. She does a lot of crazy stuff," Junior said. She glanced at her dad. "Trying to hurt White, I guess. I guess we all do some of that."

She slapped her dad on the knee. "Hey," she said, "Big Guy…ice cream?"

INTO THE DUSK, she brought out three bowls of mint chocolate chip and three giant multi-vitamins. Her dad's ice cream was gone in four bites. Junior wiped his jowls and said, "Ready for Poppins?"

I watched as they went inside. The TV sparked on, still set at its massive volume. A minute later I heard the voice of Julie Andrews as she sailed singing through the London sky under her umbrella.

"There," said Junior, returning to the porch. "He's all set."

She looked at me. She tilted her head. She kept looking at me.

"What?" I said.

"Well, Mister Dog, you know what I was thinking today?"

"I imagine you think about a lot of things on that tractor all day long."

"You're right. I do. Just like you and fishing. But you know what I was stuck on today?"

I didn't know.

"Eat your vitamin," she advised me.

Then, as I choked the pill down, Junior looked up into the deepening sky, where swallows flashed beyond the barn roof. The sun had slipped behind the hill she had just mowed, and a stunning pink light sprayed through the treetops. A whippoor-will was calling from near the stream, and a whitetail deer had just stepped from a woody wrinkle in the coulee and into Junior's pasture. Somewhere in there, in its groove below the closing asters and sunflowers, Black Earth Creek flowed timelessly on.

"That yellow sally hatch," Junior said. "It must be pretty special."

I said it was.

"It must be a rush."

I said it was.

"Kind of, I don't know...spiritual?"

I was quiet on that one.

She took my hand. "Come on," she said. "Let's fish it."

Show me how it's done

She was clumsy with a fly rod. Everybody is at first. The stroke is not what you think. It takes a while to feel the tight little space inside of which you have to be decisive and powerful at the butt of the rod. It takes a while to feel the line, to connect the fly at the end to the subtle twists in your wrist and elbow. It takes longer than a while to get your weak hand working, stripping and feeding line on the way out, collecting slack on the way in, keeping perfect pace with the stream flow.

Junior cursed her incompetence, then shrieked and laughed when, out of nowhere, a big trout rose, green-backed and silky-silent, to suck in her sally. For an instant, the fish had her fly, but she couldn't touch it. The rod was empty in her hand, the line slack, the trout just as instantly gone. She had seen the moment of truth, but, disembodied by surprise, she had failed to connect.

"Son of a buck knife!" she hollered. "Damn it, Junior!"

The yellow sally hatch was a thick one, and as we had hurried to the stream in the minutes previous, we had seen the hatch begin in the alertness of birds. Towhees tipped on branch ends, eager as sprinters in their blocks. Barn swallows killed time, mapping their long, looping circuits across the pre-night sky. Thrushes flitted on the stream banks.

I had brought a second rod and reel. I sat on the bank to attach a leader. "What's that?" Junior, at my shoulder, asked about the knot.

"A nail knot."

"It's different than what you showed me on Daddy's line."

"Completely different," I said. "Different purpose. The one you saw before connects hook to leader, a clinch knot. It's simple. Any fisherman can tie it. This one, the nail knot, is for connecting two pieces of line together. I've got this leader butt, thin but stiff, and very slippery." I showed her the thick end of the clear, tapered, monofilament leader. "And I've got the tip of my fly line"—I showed her the hollow, orange, polymer line that performs the cast—"which is thicker, limper, and just as slick. The two have to connect in a knot no bigger than a rice grain but capable of taking about two hundred pounds of tension."

I rambled on, quoting an instruction manual from somewhere. But Junior looked enthralled. I coiled the leader butt along an eight-penny finish nail from my vest pocket, then fed the leader tag back through the coils. I took my habitual deep breath. Then I worked the orange line end the opposite way through the coils. I tucked and tamped and yanked suddenly. The nail fell free into my lap. I trimmed my ends. A nail knot.

"Wow. And you all can do that?"

"All…?"

"All you fly fishermen?"

"No. Most need it so rarely they forget how. So there's shortcuts," I said. "Braided loops, cheater knots, that kind of thing. Because most fly fishermen can't tie a nail knot. Or won't bother."

We both stopped, because a yellow sally had landed on the back of my hand. It was an odd insect—a giant in its miniature world, at once preposterous and beautiful. Like all stoneflies, it had broad, flat wings, but the sally's wings were pure gossamer, impossible flakes of tissue that caught the sunset and held it in a dozen glowing, veiny prisms. The tail strands were impractically long, flickering at the end of a plump yellow abdomen, sausage-shaped and crisscrossed with black bands like Mexican gunbelts. It stood up on six stout, jointed legs, and it goggled around with out-sized, green-hued eyes. Then it flew.

Side by side, Junior and I watched the insect flutter and climb, veering and dipping erratically against the backdrop of a pink-struck box elder and a blue-black sky. Then—*zip!*—a towhee darted from an upstream willow and got it. And the trout had begun to slurp.

"Okay," I told Junior. "Let's do it. It will be over in thirty minutes."

I put the rod in her hands, and those thirty minutes passed like five, as they always do during a hatch. Junior waded in her blue jeans, shivering, stream water wicking up her T-shirt until it was pasted pink against her skin below the wide band of her bra. When she snapped a sally off behind her on the head of an aster—and a second time on my hat—I handed her the backup rod and, under flashlight, tied on another.

Junior hung in there, spooking fish with her short, slashing casts, snapping flies off, cussing herself and laughing. Time and distance collapsed on us in the gathering darkness, and somehow I remembered past lives, remembered bicycling in the Brookline dark, around my block, my father calling me in, and how fast and smoothly the bike seemed to move in the black gaps between the streetlights. I remembered the dutiful suburban Dog, thirty years later, taking himself outside for a run, trying to work the flat spot off his ass and the baggage off his belly—gamely chugging along a tree-lined street in West Newton, feeling, in the dark, like he was *flying,* like he was *going somewhere,* like he was *hanging in there,* like *everything connected* and *everything mattered* and it was a hard but good thing to be a human being.

"Okay," relented Junior at last through chattering teeth. "Show me."

I was slow on the uptake, lost in the past.

"Show me how it's done."

I passed her the backup rod. I took hers and numbly re-energized the slush of her last cast. While the line was airborne, paused horizontally behind me, I assessed the hatch. It was nearly finished. Sated, the birds were still, though a lone bat still prospected in jagged figure eights between the stream banks. It was too dark now to see fish or insects, but as my loop rolled out behind me I heard a heavy slurp from the right bank, about forty feet up.

I laid the fly down well short, knowing the timing was off. That fish would go down, work the big insect through the sphincter at the back of its mouth, then refocus on the next bite. The current was deep and slow, and I counted to ten while Junior grunted, unsticking her boots from the mud, and moved around behind me. "Left side," I murmured. "Stay on my left side."

She disappeared behind me. I couldn't see her. I raised the fly and backcast, stripped out another twelve feet of line, and laid the sally down ahead and instream of the fish. I took one long breath as the fly drifted toward the overhanging jewelweed on the bank. I couldn't see where it went. But I guessed. I raised the rod just as the slurp came, and the hook set. I was fast to a big, nighttime brown trout.

"Oh, yeah!" whooped Junior, and she moved up tight to my elbow. I felt her hot breath on my neck. Somehow the rush of that sensation was even stronger than the thrill of the big trout digging against me for the safety of the bank. Junior encouraged me in grunts and gasps, peering along with me into the cold, flowing ink ahead. I couldn't see the trout. I could only hear it and feel it, just as I could hear and feel the woman at my back, and for the moment I felt an embrace of energies like I only distantly remembered. I felt a ballooning of joy in my heart—and at the same moment, in the service of some dark and unknown truth, I felt all heat leave me. I felt naked in the cold and streaming blackness.

Shuddering, I turned the trout and unclipped my net. The big brown shook its head across the surface and rolled away. I wagged it side to side, tiring its lateral muscles. Then I turned it abruptly and filled its mouth with the push of the stream.

Junior gasped as the trout coasted into my net. I hurled my rod to the bank. I clicked on my flashlight and fit it between my teeth. We gazed at the fish—a giant male, more than two feet long, hump-necked and kipe-jawed, sleek and glistening, sheathed in exquisite skin with blue spots inside red aureoles. Junior grabbed the back of my vest for balance and leaned to touch the fish. She ran a wet finger along the pale scales beneath his flaring gills.

I felt calm and warm again, holding that fish. Then he thrashed, tore my thumb with his teeth. I pulled my hook, turned him into the current, and let him go.

The trout vanished instantly, and Junior's squawk filled the night.

"What? Aren't we going to eat him?"

"We just did," I said.

"What?"

"I'm full now."

I felt her eyes on me. She had a knife out. She had been ready to clean the fish. I was shaking. I felt her green eyes cutting through the night air between us.

"What?"

I stood there rigidly in the current. Indeed, What? What had I just said? *I'm full now.* Like a guy who knew something. As if a fix of animal energy, pushing water, and fleeting loveliness—as if these moments from the stream were enough not only to keep the Glock from my head, but enough to satisfy me. Since when, I wondered. What was going on?

That's when I felt Junior's arms close around me. The sensation was startling—and not because I hadn't felt a woman in so long. No—it was more like I had never felt strength like that—*sureness,* an easy, unconscious strength, the touch of someone who moved thousand-pound animals with the casual grace that came from knowing what was good for them. As she gripped me from behind, Junior felt weirdly solid, stunningly massive, and utterly undeniable. Her hands clasped around my chest. Her chest pressed my back. Her hat brim raked my ear and her cheek arrived against my neck.

I bent and staggered under her embrace. She didn't let up. She didn't know her own strength. Or maybe she did. And I didn't know where the knife had gone. This woman could kill me, I thought suddenly. This woman could drown me.

I struggled. Junior hung on. I felt her chin dig in between my shoulder blades. I pried at her hands and staggered for the bank. She rode me. She clung and muttered something against my neck. A prayer, a curse? A ferocious sweet-nothing? I couldn't make it out. Not until I hit slick clay at the bank edge and slipped underwater could I wrench out of her grip. I rolled and stumbled and came up sputtering in water-stuffed waders a few yards downstream.

Junior had already scrambled onto the bank. She looked back at me.

"I was so cold," she blurted. "Sorry. I was just so cold."

I panted at her, spitting water. She had tucked the knife back into her pocket.

"Really," she said. She looked flustered. "I just felt so cold and I just... I just kind of lost it." She squeezed water from the tail of her T-shirt. Her cap was gone. I flailed my feet at the ice-slick clay for a minute, trying to get out. "Well..." she said at last, "I can't leave Daddy there alone any longer."

Then she pushed off through the asters and I watched the white of her shirt as she hurried across the pasture. I heard her pickup start. I heard her roar off. I listened for direction. She wasn't heading toward Daddy.

She was heading toward town.

Leap of faith

And when I returned to the campground, the Cruise Master wallowed on her rims. Her tires were slashed, all four of them, neatly knifed through the sidewalls.

I had to talk to somebody.

"Harv!" I hurried into my little cell phone. I pulled it away from my ear and looked at it, still not quite believing it wasn't a toy.

"Yellow!" he repeated. "Whozit?"

"Harv," I said, "it's Dog. In Wisconsin. I think I'm into something here."

My tax guy chuckled. In the background, I heard a woman's voice, and the whir of a blender.

"No. Harv—listen. I mean really into something." I was still in my waders. The blender stopped. Knowing Harvey as I did, I formed a picture. The old bean counter had probably lured some sweet girl from his yoga class to his place in Back Bay for a wheatgrass smoothie.

"Somebody did a Roxbury tattoo on my tires," I told

Harvey. "And this young woman who… I'm kind of working for her…but she's got a few things going on."

"Excellent," he purred. "Excellent."

I looked at the phone again, like it was playing tricks on me. The blender started up again. My tax guy nickered something away from the phone. I think he said *wheat germ*.

"No, Harvey. What I'm saying is that she may not be what she seems to be. She may be playing games with me."

Harvey cleared his cluttered old throat—the sound he always made when he was just about to steer me in the right direction. But as I waited for him to speak, something caught my eye across Lake Bud. "Uh… Harv, hang on…"

Far out toward the opposite shore, a ghostly light panned the water's surface.

"Hang on, Harvey."

Of course he ignored me. "Hey Dog," he said, "you say this gal's playing games? So what's wrong with playing games?"

I scrambled into the Cruise Master and found my binoculars. I aimed them about in blackness, seeing nothing.

Harvey said something I didn't hear. He called my name through the phone's tiny earpiece. The woman in his apartment laughed giddily: *Dog? His name is Dog?* I focused on a building window on the far side of the pond. From there, I found the light over the lake. My hands jumped and blurred the image, but I breathed again and calmed them.

The light was aimed down, at a pair of feet swishing cautiously along just under the water's surface. I held, followed. I stared until I was entirely sure of it. The ankles, the lower legs—they had been bare before, last night, when I had ventured out to sink Jake Jacobs' ponytail. Now they were clad in boots and blue jeans. I put the binoculars down. There came a faint swish and pitter-patter, like hail over water. Then the light retreated and went out.

"Harvey," I said, "she's…she's…"

My tax guy interrupted me in a stern near-whisper.

"She's human, Dog. For chrissake. Enjoy the ride."

"No, Harv—I think she's out there, walking on the water—"

"You're in love," he told me, and he laughed happily.

"Damn it," I said. "Can you listen to me?"

"Is she cute?"

"She's plain. And she's built like a fucking linebacker. She could break my back."

"Mmmmm." The old man breathed in deeply, like he was smelling good soup.

"Harvey, listen to me."

"Why don't you listen to yourself?"

"Harvey, somebody slashed my tires. At night, somebody walks on the lake. The trout are way too goddamn big for the stream. And some guy named Jacobs gets dunked in it. She says her daddy didn't do it. But the old man's a nut case, Alzheimer's, something. But she has this total faith in him. He can do no wrong. And this strange faith in me, too. But—then she nearly drowns me—do you see, Harvey?"

I thought I was making sense. Perhaps I wasn't.

"Dog," he cut in, using the gravelly whisper again. "I appreciate the call. It's nice to hear from you. I'm glad you're having fun. But can this wait just a few hours?"

Headlights panned the far side of the lake. Then tail lights receded.

"See, Dog, I've got someone here. Someone really special. She's not perfect, in fact I'm sure she's playing the old Harvster for something. But she's special. And you see, when you're with someone special, and you've opened everything up, all the doors of the heart, there at last arrives a *certain moment*. A certain *leap of faith*. Okay? Dog? You know what I mean?"

I was silent. I was thinking.

"Dog?"

He hung up.

The time was now

The party at the pop-up camper started just about the time I had juiced myself with enough vodka to drift off. The first sounds were a pickup engine, doors slamming, giggles, and then the unmistakable sound of piss against a tree. But not just any tree. *My* tree. Somebody was pissing on the tree I was parked under.

I sat up and looked at my watch. 2:15 a.m.

"C'mon, Ronnie," called Shelly Milkerson, "leave 'im alone. He's leepin'."

"I'm jus checkin' it out." He zipped and took a deep breath. "Massa...massachewshits," he slurred, and I fingered back my curtain in time to see a heavy man in a golf shirt and slacks stagger back toward the popup.

I lay back and listened to the party gather force: someone had cut the chain around the campground gate, and two tall pickups rumbled in. Next, a radio, and one particularly gnawing voice—fucking this, fucking that, gimme another beer, haw-haw-haw—hardly enough noise to hold down a

Boston street corner, really, but in the quiet country night, it was plenty. I listened until the voices began to repeat themselves and take on a rhythm that I could sleep to. But just as I was finally drifting off, a new voice—nasal, twangy—began to contest for air space, and a new rhythm shook up the night. In no time at all a fight had broken out. I rose to watch dark shapes flail inside the arena of pickups—I made out three men, one trying to break up the other two, with Shelly circling, heaving beer cans at the fray and shrieking, "Assholes!"

It lasted no more than thirty seconds, ending at precisely the moment when the heavy guy in the golf shirt howled, "She's got a knife!" Then three pickups started up and roared away. Shelly shrieked after them, full-throated into the night, "Assholes!"

I lay back and watched dawn creep into the Cruise Master.

WHEN THE KNOCK CAME about an hour later, I put on pants and opened the door. There stood Shelly, barefoot in the dewy grass, open beer can in one hand, closed beer can in the other. "I notice your tires are slashed," she slurred at me. Her voice was hoarse. "Thassa a real bummer." She raised the unopened beer and smiled.

I sat her at my galley table, where she sipped warm beer while I whipped up some Tang. But Shelly kept getting up, lurching in tipsy excitement around the Cruise Master, showing me her young body from every angle.

"This is so cool!" she croaked, twirling, opening cabinets, squeezing past me and looking back from the driver's cab with her arms spread from bucket seat to bucket seat and her heavy breasts lifting the thin blue fabric of a halter top. "This is so perfect!"

"Have some Tang," I urged.

She downed it. "Yuck," she said cheerfully, and looked around again. "This is so excellent!"

It was like she knew the Dog had spent the night anchored to the vodka bottle, having visions of Junior. Like she sensed the drift of Harvey Digman and knew just how to ride it. She stood on the galley bench and peered into my pantry, giving me the run of her suntanned thighs, all the way up to the white curve of underpants beneath her cut-off jeans. Then she dropped down on the seat and leaned over the table toward me.

"Will you lemme drive it?" she said, barely in control of her words. "Fi fixem for ya?"

"Fix what?"

"Your tires, silly."

I wondered how.

"I knowaguy, okay? I get the tires. I put um on."

I must have still looked skeptical. She climbed halfway over the table, knocking over her beer, and grabbed me by the shoulders. "I grew up fixin stuff," she announced. "Every kind of stuff. Okay? My dad made me learn all this shit. So I know how. Okay? Now don't be an asshole. I had enough assholes. I'm fixin your tires."

She slid back through the puddle of beer into her seat.

"Hey," she said. "Hey wait a minute. You know what today is?"

She was still wearing her drunken smile, but her good mood had abruptly slipped. She was re-focusing, zeroing in on something. While I waited, studying the pout on her Milkerson face, I understood the fight at the pop-up as the basest kind of male instinct. The daughter of White Milkerson was never going to get any healthier, any cuter, any easier. In the blink of an eye she was going to be crazy, bitter, knocked up, ugly, dead. The time was now. Now, now, now.

"Today is Jake's wake," she said. "Ten o'clock."

She righted her beer can. She took a half-hearted sip.

"So I fix your tires," she said, reaching for the Tang, "and you do something for me."

Jake's wake

By the time we set out for the funeral home, Shelly Milkerson was half-sober and nervous, shivering on my arm. The sun had shone for about an hour after dawn, and then black clouds and cool air had bubbled up out of the southwest. Another thunderstorm was brewing, the sky rumbling distantly, and Shelly was clinging to my side like a sparrow seeking shelter.

Having no other way, we walked into town. She had stopped by her pop-up camper and grabbed her reunited pink flip-flops and the dirty macramé purse. Halfway in, she surprised me by fishing a cell phone from the purse. She called someone about the tires. Whomever she called didn't seem to welcome the call. But Shelly hung in there, got a promise for four RV-grade radials by afternoon. She knew what kind of tires I needed.

"That was Ronnie," she told me stonily.

"Who's Ronnie?" I asked her.

"A friend. Ronnie Hellenbrand. He's sort of a big guy in the county. I've got a lot of friends," she assured me.

"But you need me to be with you at Jake's wake," I observed.
She didn't get it.

"I'm a stranger," I said. "You feel better with a stranger."

She held on tight as we crossed Main Street near the village office and headed past the *Pêche Tôt*, then down a side street to the block east of Main.

"Okay," she sighed, relenting to an explanation. "*Boyfriends*. Mostly married guys. Not the kind of guys who are going to stick up for me. And Ingrid's going to see me and freak."

THE FUNERAL HOME WAS a low brick structure, new and soulless. The lot was jammed, and the parking had spilled out along the surrounding streets. The mourners seemed mostly from elsewhere: they had lined three village blocks with their minivans and Saabs, Volkswagen campers, a sprinkling of Beemers, a lot of Trout Unlimited and Sierra Club stickers, and more than a few out-of-state plates.

Shelly found lip balm in her dirty bag and put it on. She finished and dropped the tube into the bag.

"Poor Jake," she whispered, shivering into my shoulder.

Inside, at the back of the receiving line, we turned heads. A good share of the attention was for the sight of Shelly, who was the only one there in cut-off jeans and a halter top, exuding the hung-over version of her now-now-now look. And then there was the Dog, looking sexed-up and guilty. And it didn't help that Shelly, in her sparkly strawberry lip balm, clung to me like the two of us had been screwing all night. We smelled like a few kinds of booze, too. In the eyes of Jake Jacobs' friends and family, I'm sure, we had wiggled straight out of the wormy local woodwork.

The natives, the Black Earthlings, stared at us differently. "Hello, Dad," said Shelly coldly as her father turned inside a musty tweed sport coat and raised his moustache in a woebegone smile. White Milkerson gave me a nod. "You can turn around now," she told him. When he did, she rose with a snap-snap of her flip-flops and whispered in my ear, "See? He doesn't even care about me. I hate him."

I whispered back, "What did you want him to do?"

"Punch you," she replied. "Like he used to punch me. Anyway, you're old enough to be my father."

I put my voice back into the faintly musty curls around her ear: "Maybe he's trying not to be an asshole."

"No," she hissed. "Everybody's an asshole. Especially him."

I looked up to catch a smirking glance from Bud Lite, who was in uniform and engaged in a murmuring little clutch with Bud Heavy and another large, middle-aged man in a suit. Standing by was that man's pasty, small-eyed wife. The wife was looking at us, too. Shelly jabbed me. "That's Ronnie," she whispered. The woman looked away. Then the man turned to us—and away quickly. But not before I figured out he was the guy who pissed on my tree last night. The guy who was getting my tires today. The county supervisor who had invited us all to the Jet Ski Jamboree. Ronnie Hellenbrand. Now there, I felt fairly sure, was an asshole. He glanced at me again, as if to say, *Takes one to know one.*

The line moved slowly. Mourners stopped one-by-one to console the small and broken mother of Jake Jacobs. They were then received in a double hand clasp by the father of Jacobs, who appeared to talk a lot in his grief. Then the mourners moved on to Ingrid Jacobs, who looked stunning in black. I watched the widow. Her lips fought to stay closed in a tragic grimace over her braces. Her eyes were liquid and unsteady. She embraced each mourner slowly and silently, with a kind of old European formality, then released them to the horror of three steps across empty floor to the casket, which stood open before an arrangement of wildflowers from the banks of Black Earth Creek.

The murdered man seemed to captivate people, even in death. Mourners lingered—fondly, or in shock, I couldn't tell—before moving on. Then I was surprised to realize I had been watching Junior perform the ritual. I hadn't recognized her. She was dressed in a grey pantsuit and heels. She had worked the hat dent out of her hair. She looked good, even with the dead watch hanging from her neck. She crossed herself over the body of Jake Jacobs.

"I gotta pee," whispered Shelly, and she wiggled away toward the lobby of the funeral home.

When I turned from watching her, Junior was beside me.

"Thanks," she whispered. "For taking me fishing last night. I'm sorry about the little incident. Just forget it. Okay? I was so cold my brain stopped working." She had put on eyeliner and lip gloss, and she looked a little raw up close. "And it's so nice of you," she said, "to be with Shelly."

"I'm not—" I stammered. "I mean, I wasn't…really with her. She asked me."

Junior gave me her crinkly grin. Her sunburned nose was peeling beneath foundation cream. "Relax," she said. "I know you're okay."

Her eyes darted away. I followed them and saw Dickie Pee wheeling himself out of the line to try to join us—but with the chairs and the long, slow-footed line of mourners, he was trapped.

Junior put her hand on my arm.

"You know how I know you're okay?" she said. "I drove into town last night because I realized I was out of diapers for Daddy. I bumped into Willis Schultz from the co-op. He told me I got top dollar for my bull. Gareth Kaltenburg gave me two hundred above the index. And the next day the price collapsed." She looked at me earnestly. "That's a sign," she said. "Things happen for a reason." She smiled. "Forget last night. Mostly, good things just keep happening with you and me."

I looked away again. Dickie Pee was still trapped. Ingrid Jacobs was embracing President Bud. Her face looked sick. I knew how she felt: *rubbernecks*. Death walks into your life, and suddenly everybody cares. We shuffled a few feet forward. After a moment Junior said, "But listen. I hope you're making progress. I think they're going to come after Daddy any minute."

I waited. Junior chewed her glossy lip. She took my arm and gripped it like a shovel. She leaned closer and I could smell her shampoo, mingled with maple syrup and a slightly gamey, barn-like smell. She lowered her voice.

"B.L. came to the house last night with a warrant. Middle of the night."

I snuck a glance ahead. White Milkerson rocked sedately on his heels. It was B.L.'s turn to embrace the lovely Ingrid. She grimaced. He got her pretty good.

"And?"

Junior leaned so close our shoulders brushed. "He was looking for Jake's ponytail," she whispered. "He's figured out I took it. Not that it was too hard. But President Bud was giving him hell all the way. It sounded like B.L. couldn't talk the judge into giving him a warrant for your RV. But he was looking for Jake's fly rod, too. I guess he went into the *Pêche Tôt* earlier, because Ingrid said the yellow sally was on it, but when he went to pick it up yesterday, the rod was missing. Ingrid said she didn't know what had happened to it."

We shuffled a few more feet.

Junior whispered, "So then… guess where B.L. found the

rod." I looked forward. Black Earth's police chief had taken up an official pose a few yards beyond the coffin. His arms were folded across his gut. His mirrored shades where up on his shaved head. I knew where he had "found" the rod: in Junior's barn.

"Clever, huh?" she whispered. "So they can claim I took it from the start."

Now B.L. looked our way.

"When this is over," Junior said, "I'm going to kick that boy's fat little ass. But listen," she went on, "this morning Dad told me something that I think we need to check out."

The receiving line gave the illusion of movement. I stepped and bumped into White Milkerson, who seemed in a daze. The woman behind B.L. snuffled loudly as she embraced Jacobs' mother. I caught Milkerson nipping at a flask from his breast pocket. Meanwhile, Dickie Pee had worked his way around the far side of the floor, moving chairs with one hand and wheeling with the other.

"Dad is lucid about two or three times a week," Junior told me. "It's like he wakes up out of a dream. This morning he told me his friend Einar from the cheese factory has been seeing Jesus."

I slid a questioning look at her.

"Regularly," she whispered adamantly. "From the window in the back room, looking out on the lake."

I wondered about the term: *lucid.*

"I know," said Junior. "It sounds nuts. But sometimes Daddy is just like old times. He comes in and out. He said his friend Einar had dropped by yesterday while I was cutting hay. Einar works nights at the cheese factory. He's been watching someone walk on water, out on Lake Bud, and Dad's real religious, so he thinks it must be Jesus."

I bit my tongue. I wondered how deep this belief thing went with her.

"But what I think," she said, "is it's something related to Jake's murder. Something Jake might have known about."

Imagine my relief. She wasn't going to ask me to confirm the second coming of Christ on Lake Bud.

"It's over on the Bud's side of the lake," she said, "where he's got everything all fenced off. But I guess from the window of the cheese factory, the storeroom in back, Einar got a pretty good view."

"Can we talk to Einar?"

"Done," she said. "He'll be waiting for us at the cheese factory tonight at eight." She squeezed my arm again. "I'll pick you up."

The snap of flip-flops announced the return of Shelly. She smelled of pot smoke. Junior gave her a quick smile, me a somber nod—"Gotta get my calves in before the next storm," she told me—and she moved away toward the lobby.

Shelly gripped my arm. A gust of dirty curls passed beneath my nose as she turned her head to watch Dickie Pee circumnavigate the back of the room. He was nearly to us when suddenly it became clear he never meant to join our party. All along, he had been trying to reach the two men in suits behind us.

The men greeted Dickie with a grave and familiar heartiness, like they had known him all their lives. Then they introduced themselves.

"Mark Martin, Jake's attorney," said one, bumping me as he made space for Dickie.

"Blake Langdale," said the other, "Sierra Club. Regional Director. Remember us? The new guys on the Friends of Black Earth Creek board."

I glanced back to catch Dickie Pee flicking hair from his eyes like a high school kid. He had on a brown suit that might have served for his graduation. His left pant leg bulged over the electronic-arrest bracelet. He held an unlit cigarette in one hand, a lighter in the other.

"Dickie," said the attorney, "Jake was really getting somewhere on this dam lawsuit. You know he had Hellenbrand—"

Jake Jacobs' attorney stopped and looked toward the casket. Ronnie Hellenbrand was getting his moment with the new widow, so it was safe to talk about him. The Sierra Club guy jumped in. "He had Hellenbrand by the balls. I don't know how he did it exactly, but Hellenbrand was talking. Jake found out that the village president had been bribing him to keep Lake Bud in the county historical site program. Plus Jake had the studies—"

"He had that shit cold," joined the lawyer as we all shuffled forward. "That dam has been messing up the stream big time. Hellenbrand's been working with the state to keep it under the radar for years. There's bigger fish, but a lot less of them. And the brookies are almost gone. Christ, someone caught a *pike* in the headwaters this spring. So Dickie—Friends of Black Earth Creek—the organization has gotta survive. Somebody's gotta carry on Jake's work."

The Sierra Club guy stepped on my foot—I glanced at him: shirtsleeves and a neat red beard—then he lowered his voice and said, "Dickie, you could be the man. You know the creek, you know the village. What do you say?"

We shuffled forward, nearly there.

"Friends of Black Earth Creek President," urged the lawyer. "Ingrid's not going to do it," he added. "She's got her daddy's place in Wyoming. She's going to blow this town." Dickie glanced from one to the other. He looked pleased.

"Or maybe," said the Sierra Club guy, suddenly reconsidering, "maybe Brad Hughes from Saint Paul could come down here and take the top spot. FOBEC president. You know, logistics-wise, maybe that would be easier."

"Hmm," said the lawyer. "And Dickie helps out. Kind of a community liaison-type thing. Fund-raising, web site. Interesting thought."

I saw Dickie's face darken before Shelly squeezed my arm. She wanted me to go before her. I heard the clattering of a wheelchair through the maze of chairs as I stepped unprepared into the weepy purview of Jake Jacobs' mother, who grabbed my hand and said, "And you must be...?"

"Just passing through," I said. When that didn't register, I said, "I was the one who found Jake."

But the old woman had lost interest and passed me along. "And sweetheart," she was saying to Shelly, "you must be...?"

Before I was ready, Jacobs' father had me down low, by the belt. He pulled me in—all hairy ears and shining head, a soft old man empowered by rage—and he growled, "You sure you didn't find my boy's ponytail stuffed in his mouth—like that old bastard said he would?"

Once more I lied for Junior—this time in the burning gaze of the dead man's wife, who took me next in her fierce hands and said "Thank you" before I could get a word out.

I drifted away from Ingrid toward the casket, aware of the stillness behind me as Shelly moved into the sights of her former employer. I stared down at Jacobs and saw a handsome man. He seemed to be smiling faintly, calmly, sure of himself even in death. Then Shelly, unscathed, bumped up against me. I watched her raise her little macramé purse and dip a hand into it. She brought something out, and as she reached into the casket to lay the object on Jake, Ingrid shrieked, "No!"

Shelly jumped. "You little witch!" screamed the widow, flying to her. "Don't you touch him! Get your hands off! Get out! Oh, god, why is she here?" Ingrid's mouth was ripped open, teeth and braces bared. She gasped about, looking for some explanation. "Why is this girl here?" she howled. Her mother-in-law had come to her elbow. "She said she's a friend of yours, dear. She said you let her stay upstairs of the coffee shop..."

Ingrid threw off her mother-in-law's hand. "She was fucking him!"

Stoned Shelly, beside me again, holding my arm, said bravely, "No, Ingrid. Jake and I were friends." Then she stepped up again and tried to lay her object in the casket.

Ingrid burst forward and slammed her palms against Shelly's chest. Chairs flew as Shelly collapsed backward. Ingrid dove on her in a fury, punching and clawing. But Shelly had been in that spot before, it seemed. The girl could fight. She squirmed powerfully away and with a practiced hand caught Ingrid by the hair and slung the sobbing woman to her knees. Then she glared at me.

"Asshole," she said. "You were supposed to protect me."

In the next instant B.L. had Shelly by the wrist. But that didn't last long either. She kneed him in the balls, broke his grip and ran. She hit the lobby doors and vanished.

"Jesus Christ, Dwighty," came Bud Heavy's voice wearily into the silence. "You can't even hold on to a girl?"

IN THE SHOCKED AFTERMATH, the storm had cut loose outside. Rain hammered the roof and windows. Thunder moved through the bones of every mourner. Ingrid picked herself up and disappeared into a rear room with a funeral home employee, pursued by her fractured parents-in-law.

So eager was everyone else to leave that the rain didn't stop them. In a moment I was nearly alone. I stooped to pick up the object Shelly had tried to lay on the chest of Jake Jacobs. It was a small grass wreath, supple stems from the streamside, tied with elaborate knots so that they formed one thick, exquisite circle. Half dried, almost heavy, it was beautiful. The knots were perfect.

I looked around for Shelly's dirty little purse. I found it beneath a collapsed folding chair. I pushed my hand inside. Her hair brush. Her tampons. Her phone. Her dope bag.

Then I had them: her keys.

A man who could take you down

Not a minute later I was splashing down the alley behind the *Pêche Tôt* with a glossy *Guide to Bereavement Services* spread futilely over my head. This storm had twice the power of yesterday's, and I could sense the rushing of cooler, more violent air. I had braved a hundred tempests in the last thirty months, but always in waders and a rain jacket, impervious, sheltered as a bug on some streamside rock, watching the majesty of storms. But this time I was exposed, soaked to the skin, and a little intimidated. I rushed through Shelly's wad of keys and finally found one to match the lock.

I'm guessing that to step soaking wet into a warm and fragrant coffee shop would be one of life's finer pleasures. But under other circumstances. The big orange cat circled my ankles, mewing as I locked the door behind me. I stood and listened for a moment. The radio was on, but the place was empty.

I found my way upstairs. The first door I tried apparently was the room Shelly had crashed in: storage boxes, a mattress, a cluttered ashtray on the floor. The second door opened into Jacobs' Friends of Black Earth Creek office.

The man was alarmingly neat. I had already figured out that Jake Jacobs had been a powerful personality. Now he was officially one of those people who made me wonder exactly how much was wrong with me. The walls were perfectly balanced with framed piscatorial artwork. His furniture was arranged in such a way that the square room had a shape and flow that made you *experience* the space as you entered it, even when you were soaking wet and trespassing. His desk faced the door, which led you to understand that he expected an audience for his conclusions in regard to the handsome piles of documents arrayed across it. I knew the faces in the photo-portraits behind the desk: John Muir, Papa Hemingway, and Chief Seattle. A Mac computer blinked at standby on one corner of the desk. Suddenly I understood a bit of President Bud Bjorgstad's reaction—and of Dad O'Malley's—and Lumen Bostock's—and maybe of a lot of other people in Black Earth. The ponytail was a tease, a coy vanity, an irritant. Beneath it, Jake Jacobs looked exactly like a man who could take you down.

Ingrid had piled his fishing gear indecorously in a corner behind the desk. As Junior said, the beautiful bamboo rod was gone. Jacobs' waders were humped against the wall, his hat tossed on top. I went straight to his vest for his fly boxes. His stonefly box had eleven standard yellow sallies—none of the special upside-down Jake's Sallies that Dickie Pee claimed to have tied for him.

My fingers scrambled through the other vest pockets: floatant, split shot, leader butts, tippet spools, flashlight, sunscreen, insect repellent, a package of braided leader loops, a pack of matches—and then, inside a baggie, inside a breast pocket with his license, a small spiral notebook. As I paged through it, a vehicle stopped in the alley below. When I rose, keeping my eyes on the obscure notations in the little book, I bumped Jacobs' desk chair. Something heavy thumped to the oak floor beneath the desk. I slid out a long, rectangular UPS carton, taped shut and addressed to Jacobs from a taxidermy firm in Poynette.

A humming sound carried faintly beneath the rumble of the storm. A sliding door slammed shut.

I put the box back the way it had been, barely fitting it lengthwise beneath the desk. I dropped the notebook back into the baggie, crammed it all into my hip pocket and rose to the window.

Dickie Pee was wheeling through the slashing rain toward the back door of the *Pêche Tôt*. He had something on his lap—a heavy piece of plywood, wheels screwed onto the bottom. There was a step up to the coffee shop's back door, but I lost sight of the wheelchair beneath the window, so I didn't know how he managed it. But in no time he was inside, rolling across the creaky café floor. I heard dishes crash to the floor. Then something hummed in the wall, where a large open cabinet hollowed out the wall across from Jacobs' desk. I stared at the cabinet as the space filled with grunting and clattering from below.

Then I had it. A dumbwaiter. Dickie Pee was coming upstairs in a dumbwaiter.

I stepped back into the closet behind the desk, pulling the door shut on the smells of sawdust and drywall mud. This was where Shelly had been with her tools, making a space for Jacobs' fishing gear. I stumbled across an impressive collection of extra rods and reels, all cased and labeled *J. Jacobs*.

The dumbwaiter rattled to a stop. Through a crack in the

door I caught a fleeting slice of Dickie Pee as he scooted past, cross-legged on his wheeled square of plywood.

He shoved in behind the desk, knocking the long box to the floor again. I heard a desk drawer roll open. Then another. *"Sonofabitch,"* he cursed. He pawed. He dropped things on the floor. Then the sounds stopped, all except the delicate sound of pages turning.

After a minute, Dickie Pee scooped papers back into the desk drawers and closed them. He scooted past the door crack again. As the dumbwaiter rattled down, somewhere in the wall between the first and second floors, a lighter snapped. Cigarette smoke drifted up into Jacobs' office. A minute later, the outer door slammed. At the window, I watched the blue van pull away into the storm.

As I made my way back toward the desk, I saw them. The Jake's Yellow Sallies, tied by Dickie Pee, were in a small, clear, plastic box atop a filing cabinet between the desk and the window.

Jacobs hadn't used them. He had received them. He had set them aside. Maybe he had forgotten them. *Jake and me had cracked the hatch,* I recalled Dickie Pee telling me on the road the other day. Like he and Jacobs were a team—in Dickie's eyes. But maybe they never were.

Dickie's gift, the box of Jake's Yellow Sallies, was well beyond the sight and reach of the man on wheeled plywood. Beside the plastic container was the empty box and spool of a brand new line—a top-drawer Orvis Wonderline and the receipt for it, dated August 10, 11:17 a.m., the morning of Jacobs' death.

So Jacobs, that day, had bought a new line and gone fishing with it. But he had left his special sallies at home. All six of them.

Both the first and second Jake's Sallies had come from somewhere else. That is, if Dickie Pee told the truth.

A twenty-eight-inch brown

The thunderstorm was on full wash when I left the *Pêche Tôt*, and my walk back to the Cruise Master felt more like sailing. I had to flatten out, bend into the wind or it would knock me over. If I caught it just right, I was carried along at a dangerous speed—eyes nearly closed against a new onslaught of hail. I hit the ditch twice. Then I saw color—real, alive color for the first time—when lightning struck the road ahead of me.

Shakily, I stripped inside the Cruise Master. There was my shower for the week, I decided. As my home-on-wheels rocked and rattled under driven hail, I toweled off and looked out the back window. My chance to see a tornado on the approach had passed. The sky was on the ground. The air was black-green. Trees thrashed and broken branches cartwheeled through the air.

I could see no further than Shelly's pop-up at the far end of the campground, and as I watched, the wind got beneath it, snapped the ropes of her little awning, and slowly tipped the little trailer onto its side. Suddenly comprehending my own fate, I scrambled naked into the driver's seat and buckled myself in. It was all I could think of. I was on my way to Oz, but at least I had my seatbelt on. Christ, I thought next, they'll find me dead—dead and naked.

Jesus, Dog.

Then the storm abruptly stopped. It just stopped. What seemed like a lull, a pause for wind-shift, simply and neatly attenuated to a clean-scrubbed nothing, into a revelation of still, fragrant air and a spray of sunlight over the western bluffs. Then a gleam caught my eye, and the sight of a silver milk truck, bouncing and splashing down the campground road, gave me ten seconds to get my bare butt out of the driver's seat and put some clothes on.

Stumbling into trousers at my rear window, I watched Lumen Bostock pass me by and park his rig down by Shelly's pop-up. He left the engine running. He hopped down and strode like a bantam through the soupy, stick-littered grass to the rear of the upended camper. It was tipped back at a forty-five, supported precariously by the decomposing picnic table behind it. Bostock sprang nimbly on top of the table and pushed the camper back onto four wheels. Then he strutted back to the front and hammered on the door. Almost instantly, the door flew open and out tore Shelly, clad in a plaid bathrobe, cursing and flailing, knocking Bostock's hat off and screaming, "Asshole!"

Bostock was pale bald on top, and his head appeared strangely small. He puffed his little chest and twanged curses back at her, strings of cancerous little words that inspired Shelly to haul back and spit in his face. Then, wild-haired and puffy-faced, she lunged to the brink of a fire pit and picked up a large, charred stone. Bostock began to backpedal. He stepped on his hat. Shelly kept coming.

"You touch me with that, I'll kill you," warned Bostock, his back against the milk truck. "You hear me, girlie?"

"Go ahead!" wailed Shelly, and she hurled the rock with all her strength.

Bostock ducked, but he didn't need to. The rock missed broadly and clanged off the silver tank. Bostock sneered. He said, "Gimme them keys."

Shelly glared at him, at once enraged and bereft. She glanced toward the Cruise Master—or toward the fire pit again, I couldn't tell. She drew in the plaid robe and put her arms around herself. Her shoulders slumped.

"I don't have them."

"You gimme them keys, girlie. I asked your old man. He says you got 'em."

"I don't have them. I lost them. That bitch attacked me at Jake's wake and I lost my whole fucking bag."

Bostock sized her up. He shook his head in disgust.

"Well that's just too bad for you," he said finally. He recovered his hat and climbed into his cab. "I'm gonna be back after my route tonight. You have them keys ready. And you tell that dough-boy Hellenbrand to stay at home, so I don't have to kick his ass again."

Shelly stared at the wet grass. "Asshole."

Toot-toot, responded Bostock, backing out.

Shelly didn't watch. She turned to look at her camper. One corner of the canvas roof was torn at right angles where it had fallen back against the picnic table. The support lines for her awning were snapped.

She picked up a stick from the wet grass. She broke both ends to shorten it and stripped the leaves. Then she bent over her lines, pulled the broken ends together around the stick, and in a minute they were both repaired. She tossed the stick aside, glanced once more at the Cruise Master, and went inside the pop-up.

I believe I pictured her accurately: she was going back to bed.

I MIXED A STRAIGHT Tang and opened Jake Jacobs' little notebook on my galley table. The dead man's notations proceeded neatly about halfway in, and then the rest of the pages were blank. I backed up to the beginning. The man's handwriting leaned left—a lefty's stylish scrawl. I looked hard at the initial set of notations. They looked familiar. First, a date. Then *6 bn, 2 bk, 0 rb, 8-14, cdpup.* Jacobs was a fish counter. He meant that on a certain date—in this case, one day in the May of two springs ago—he had caught six brown trout, two brook trout, no rainbows, all in a range of eight to fourteen inches, on caddis pupae. The dead man went on like this, keeping meticulous records, until that fall, when suddenly an entry broke rank.

1 bn 28!!!! he wrote in large letters, triple underlined. *wb!!!*

A twenty-eight-inch brown on a wooly bugger. A behemoth like the one that Bostock had jugged up and slaughtered under the bridge, or like the one Junior and I had fooled into taking a sally.

Jacobs had let his big fish go, I gathered, but he had carefully diagrammed the spot on the stream. It was about halfway between the two County K bridges, in a corner that he triangulated with Junior's farm and a limestone outcrop on the west edge of the coulee.

From then on, the dead man's journal changed tone and form. It began to carry notes and lists and phone numbers and hand-made stream-section maps, terminating finally with a half-drawn diagram of Lake Bud. He had drawn a grid over the lake, as if he were a scientist, measuring something, or searching for something.

Curious, I dug out my little cell phone and called the number Jacobs had penned neatly on the Lake Bud page.

"County Supervisor's office," said a woman's voice on the other end.

I stammered. "You mean Ronnie Hellenbrand's office?" I said finally.

"Ronnie's out today," the woman said, "at a funeral. Would you like his voice mail?"

I hung up.

I chose another number randomly—a long-distance number that Jacobs had put down beside the phrase *client pool?*

"Hanson's Safari," barked a man on the other end.

"Uh, where are you located?"

"Route fifty-six west outa the city, left on Turner Road. Follow the high fence. We only take appointments."

"No," I said. "I mean what state?"

"Huh? This is Texas. You want something, fella?"

"I'm calling about Jake Jacobs."

"Say what?"

Again I hung up. I stepped outside, needing a greater space for my puzzlement. What was Jake Jacobs doing with the number of a Texas game farm? And the number of a Bud Bjorgstad confidant like Ronnie Hellenbrand? What did he mean, *client pool?* And why had everything changed after he had caught the big brown trout?

In the panorama before me, a pair of small motor boats plied Lake Bud. In my three days in Black Earth, I had never seen a boat on Lake Bud before—and now, suddenly, two.

Each boat had a driver and a person in the bow, and they moved deliberately, like insects laying eggs, leaving behind twin trails of bright orange buoys. I looked through my binoculars. There was no mistaking Village President Bud Bjorgstad at the helm of one boat, and the uniformed man in the bow had to be B.L. The other boat was too distant for a good reading. Two shapes. One in purple. That was all I could tell.

"Hey!" said a voice right beside me.

Startled, I put down the glasses. Shelly stood beside me in dry clothing, this time a ratty pair of cargo shorts and a tank top. She had a can of beer in each hand. She was barefoot. She was about half-fresh, about half-smiling.

"I checked about your tires," she told me. "I can get them here day after tomorrow. If not that, then the next day for sure. No problem."

She looked out at the scene on Lake Bud and back at me. She put a warm beer in my hand. She nestled against me.

"Which is okay," she said. "Isn't it?"

When the going gets tough

You understand by now that the Dog is no philosopher. The Dog is not, nor has he ever been, the kind of healthy, well-adjusted soul who just naturally makes the right decisions on behalf of the oneness and goodness of human kind. At the top of my game, I was a good Dog, a follower and a bet-hedger, just barely smooth enough to make it look like I knew what I was doing. I was hoping for no bad things. Which I know now is different than believing in good things. And different from truly living. But I suppose I've already revealed the psychology of the Dog.

Still, now and then a cliché comes through for you. You've heard it: *when the going gets tough, the tough go fishing.*

Granted, going fishing for three solid years is perhaps matter for another discussion. But I'm talking about the short term now. I'm talking about fishing—any kind of fishing, even ice fishing, probably—as a better use of a grown man's time than, say, accepting a head job from a drunken and desperate teenager.

Which allows me to admit that this is quite nearly what next befell the Dog. Shelly invited herself into the Cruise Master and I followed, meaning to root her out and get back to my analysis of Jake Jacobs' final notebook entries. But she barely let me clear the top step before she pressed herself against me again and mashed her lips sloppily against mine.

"Whu—?" I said.

She sloshed her beer can down on the galley table and went incisively at my crotch with both hands. In no time flat she had my zipper open and my woebegone member was rising nicely in her beer-sticky little hands.

Then I pushed her away. I was honestly, foggily puzzled. Funny thing, though, so was Shelly, it appeared. Puzzled. We stared without comprehension at one another for a long moment. Then she went back to work.

"What are you doing?" I asked her.

"I'm going to get you off," she replied matter-of-factly.

"But why?"

She shrugged, dropped one hand to cradle my nuts. "That's what I do," she explained. "Guys want to fuck me at first, especially older guys, but usually I don't even like them, and anyway I don't want to get knocked up or get some disease. So I just give them head and everything works out fine." She looked at me quizzically. This whole intermission was making no sense to her. "I'm not even charging you. You mean you don't want me to?"

I'm not sure what I said. But Shelly didn't believe it, whatever it was. I guess she must have heard all the perfunctories before. Anyway, the next moment I was looking at the back of her head, and I was slipping, sliding, feeling good and feeling awful…and then suddenly I had hold of something so solid I could pull myself to safety.

Just like that.

It was Junior. It was Junior's weird faith in me. Maybe it was crazy, delusional, a fantasy of health, like Harvey's wheat grass smoothies, like dream catchers and multi-vitamins. Except there it was suddenly, real enough to use. Junior thought more of the Dog than this. And so the Dog *was* more. It was that simple.

I separated as gently as the girl would allow. She looked up in bafflement edged with a trace of orneriness. "What's wrong?"

Nothing, I told her. I zipped up.

"Come on. You got a wife, right? So what? Everybody's got a wife."

I told her, "No wife." I guess that was an insult. She rose in a fury and grabbed her warm beer off the galley table. She leaned against the bench back and chugged.

"Shelly," I told her, "I'm going fishing."

Her eyes watered as she glared at me.

I lifted my vest and waders from their hook behind the door. There would be high and muddy water from the storm, I imagined, but what the hell. I reversed the door and tossed my gear out on the grass. Strange, but it seemed new—it seemed a celebration of something, this fishing. I gave Shelly a squeeze around the shoulders. She twisted away.

"Hey," I said to her anyway. "You wanna come with me?"

I knew how he felt

"And?" said Junior, giving me her crinkly little grin. It was eight p.m. We were bouncing out the campground road in her mud-spattered blue pickup, en route to our stake-out of Jesus at the cheese factory. I had related an abridged version of my afternoon, throwing in at the end that I had bumped into Shelly in the campground and invited her along.

"She came along for a while," I said. "Grousing about the heat, the bugs, the mud. She'd already done too much of that with her dad, I guess. Said she hated the creek, hated fishing, hated water—and especially hated her dad. I've always heard that's how grown kids behave for awhile. They go opposite."

Junior pulled out toward town on County K. Then she slapped me on the shoulder in a congratulatory way.

"But she went with you. That's great."

"For a while," I answered. "We ran into her dad sampling fish upstream a ways and she took off."

Junior sighed. "How was White?"

"Tipsy," I said. "And sad looking." As Junior sped her

pickup toward the village of Black Earth, I thought back to my second streamside meeting with White Milkerson. Shelly and I had come upon the biologist fumbling with a large brown trout in midstream. The water was soupy and high with runoff, and Milkerson's elbows were dripping. He wore his yellow electrofishing backpack. The probe trailed him in the current. His net was twisted across his shoulders and under his arm. He was cussing as the trout thrashed in his hands. Then he lost it. He raised up, his vest attachments swinging and flapping.

"Hey, Babe," he said, surprised to see his daughter.

"Screw you," Shelly retorted from behind me.

I turned to watch her flip-flop off through the high grass and disappear into the cornfield between us and the road.

"Thanks for bringing the car back!" her father called after.

He chuckled morosely around a cigarette, snapping at it with a dying lighter.

"If she visits me," he said, "stays overnight, takes care of herself for just one damn night, then she gets to have the car for a day." We watched her crawl under the fence at the other side of the cornfield and set off in a jerky, hurried stride back toward the Lake Bud campground.

Now, to Junior, slowing her pickup for the village limits, I said, "White Milkerson asked about you and your dad. And he worried about Ingrid Jacobs, too. He seemed real upset by this whole thing."

"He and Jake were pretty close," Junior said. "Jake was working with him on stream studies. And this evening, when I came in from milking, White was sitting with Dad on the porch. Had his arm around Dad. Neither one of them saying a thing. Just staring at Dad's bobber in the grass, kind of like old times. White's an emotional guy. I guess that's why he drinks so much."

"Shelly, too," I said.

"Yup."

"She fought with Ingrid today."

"I heard."

"And a little while later I watched her have a fight with the poacher. The milk truck driver. Lumen Bostock."

Junior was quiet about this. I asked her what she was thinking. We were nearly downtown, such as it was.

"That little prick," she said quietly. "He torments Shelly. He lets on like he knows something about the way her mother left town. So he can jerk her around, make some kind of claim on her. Shelly goes for it every time."

We were on Main Street now, taking the right-hand turn over the creek that would allow us to drive up the opposite side of Lake Bud to the cheese factory. It was just now dark. Pink and blue tavern lights spread their glow in the heavy air.

"Just out of curiosity," I asked Junior, "when did it happen? How old was Shelly Milkerson when her parents split up?"

Junior thought about it a while. The stream sparkled behind us up to the frothy plunge pool below the dam. The algae-stink of Lake Bud filled the air. I could see the Cruise Master far across the way, a momentary silver speck in the headlights of a car on the county highway.

"Five," Junior concluded. "About five years old. And there was no split-up to it. Nothing like divorce. I told you Shelly's mom was about twenty years younger than White. Turns out since Shelly was about three, Nanette Milkerson had been seeing this farm equipment salesman, and one day she just packed her bags and disappeared. Both of them. People say they went somewhere in Arizona, some kind of patriotic cult compound, but Shelly ran away down there when she was in high school and found nothing."

I rode quietly a while. I pictured Shelly in her bathrobe, heaving the fire pit rock at Lumen Bostock.

"So what's Bostock know about it?"

"Nothing, probably," Junior said. "He's just a prick. That's just his way of trying to get laid."

She turned onto a gravel side road. We rounded a birch-shaded curve and the cheese factory surprised me. I guess I had expected something grander, given all the hoopla one suffers elsewhere about the wonders of Wisconsin cheese. I guess I had expected elves in lederhosen, yodeling outside a gingerbread chalet. But Junior pulled up to a little low-roofed cinderblock rectangle that sat inside a weed-lined chain link fence. Various other structures had been appended lakeward to this windowless base, apparently over time and according to trends in bargain construction. A pair of good-sized trucks idled at the maw of a loading dock. A small sign near the door said Kussmaul Butter Käse. To our left, the woods along the shore of Lake Bud were lined with NO TRESPASSING and LOTS FOR SALE signs. The phone number on the sale sign, I guessed, was President Bud's. Or his realtor's.

"So one day," I recounted, trying to sum up the Milkerson story, "things are normal enough for Shelly. And the next day she has no mother."

Junior agreed.

"Messed her up," I said.

"It messed them both up. She and her dad. They never really dealt with it. You can see how it messed them up. They don't talk to each other."

I sat there a long time, grinding on this, staring near-sighted at the flaky white paint on the side of the cheese factory. In the stream that afternoon, watching Shelly stalk away down County K, I had heard a grunt and a splash and looked behind me. White Milkerson was awkwardly reaching out, cigarette in his trembling hand, trying to touch me. Poor guy, I thought. Poor, ruined father. I knew how he felt.

"By the way," said Junior finally, shaking me, giving me her grin. "That's Dad's friend, Einar. We're here."

Jesus at the cheese factory

Roly-poly old Einar, thumbs in suspenders, limped ahead, giving us the tour in his high, wheezy voice. The curing vats, the curd separators, the presses, the knives and rollers, the packaging room, cold storage, and the dock, where the last of the trucks had just pulled away for an overnight run.

"Now, Mister, uh…"

"Dog."

He shook his lumpy bald head. "Come again?" he squeaked.

I told him again, and he gamely called me "Mister Dog" as he limped ahead into what appeared to be part storage and maintenance room, part office. There were tools, an air compressor, janitorial supplies, an old television, a pair of huge stainless steel coolers, and a ratty old sofa. The sour smell of milk solids permeated everything. I looked around. Einar was a Jesus-and-*Popular Mechanics* guy, the Good Lord on a crucifix above the tool bench alongside the pipe wrench. Then I took a side view of Einar. He was short, small framed. Meant to weigh one-fifty, tops, but he had sculpted himself up to twice that and seemed perfectly old country about it. He had gotten himself fat on cheese. His earthly work was done.

"Now, Mister Dog, out there is where I seen the light," squeaked Einar, as if his windpipe were impinged. He indicated the view through a dusty little garage window above his sofa. "I figure it's somebody night fishing. Off and on over the last couple months I see it and don't think nothing of it."

He grunted and hauled open one of the cooler doors. His pudgy little hand was deft enough to grip two beer cans and set them on his workbench.

"Then," he said, "the other day it's too windy to fish and I see that light anyway. So I figure President Bud and his people are out there laying the buoys for that noisy snowmobiles-on-water thing—doing it at night for some reason."

Next out of the refrigerator came a huge yellow onion, halved and festered on the open end.

"Next day, though," Einar said, shucking the half-onion on a cutting board and slicing off the bad end, "there's no buoys out there. That's when I got curious." He pointed the knife at a large binocular case. I had mine, too. Einar nodded with approval. He cut a couple fat disks of onion and laid them on a plate beside the beer cans.

"So last night I laid in here with the lights off and them glasses ready."

He took a deep, wheezy breath.

"About nine o'clock… I seen… I mean there appeared to me… gosh, I don't know how to say it…"

I realized Einar was puffing now. This had suddenly gotten emotional for him. He was staring intensely from me to Junior and back again. "I seen…"

He trembled.

"Gosh I'm glad you're here, Junior. You've always been

such a good girl. Mel done right, raising you. And your Ma, too…"

Junior gave him a slightly impatient version of the crinkly grin.

"I seen Him!" burst the old man finally in a breathless squeak. He thrust a trembling finger toward the crucifix beside the pipe wrench. "Walking on water!"

He stared into my eyes with jowly distress.

"Walking toward me! His hand out!" He pointed out the window. "Right… out… there!"

Perhaps I didn't respond properly, because Einar switched his beseeching stare to Junior. His voice rose to panic.

"And I'm thinking He's going to speak to me. I'm thinking He's going to ask me to do something, you know, go to South America and teach orphans or something, and I'm only six months from retirement! I… I…"

Junior steadied the old fellow with a hand to the shoulder. "You came up and told Dad."

"I ran like the dickens!" squeaked Einar. "Six months, I got a pension here! It wouldn't be fair. I mean, let Him appear to someone else. Someone, you know, who ain't doing as well as me…"

Junior looked at me. "That's why he came up and told Dad," she said. Then to Einar, "But Dad couldn't come tonight, Ein. He's home with Missus Sundvig watching him. Now why did you think it was… you know… Him out there?"

He made bloodshot old goggle-eyes at her, like she had gone nuts.

"Walking on water?" he squeaked. "You know anybody else?"

"What did he look like?"

The cheesemaker pondered this. "Kinda hard to say," he

decided. "His light was pointed down, around his feet. So up above that he seemed kinda heavyset, dressed in purple— robes and shadows is what I figure. Lotta hair." He gave a little jelly-bowl shudder. "Nice and friendly looking fella. Don't worry about that."

He looked from one of us to the other. He was hoping, I realized, that the Lord would appear to us, instead of him, and that Junior and I would be the ones stuck with the South American orphan gig. As if in appreciation for our sacrifice, he opened the big stainless steel cooler again and brought out a wheel of the smelliest cheese I had ever encountered. He cut out two massive, reeking wedges and laid one atop each disk of raw onion. Handling the cheese seemed to calm him. He snapped the beer cans.

"Okay then," he announced. He gave us a big sigh and a smile. "You kids are all set."

He leaned toward me as if in confidence. "Don't mind the smell. It's Limburger. Best cheese ever made. We're the only place in Wisconsin that still makes it."

He grabbed my arm.

"You ever think I'm dead, Mister Dog, you put some of this cheese on a plate and pass it under my sniffer. At my funeral, you go right up to the coffin and do that. I don't move to the smell of this Limburger, then I'm dead."

Einar snatched up his lunch bucket and a newspaper. Then, noting that Junior had gone to open the window, he gestured at me to come close again and wheezed, "Hey, Mister Dog."

The round old cheesemaker bumped his belly against my waist and pulled down on my shoulder. He leaned his lumpy head toward Junior. "Look sharp," he whispered. "I heard she's getting over Darrald."

Go ahead, ask me anything

The Limburger smelled like the insides of an old pair of rubber waders after a hot day on the stream. Worse, actually.

Junior turned from the grimy little window. "Those buoys are out there now," she said. "The Jet Ski Jamboree is tomorrow, I guess."

"You don't get involved in that?" I asked her.

She flopped on Einar's old sofa. A cloud of dust rose, but she didn't seem to notice. Anything was cleaner than a barn, I guess.

"Too much work in summer. I'm pretty good on a snowmobile, though. Winter, I get to play a little. Or I did, before Dad got so messed up."

She seemed to catch herself being wistful. She shook it off and gave me a grin.

"So, Mister Dog," she said. "Are you going to tell me your real name?"

I said no.

"How did you get called Dog?"

Grade school, I told her. It came from my real name. But

lately I'd embraced it. Accepted it. Become the Dog—and then gone feral.

"I see," she said, clearly unconvinced, and then she stood back up. I guess as only a farmer could, she put both hands on my shoulders, turned me around, trapped my arms, and bent me over—just like that. She could have shaved my back, or branded me, or gelded me. She had that much control. She was that strong. But instead she took my wallet.

She studied my driver's license. "Ned Oglivie," she said. "I see the D...O...G in there, in the middle of the first and last names. Is that how it happened?" It was, but she had already moved on. She was raising the wallet, squinting at the license, and suddenly I understood she was probably trying to place the face in the picture. Sad, pudgy, pasty—the domesticated Dog, five years ago—in for his renewal photo, sleepwalking. I hardly recognized myself.

Junior's eyes bounced from me to the picture and back.

"You look a lot better than this. Do you realize?"

I shrugged.

"I mean it," she said. "A damn sight better." Then, "Forty-two," she mused. "I had you at closer to my age." She eyed me. "You don't weigh anything like two-thirty, either. You go about one-eighty now. There's a story here, isn't there?"

I shrugged again. She smiled and sat down. "You're just like Darrald. You're not going to tell me a damn thing about yourself. I have to dig for it."

I came over and sat on the other end of the sofa. Junior seemed to read my mind. "Go ahead," she said. "I'll tell you my story first. Women like to talk about themselves. Ask me anything."

She faced me. She looked lovely in her work boots and jeans, her T-shirt with the dead watch hanging around her neck, her stumpy little ponytail sticking out the back of her

John Deere cap. But she didn't look quite the same as usual. There was something different about her that I couldn't quite place. I asked her where she got the watch.

"It's Darrald's watch," she said, and stopped cold.

I teased her. "That was a big bunch of talk right there. We'd better slow down."

"I answered your question, didn't I?"

"You miss Darrald?"

"Of course I miss Darrald."

She was looking straight at me. Like she was daring me.

I cleared my throat. "There's a lot of talk around town about when you might get over him." I paused. "I guess never, huh?"

"No," replied Junior. "I said I miss him. Missing someone and staying stuck on someone are two different things. It takes a while to separate them. I'm trying not to be stuck on Darrald," she said. "But the missing part just goes on and on. And that's okay. I mean, it has to be okay."

I sat a while and digested this. She hadn't used any new words. She hadn't expressed a single new idea. I had heard it all a hundred times before. Why then did Junior's simple explanation make so much sense? Why did it make me breathe all the way down to my tailbone and then let the air go slowly and gently across the empty space in Einar's hot little shack?

"What I have trouble with is letting go of the baggage. Dickie Pee, for one thing, never said he was sorry for his part in taking Darrald away from me. That makes it real hard."

I nodded. I waited.

"So when did Darrald's watch stop?"

She tipped her head and smiled again. "Thank you."

"What for?"

"For asking." Then she sat up straight, squared her shoulders and shivered slightly. "We were making love," she told me. "Darrald said this was going to be the one-hundredth time we had done it. I was laughing at him. Darrald was so bad at math. Any time that big old boy came up with a number, you had to just shake your head. We'd only been going out for a year at that time. And a hundred was way too much nookie, even for Darrald and me. But when we were done that morning he looked over on the nightstand and saw his watch had stopped. He just freaked. He was so happy. He thought it was so special. He said it meant we were on the right track. We were supposed to be together. He gave me the watch. He asked me to marry him. I said sure—as soon as…as soon as…shit, I don't know what I said. My mom was still healthy, and she had her job at the clinic. Dad was fine. Darrald was the guy we hired to milk. He lived in that old summer kitchen out back. But I still had thoughts of going somewhere besides Black Earth."

She sighed and fingered the watch.

"Three years later Mom was dead, Dad was sick, and Darrald and I weren't married yet. Then one morning Darrald milks early and goes out hunting with Dickie Pee." She made a long pause. "But anyway I kind of hung on to the watch."

"Yeah," I said. "Kind of."

We traded shy and slightly maudlin grins.

"Darrald wasn't the quickest fly in the barn," she sighed, looking off toward the window and Lake Bud, "but he could sure ring my bell."

She scared me with that. After a quiet minute, both of us looking off in our own directions, she waved my wallet and said, "Okay, Ned Oglivie. My turn. Who's this?"

It was a picture of my son, Eamon.

"And where is Eamon now?" she wanted to know.

"Eamon is nowhere."

"What do you mean nowhere?"

"I mean I don't know where he is."

She scooted closer to me. I felt a rough hand on my own. "You're divorced, aren't you? Your wife has your little boy."

"I'm divorced," I said stiffly. "But my kid is wherever kids go when they die."

Junior gasped. "You mean heaven. Your little boy's in heaven. Oh my God."

She reached out her other hand and took my wrists. My answer to the touchy-feely he's-with-Jesus statement was always the same. I met that crap with the cold hard fact. I thought the fact would keep me sane.

"He drowned in the bathtub," I told Junior.

She slumped back. "You don't have to tell me anything more. Don't tell me. I'm not even asking."

She gave me back the wallet. It was Eamon's pre-school portrait photograph. He was wearing his favorite striped shirt and looking a little subdued because he hadn't been allowed to wear his Red Sox cap, which he liked to yank down over his eyes. No hats. School rules. He was four years old.

I owned Oglivie Security back in those days. We did mostly physical security, guarding places, checking worker IDs at gates, video monitoring, fencing and lighting, that kind of stuff. I was working like a dog, right? Mary Jane, my wife, was working hard, too. She was a vice president in human resources for an insurance company. We both spent a lot of time talking about security, safety nets, guarantees, the social fabric, that whole bit. But somewhere in there we stopped connecting like we used to. I mean, if we had ever really connected. Not much social fabric between the two of us. So we had Eamon. That's when things got *real* tricky.

From the look on Junior's face I realized I was talking aloud. She wanted me to go on. But that didn't matter. I was going on.

"Time and energy," I said. "They came to be such scarce commodities that Mary Jane and I began to barter them."

I paused. Did she know what I meant? Junior gave me a sympathetic smile.

"We'd have these short, intense conversations—in places like both of us standing in the driveway with the car running, Eamon belted up and eating a Pop Tart in the back seat. We'd exchange scheduling information, negotiate, decide who was going to pick up supper, who got to go to the gym after work, who was putting Eamon to bed that night… and I thought I was handling it… I was a civic whirlwind. I was a dog in the pack—school board, Cub Scouts, pee-wee soccer, you know, the whole world was created for my kid, and I was out tending it, guarding it…"

I stopped, feeling sick.

"Sorry. This is a boring story. It's stupid. Everybody in America goes through this."

Junior didn't bat an eye. "Not me," she said. "I milk cows." She expected me to continue.

"We did okay," I claimed about Mary Jane and me. "We processed a lot of decisions. We coped. Of course things flared up now and then. Then the fights started coming more and more often. Suddenly it seemed like no one was happy.

"We had a fight one night after dinner. I wanted to leave the dishes. She said it was my turn to wash them. I said I know it's my turn to wash them. That's why I'm leaving them. If it's my turn to wash them, it's also my turn to decide when they're going to get washed—that kind of thing."

I felt Junior squeezing my hands. She was looking at me with teary eyes. From her distance, I'm sure it all looked so small, so quaint, so cozily tragic—but the moment itself was infused with inexplicable rage.

"So… Mary Jane went up and ran a bath for Eamon. He loved to play in there. He had this whole zoo of water animals. Then she came back down mad as a hornet. I dug in and fought back. Mary Jane had a real temper by then. She yelled. I stayed on her. I got logical. She wasn't making sense. Eventually she tore out of the house to take a walk. I went upstairs…to take a leak. And my…our boy…he…well, I told you."

Junior was releasing silent tears down her sunburned face. "He fell? Or something?"

I shrugged. We had no idea. He was just dead, his little body curled on its side in five inches of water. And everything came apart after that.

I'm not sure how much background I gave to Junior, but Eamon's death came just at the time when corporate security was getting real techie—server security, internet firewalls, email snooping. I just didn't have the heart for it. I let myself get bought out, then marginalized in the new company, and finally, when the market crashed, I was downsized. Mary Jane and I— there just wasn't any point in being together anymore. She wanted the house, the cars, everything. Because *I* was the one at home when Eamon drowned. I just didn't care anymore. She could have it all. Things, objects, didn't matter. People didn't matter. They all looked ugly to me. I wanted nothing to do with the whole idea of human connectivity—this web I thought had so much meaning just meant nothing without Eamon. I could take every human relationship and dissect it to its shallow, selfish, pathetic core. I could look at every past action of my own and break it down into its components of greed, fear, and stupidity. Only one thing, I told Junior, made me feel calm and positive.

"And what was that?"

"Ah, shit," I answered, "nothing really."

"But you like fishing."

"It fills me up," I said, "and tires me out." Probably she didn't understand. I explained about movement, water, change, the road, the cycles of insects, the feel of a wet and heavy trout in my hands—and most importantly, the exhaustion that allowed me to sleep. I told her I had a little money left after it all blew up. I explained how I saw Harvey Digman, my tax guy back when I had taxes to pay, and Harvey had saved me. Harvey had set me up.

"These last couple years, I've been fly fishing my way through the season. I bought this book, the hundred best trout streams in the country. I did them all. I'm on my way through the smaller streams now, the lesser known. Black Earth is in there. Anyway, I fish my way through the season, down to New Mexico, where I've been learning to dive in the winter."

"Dive?" Junior looked puzzled.

"Scuba. Snorkel. I got the stuff—it's all under the bench seat back in my RV. I just have to be around water."

Junior smiled. "Can you walk on water?"

Now we both looked toward the window. Nothing moving so far.

"There's something out there to walk on," I said. "A log or something. Just under the surface. I don't think Jesus would have chosen Lake Bud."

She laughed. She got up, served me Limburger on onion, with beer. I guess I had gotten used to the smell. It must have been everywhere and without contrast. Junior started eating heartily, washing it down.

"Oh, God, that's good." She looked out the window— and that's when I saw what was different. No sports bra. Different bra. And rather flattering. "You're damn right there's something out there," Junior said. "And now I'll tell you a story. Back in the seventies sometime, I was in grade school, we had a flash flood that took out three or four of our buildings, some of our livestock, washed it all right down into this reservoir. Timber, fences, corn cribs, everything west of the highway."

Jake Jacobs had talked a lot about that flood, Junior said. Jacobs said that flood reflected the misuse of land in the watershed. That was exactly the kind of thing that made her Dad furious. O'Malleys, after all, had farmed the Black Earth coulee for seven generations and nobody told them they were doing any wrong. And then on top of it, Jake wanted to take the dam out, when it was the dam, Dad said, that saved the village. What the dam was saving, Jake said, was enough water to wash the village away when it finally broke. Dad said, hell no, the dam broke before, in '35, and all it did was fill up Sundvig's pasture and drown a bunch of cattle. Then how, Jake countered, was the dam protecting the village?

"They had some doozies about it, when Dad was still a little more with it," Junior said. "But you're just looking at my tits."

"No," I claimed.

"Yes," she countered. "And thank you."

In the awkward space after that, I tried the cheese. I bit, spilled Limburger and onion down my front, then doused the shocking taste with too much beer and came up choking.

"Damn," I said. "That is good."

Junior broke out laughing. "Hallelujah," she cried. She reached out her beer can and bumped mine in a toast.

"What?" I said.

Her crunchy grin seemed as wide as Lake Bud itself. "You know what? Sitting here, listening to you, looking at you, looking at you look at me, seeing you try to eat… you know, I think I just got over Darrald."

OUR LOVEMAKING WAS about what you'd expect for a man and a woman who hadn't done it for a combined twelve years. We had to undress ourselves, seeing as the other party was too clumsy to do it right. For a long time we just stood together, ribs against ribs, patting each other on the back like long-lost relatives. Finally Junior had the sense to walk me back to the sofa, park me there, and turn off the lights.

That eased the harshness somehow of being a forty-two-year-old born-again virgin, buck naked on a strange and nappy sofa. Junior lay out beneath me, solid and shapely and hungry as a woman could be. She was no linebacker in this view. I matched up and tried not to gouge her with my elbows. And we started.

But our bodies were too long for the sofa. I bent one leg up and hung the other off. I must have been pushing with it, though, because the next thing I knew the sofa was all the way across the floor and hammering against one of the stainless steel coolers.

That's when Junior saved us again. She had the common sense to sit me down and get on top. "Oh," I moaned, and I nearly settled down. But then she bore down with her arms around me and nearly broke my neck. I had to fight her, fight for air, and in no time, raggedly, in the midst of our struggle to get comfortable, we both erupted.

For a long time after, Junior pressed my head to her chest and sighed through the top of my hair. She was facing the window.

"That could have been different," she said after a while. She paused a long time. "But it couldn't have been better."

After another minute she sighed again and said, "So now, who's going to get up and get the binoculars?"

You're not going to believe it

Junior and I had developed a plan for the moment the light appeared on Lake Bud, but that plan didn't include being naked. We watched long enough to realize the feet were heading back towards shore. The light had appeared long before we noticed it, and it was too late for binoculars. "Keep your eye on that spot," Junior said, kissing me on the lips one last time. Then she hurried out the door carrying her hat and her boots. Her job was to get out to the road and see who drove by.

I felt almost too good to move. But my job was to fix the spot on the lake where the legs were now retreating and get to it. As I struggled into my pants, I noted some kind of a brushy lump near the shore, caught in the beam of the light as the legs came out and disappeared into the woods.

But by the time I had found my way around the back of the cheese factory to the shoreline, I had lost my bearings. I was facing a blank, black lake and a muddy, tangled shoreline. An engine started up a quarter mile away. I stumbled along until I found what might have been the black lump, and from there I felt my way into the water. About knee-high in, about fifty feet out, I bumped into something warm, slick, and wide. I stood on it. Barely stood on it. It felt ribbed, corrugated, rounded—but I couldn't quite find the center of it. I took a step forward.

Then another.

Then I fell.

BY THE TIME I slipped and squished my way back to Kussmaul Butter Käse, Junior had returned from the road. Her blue pickup was waiting for me in the lot out front.

"You ready for this?" she asked me. "You're not going to believe it."

I got her seat wet and muddy. She didn't notice.

"That was President Bud's red Suburban."

Sure I believed it. Why not? Why didn't she?

"Okay," said Junior, gunning down the factory drive to the road and turning left. "Right. But now think about what Einer said: heavy-set, purple, lots of hair."

That part I didn't get. Junior let me muse on it while she attacked a dark country road at eighty miles per hour. Just to help me think.

"Who does all Bud's dirty work?" she asked me.

"B.L.?"

"Besides him," Junior said, sending me into her shoulder with a hard right. "Tonight, it was Mary Malarkey, the village clerk." She passed another pickup. "You know Mary?" I didn't. "Mom's old bud," she said. "Nice lady. But she'd do anything for Bud. *Anything*."

Junior tore down the last straightaway and rattled to a stop at Main Street. There, at the stop sign, her hurry dissipated.

"Oh," she said. "All Mary did was come back to the village office. Bud must be in there."

She cruised by. The lights were on in the clerk's office and also behind, in Bud's office. The red Suburban was parked in the back beside B.L.'s police cruiser. Junior turned around and pulled to the curb next to the *Pêche Tôt*.

"It's almost ten o'clock," she told me. "Listen—I'm going to dash home and check on Dad. I'll see if Missus Sundvig can stay and watch him a little longer. I'll be back in twenty."

I got out. Junior reached after me, her hand scarred and chapped, straining for a final touch. I squeezed it.

MY FIRST STOP WAS the air conditioning unit on the north side of the building. With my pocket knife, I took the cover off. I tripped the shut-off switch. On a sweltering night like this, fifteen minutes and somebody would be outside looking to see what was wrong with the cooling unit. They would find nothing they could fix. Five minutes after that, the windows would be open. It was a classic corporate break-in scheme.

I spent my first five of the fifteen minutes in the back lot, checking the doors on President Bud's red Suburban. Mary Malarkey had left the rear gate unlocked. I moved fast over the back bench and into the driver's seat, where I turned off the interior lighting. Then I slowed down. I had a tiny LCD flashlight on my keychain, and I used that to scan the contents of the president's glove box. Nothing special. Then I went through the door pockets, under the visors, beneath the seats. Nothing but car wash coupons, road maps, ice scrapers, the usual stuff. I checked the ashtrays, cup holders, wheel wells. *Nada.* I scrambled over the back seat into the trunk space, landing on a thick plastic bag half-stuffed with something of a gravelly texture.

I backed off the bag, glancing out above the sidewalls to make sure no one was watching me from inside the village president's office. Then I drove a hand into the heavy contents and lifted out a streaming handful of pellets—pill-sized, oily, smelly, dark-colored…fish food.

I stuffed a handful into my wet hip pocket. Then I snuck out of the Suburban and into the landscaping behind the back door to the village office. It was time. From inside, I heard President Bud bellow, "Mary!"

In a minute more, the village clerk came hulking out in wet purple stretchies, puffing and muttering, propping the door open and aiming a flashlight toward the air conditioning unit. As she angled across the crushed stone, fighting the spider webs knit between the shrubbery, I slunk in behind her. I was inside the Village of Black Earth office.

I took the first dark doorway and found myself sitting in the village board meeting room, staring up at a plat map and hearing Bud Bjorgstad in the next office, grumbling profanities.

"I don't give a good goddamn what they said in cop school," the village president was telling someone. "You're not working for the damn ACLU. You're working for me."

It was B.L. He sounded sullen. "I'm not supposed to break the law," he said through gritted teeth. "And we have to make sure it's his first."

"It's his, for chrissake."

"I know that. But I keep telling you, if we get it illegally, we can't use it as evidence…"

"Mary!" bellowed the president.

The clerk trundled in, the heavy door slamming behind her. "That's my name," she said sourly as she passed the meeting room door. "And the unit's busted."

"Then open some windows," Bud ordered her.

"You mean there's too much hot air?" she retorted distantly, from the front as a window crank squeaked.

Bud and Bud Lite were quiet as she made the rounds. I knew when she had reached Bud's office, because B.L. said, "Ouch!"

"Then move," said the clerk. "You seen me coming."

She cranked open a window.

"What they do on *NYPD,*" she said, "is they add somebody intelligent to the plot." Her voice trailed away to the front reception area, then came back down toward the rear door. "So anytime you guys feel like telling me what's going on, I'm available. Good night, now."

They let her leave without comment. A half-minute later, she poked her head back in the door. "I forgot to ask," she said. "You fellas want Danish in the morning? Or kringle?"

B.L. was silent. Bud said kringle. B.L. sighed.

"Now listen," said the president, moving his boy past me down the hallway, "you let me worry about the right and the wrong moves. That's my department. I got lawyers. You get the county in behind you, close in, and you do it. I'll be waiting over at the Dew Drop Inn."

The door slammed. Engines started. I was alone.

A perfect nail knot

I studied the plat map for a while. My eyes had adjusted, and in time I could orient myself by using the stream, which flowed out of the north, swelled into Lake Bud, then continued along the west flank of the town and into the Mallard River.

It was easy to see both the past and the future of Black Earth. The simple sketch of blue lines on white paper told it all. The properties around Main Street were small, mostly square or rectangular lots that could hold a hardware store and six parking stalls, or a two-bedroom cracker box house and a yard with a maple tree and a swing set. On one street there were some double and triple lots—where the half dozen wealthy Black Earthlings had built their clapboard castles at the turn of the century. These would house the gentry now. Jake and Ingrid Jacobs. Those folks. Plus maybe an antique shop and a bed and breakfast.

The outskirts framed the action. The big farm plats south of town had been annexed—marked in red—and carved up into cul-de-sacs with vast, pie-shaped lots fed by sewer and water and cable TV lines. The streets were wider. The geometries were sleeker. Up on the north side of town, President Bud had done the same thing. His side of Lake Bud was all pruned up into long "lakefront" lots, with the roads, sewer, power, everything all drawn in. The red line of annexation strapped his parcel to the village, straddling the gap of Sundvig's pasture below Lake Bud and hooking in Junior's place to the northeast.

When I was sure no one was coming back into the village building, I rose and entered the president's office. My first inspection took in an array of big-game trophies on the walls. There was a cape buffalo, a boar, some kind of a mountain goat, a kind of African deer, a bighorn sheep. I wondered if Bud had bought them at a flea market. I pulled a chair over and stood. I lifted the goat head from the wall and squeezed my little keychain light onto the back of the mounting plate. It said, *Hanson's Safari, Turnerville, Texas.*

I placed the goat head back against the wall. Jake Jacobs had written the Hanson's Safari phone number in the notebook I had found inside his fishing vest. I had called that morning from the Cruise Master. But the man answering the phone at Hanson's hadn't seemed to know Jake.

Musing on this, I stepped down off the chair and began to open desk drawers. What was on my mind, funny thing, was not Bud Bjorgstad or Bud Lite, but more Mary Malarkey, the village clerk, and her comment about someone intelligent coming into the plot. Jake Jacobs had come into a plot, I felt certain. And now the Dog was sniffing his way down the same path.

President Bud's top drawer held a copy of Jake Jacobs' lawsuit against the Village of Black Earth for concealing insurance premiums as ancillary maintenance costs in the village budget. I read with an open mouth. A million dollars in premiums over the last twenty years, for what the company described as "coverage against flood and other damages potentiated by an unsafe, unfit containment structure upstream from the village." The suit had been filed three months ago. The village had petitioned for time to respond. The case was pending.

Someone intelligent. The phrase kept running through my head. The next thing I found, midway through an IN basket on top of the president's desk, was a copy of White Milkerson's study, *The Effects of Lake Bud on Black Earth Creek.* I flipped through it. Not that I knew anything about scientific methodology, but Milkerson seemed to know what he was doing. He talked about his data from his many years of shocking the stream. He described his process in layman's terms—his variable voltage backpack unit, his wand-electrode, the way the fish rose stunned but unharmed to the electrode and could be measured, tagged, whatever was necessary. Since the dam was raised and reinforced in 1985, he reported, naturally reproducing brook trout had declined precipitously, followed by an increase in brown trout, followed next by a decrease in all types and sizes of trout and an increase in rough fish like suckers, chubs, red horse, and, lately, bluegill and pike. As Lake Bud filled up and spread and became a shallow, muddy pond, its continued presence had increased stream temperature, siltation, heavy metal and phosphate concentrations, and it had decreased overall dissolved oxygen. The dam, and Lake Bud, were slowly strangling the stream.

I flipped ahead to the end of Milkerson's report. My eyes were drawn to a circle in red pen around a single phrase from the Summary and Options section. *Smallmouth bass fishery.* "While dam removal is risky and its effects on the stream uncertain," wrote Milkerson, "current conditions, projected into the future, appear ideal for the development of a hatchery-supported *smallmouth bass fishery.*"

Out of the entire report, one phrase had caught the attention of village president Bud Bjorgstad. *Smallmouth bass fishery.* The stream could warm up, silt up, weed over, suffocate its natural trout population. That was okay with him. Just pitch a bunch of bass in it and watch them grow. *Lakeside lots on a trophy smallmouth bass fishery.* I supposed that sounded just dandy to President Bud.

Grimly, and wondering if Jacobs had been killed on behalf of the smallmouth bass, I opened a door between the restroom and the rear exit and found a stairway to the basement garage. It was a mess down there. Two car bays hosted an extra patrol car and a massive snowmobile. Cluttered around the margins of the room were traffic cones, yard tools, sidewalk salt, lost-and-found bicycles, backlogs of LOTS FOR SALE and BJORGSTAD FOR VILLAGE CHAIR signs.

B.L.'s evidence locker was just that: a locker. A pair of them, actually, looking like they had been salvaged from a grade school remodeling project. The left-hand locker had a combination padlock on it, and through my mind ran *Havlicek, Silas, Havlicek...* 17-35-17... the Celtic jersey numbers that opened my high school gym locker.

That didn't work, though. I pinched my LCD and shined it in through the grid of the door. B.L. had impounded Jake Jacobs' fly rod. I scanned up and down to be sure it was the right one. It was the beautiful bamboo rod, with the Orvis reel, the brand new Orvis Wonderline. I winked my light at the fly. It was the upside down Jake's Sally—the eighth of those in existence, if I could believe Dickie Pee. I slid my light up the leader. There I was startled. I hadn't noticed before. The leader was tied onto the line with a nail knot. A *good* nail knot. A *perfect* nail knot.

As I registered this, I began to smell the fish food, dissolving in my wet pocket. The other locker was unlocked and I opened it. More fish food—bags more of it, crammed and slumped like small fat bodies in the locker: *Fred's Grow-Boy Fish Feed.*

President Bud was growing smallmouth in the lake. That's what I figured.

And Jacobs found out.

But as I came back up the stairs I couldn't hold the thought. And as I looked fruitlessly up and down Main Street for Junior, my mind rebelled.

Jake Jacobs discovered smallmouth bass? I wondered. *And died for it?*

A friend of the Dog

He saw me coming. As I pushed into the Dew Drop Inn, President Bud gave me a nod and a smile and hitched his stool back a notch.

"Hey, fella," he said. "Good to see you. How's fishing?" Elbows braced against the bar, back swayed, he swirled a cola-colored highball. "Milt," he said, getting the attention of the elderly bartender. Milt looked away from the television. President Bud nodded my way. "Set the fella up."

I sat. I asked for a beer and Milt didn't ask what kind. He just tapped one up.

"Guy who found the body," Bud told anyone in earshot.

Milt set the beer in front of me. I'd seen urine specimens more appealing. But alcohol was alcohol in the Dog's world. Over the rim of the glass I saw a half dozen other drinkers looking my way. Beyond the bar was a dark lounge with high-backed, black-vinyl booths and a pool table under a plastic Grain Belt light. Domestic game trophies, deer, ducks, pheasants, lined the walls, and the Packers were playing a preseason game against the Jets on the television. Along the bar were arranged warm little lamps from Coca-Cola and Jack Daniels, set up alternately, each beside a Grain Belt ash tray. That's what I was having, I decided. A Grain Belt. And President Bud was having a Jack and Coke. The guy at the end of the bar was playing bar dice. Rattle, rattle, rattle... WHAM!

"So you like fishing?" said the village president. "Hell, now there's a dumb question." He laughed. "But I'm gonna ask it anyway. Milt's used to my dumb questions, aren't you, Milt? You really like fishing do you?"

I told him I liked fly fishing.

President Bud wet his lips on Jack and Coke.

"Yup," he said. "Yessir, I've heard that's the real deal. Fly fishing. Really catching on lately."

He watched a replay. Fumble. He turned back to me. *Rattle, rattle, rattle...*

"So you must like fly fishing for—" WHAM! "—for smallies, too."

No, I said. I didn't care much for smallmouth.

The president cocked his flabby head like I'd said something deeply ironic.

"But he don't like fishing for smallies, Milt."

The bartender ambled over and laid a long cigarette in my Grain Belt ashtray. He gave the bar a wipe, leaned on it, and looked to his right out the neon-cluttered window.

"They'll fight," he said. "Smallies. Harder than largemouth."

Rattle, rattle, rattle... Bud said, "Now bluegill are—" WHAM! "—I'll bet if you like fly fishing, you like to fish for gills. We got a real nice crop of them on the lake out there."

I said I'd pass on the bluegill, too.

Now the president put on a look of dismay. He swirled his Jack and Coke and took a sip.

"Now you're confusing me here," he said. "Milt, he's confusing me. Says he likes to fly fish." Bud reached out with his fingertips and gave my beer a nudge, reminding me to drink. "But it don't sound like you're all that crazy about it after all. Hell, a guy with a fly rod can take thirty, forty bluegill off that lake out there, one-pounders, do it in a couple hours. They'll hit anything that moves."

"They fight good, too," said Milt. "In circles."

"And good eatin'," said the president.

Rattle, rattle, rattle...

"I'll have a glass of water," I said.

WHAM!

Milt moved off to hose seltzer over ice. The village president said to me, "Something wrong with your beer?"

Actually there was, even by the Dog's standards. "It sat around," I said. "Like that lake. It got flat."

"So you're a pretty sensitive fella, it turns out."

"If you say so."

That made him laugh. He wet his rubbery lips again with the drink and slapped my shoulder.

"See, what I'm saying here is that for a real fly fisherman, it wouldn't matter. Smallmouth bass, bluegill, trout—makes no difference to a guy that really loves fly fishing. Ain't that right, Milt? Fella, you see what I'm saying?"

"I do," I said. "You make a good point."

That seemed to please him.

"What I like is fly fishing for trout," I said. *Rattle, rattle, rattle...* "In places like this, Black Earth, where it can still happen on its own. Because it—" *WHAM!* "—because it means something. The existence of a trout here means something."

President Bud guffawed. "God almighty you sound like Jacobs!" He looked down the bar. "The soul lives on, folks. Another nut job like Jacobs."

The rattling stopped. The guy with the bar dice—big guy, clumsy-looking, thick glasses and a beard—said, "Jacobs got murdered, Bud. That ain't funny."

Chastened, the president drained his Jack and Coke and shoved it out for a refill. He looked hurt. I leaned in to console him.

"You know," I said, "I don't believe you really thought Jacobs was a nut job."

His small eyes darted to mine.

"No," I said. "I think you were afraid of him. I think he kind of had your number. Am I right?"

That shifted his gears. He looked past me toward the window. "So who the hell are you?"

I pondered that. I guess I had been pondering that for a couple of years now. Funny I should feel like answering suddenly. "A friend," I said.

And we sat there, eyes locked, both of us wondering, *friend of whom?*

I could have said Junior. I could have said Jake Jacobs. Both felt true suddenly. But I leaped over all that. Or I went back. Christ, suddenly the social fabric was all over the place, and it all webbed back to one center.

"A friend of the Dog," I told the muttering old man beside me. And then *I* laughed.

Because there I was, getting something right, finally, something that had eluded me, and I was doing it in front of exactly the kind of asshole who could never appreciate it.

"Don't tell me," he said out of nowhere. "You're gay. You're a goddamned pervert. Jacobs, too."

"If you say so."

He shook his head sadly.

"Now I'm *all* confused," he said.

I put my head close to his. "You're about as confused as a coyote with his foot on a jackrabbit," I told the Black Earth village president. "Jacobs was making life real difficult for you. And now he's dead. That's not too confusing."

He took a long drink and looked into the mirror behind the bar.

"I didn't do nothing to Jake," he said. "I was at the meeting. In fact, that night, me and Ronnie Hellenbrand were planning on Jake being at the meeting, too. The minutes'll prove that. We had a group we wanted him to join. Hell, we were *at the meeting*."

"I know what you're trying to tell me."

"Damn right," he said. "The sally hatch. Eight o'clock. And Jake had a sally on to prove it. Meanwhile, I was right over there in the president's chair. You can read it in the minutes."

"I read the minutes." He didn't like the sound of that. "But who's to say someone didn't kill Jacobs at five o'clock and just retie his fly? Seeing as the whole town seems to know what time the sallies come up."

He nodded. He worked his rubbery lips at himself in the bar mirror. "Say," he said, turning to me with an eyebrow raised. "That's clever." He rattled his Jack and Coke and tossed a wink at the Milt bartender. "You'd better tell that to the police chief."

"Oh," I said, and I dribbled a smelly handful of fish food pellets across the bar. I set down my special Jake's Yellow Sally amidst them. Then I snatched the fly back. "My guess is the chief knows all about it."

Something was amiss

Junior hadn't returned in twenty minutes. Or even thirty. Hurrying up the hot county highway in the dark, I knew something was amiss, and I began a stiff-kneed trot that broke down opposite the campground, when I realized the Cruise Master had been torn apart.

I rushed across the black, dew-soaked grass. Someone had gone through the rear door with a tool that had worked to the effect of a giant can opener. Out onto the dark grass were strewn various of my meager possessions—including my quaint little strong box.

I rushed straight to the box. Beside it lay the campfire rock that had smashed it open.

I knelt beside it. I was startled to find my cash still inside, all eight hundred. And my Glock. Only Jake Jacobs' ponytail was missing.

No.

The ponytail and the earring from the big trout's gut.

They were both gone.

Coming up Junior's driveway, I could see the lights were on and the front door was wide open. From somewhere within or behind the house came a sizzling sound, followed by a curse.

I climbed the porch. The television played Dad's video. Mary Poppins was just leading her brood on a mad carousel ride. A tub of vanilla ice cream lay upended and leaking across a threadbare throw rug. A patch of knitting hung discarded on the runner of the rocking chair.

"Junior?"

I continued into the kitchen. Soap bubbles popped in the sink. The bathroom was dark and empty. I pushed open Junior's bedroom door. Three hundred angels—dolls, ceramics, ornaments—watched from shadowy perches around her perfectly made bed.

"Junior? Hey—anybody home?"

I continued to the back porch and from there beheld a bizarre and wholly unexpected sight. A stocky old woman—this had to be Mrs. Sundvig, Dad's babysitter—stood braced at the dark maw of the barn, holding someone at bay inside with a cattle prod. And that someone was dodging and feinting about—in a wheelchair—trying to get out.

So it was an old woman with a cattle prod versus a sad case in a wheelchair. Not being sure which side to take, if any, I watched in horror for a moment. Dickie Pee's entire upper body was straining and thrashing—which gave him an outside chance against Mrs. Sundvig, who wielded the prod with authority.

She zapped him squarely in the chest, turning back a charge. Dickie Pee spun and disappeared into the barn. A moment later he reappeared holding a shovel. They jousted for a frightening moment. Then the prod clattered down and Dickie Pee spun past into the open drive, bouncing madly over tractor ruts. I saw he had something pinched between his legs. When he hit the county highway, heading downhill, he let the wheelchair roll—down the coulee, around a corner, out of sight.

As I approached Mrs. Sundvig, she aimed the prod at me.

"I'm a friend of Junior's," I said, raising open palms. "What's going on?"

She looked me over—small, black eyes, squinting for lack of eyeglasses—and lowered the prod. I could hear her lungs working, each breath like water over gravel.

"You ain't the other one," she told me.

"No, I'm not."

"The other one…was little. Ran out the back of the barn. Now they both got away."

"What happened, Mrs. Sundvig?"

She looked grimly toward the road where Dickie Pee had vanished. Her right hand was bleeding.

"Well," she said, "after all the commotion at the house… I stuck around to pick up. All that fighting made a mess, you know. And the police…they just walked away and left it. About a quarter hour later I heard some noise out in the barn. So I came out to check. Found them two back in the storage, messing around."

"Mrs. Sundvig…what commotion at the house? Where's Junior? Where's her dad?"

She eyed me. "O'Malleys you mean?" She wiped a bloody knuckle on the hem of her faded house dress.

I nodded.

She looked toward the empty house.

"Them two," she said, "been arrested."

Some trouble now

"Ya," said the old woman. Her knuckle wouldn't stop bleeding. She looked at it dispassionately, then dismissed the whole hand to drip onto the barnyard dirt.

"Them two." She shook her balding old head. "Some trouble now."

I asked her what happened. She turned and aimed her cattle prod toward the end of the driveway.

"Police chief," she told me. "Come up here on foot, looked around in the barn for a minute. Then he come banging on the door and cussing. But Mel don't take cussing. He don't like his video show interrupted either. Mel tossed that kid right off the porch." She seemed proud of the old man. "Then all them sheriff's cars came in."

"Mrs. Sundvig, you're bleeding pretty badly there. Let's get you into the house and wash that."

I steered her into the kitchen. The wound was deep, and I realized that Dickie Pee had caught her with the blade of the shovel. As I cleaned and bandaged Mrs. Sundvig's hand, she told me the story of Mel and Junior's arrest. After Dad had shoved him off the porch, B.L. had gone away and come back later with a pair of deputies from the Dane County Sheriff. They had just gotten Mel subdued on the porch when Junior arrived home from our date at the cheese factory. Mrs. Sundvig sounded proud again as she described Junior's reaction, the upshot of which was that B.L. had a bloody nose.

"But Missus Sundvig," I said, "You don't hit cops. You never hit cops. No—not even if you grew up with them. No, Missus Sundvig. Not even if you've been slapping their red asses around since third grade."

A sheriff's deputy had pepper-sprayed Junior and led her away in handcuffs. Then B.L. and the other deputy had searched the farm, and they had carried away what Mrs. Sundvig described as a "small, furry-looking black thing." She looked at me, suddenly bug-eyed with worry.

I guess we both knew what it was.

B.L. had "discovered" Jake Jacobs' missing ponytail.

I RACED TO TOWN in Junior's pickup. Finding no one at the village office, I backtracked to confirm what I thought I had seen as I passed the *Pêche Tôt*.

I had seen right. Ingrid Jacobs was at the table in the back, tying flies. I banged on the glass.

She was dressed in a man's button-down shirt and a pair of jeans. Her breath smelled like coffee. She said, "Yes, I heard it from Bud, who just came over from the bar to give me the news. He said B.L. got a tip. Someone called him, said look in Mel O'Malley's barn, by the milk cooler." The dead man's wife gave me her closed-lip smile. "Did you want to come in?"

I followed her back to the fly tying table. She picked up her bobbin where it hung and began to tie down deer hair on a large stone fly imitation. Ten or twelve finished flies were stuck around the rim of a foam coffee cup. I stared in disbelief: *Ingrid Jacobs, tying flies?*

"So," she said, sticking another fly to the cup. "It's over now. Jake can rest."

I squawked: "Someone gave B.L. a tip?"

Ingrid nodded serenely, gripping another hook in her vise.

"Ingrid," I said, "if Mel O'Malley killed your husband while everyone else was at the village board meeting, then how does anybody else know about it? Who else is available to know where the ponytail is? How does someone else tip off B.L.? And why does B.L. believe it?"

She wound her thread to the hook bend and tied in an orange polyfiber butt. She said, "Don't ask me how things work in this town. I never did get it."

"And excuse me," I said, feeling my brain jump a rail. "But you're about the last person I expected to see sitting here tying flies."

The smile again, this time to herself. She tied down the tip of a palmer hackle.

"Was that a question?"

"You tie flies?"

"I tie to calm down."

"Jake taught you?"

"No." She reached her long arm out for a coffee mug, and she looked at me over the rim as she sipped. Her eyes sparked oddly. "I taught Jake."

I took a nice slow breath, letting things settle into their new positions. Ingrid taught Jake. I hadn't expected that.

"When did you meet Jake?"

"Five years ago," she said. "Jake's design firm bid on a project for the resort my family owns in Jackson Hole. My father's still mad that I fell for Jake. Jake was a city boy then. He couldn't even hold a rod."

I looked around the coffee shop, still trying to recalculate everything. The shop looked different somehow.

"There are none of those big orange stone flies in Black Earth Creek," I said finally.

"No shit," answered Ingrid.

"Black Earth is a little creek, muddy bottom. Not like out west."

"No shit."

"No room to cast half the time. Trees and weeds. Tight corners."

"No shit."

"You never even fished Black Earth, did you?"

"Once," she said, "and that was enough."

"But Jake loved it here," I guessed.

She sighed as if this were more true than she could bear to think about. She stuck another big orange stone fly in the rim of the foam cup. Then a voice startled me, booming down the stairwell. "Inkie!"

"My big brother from Wyoming," she told me. "Yes?" she called back.

"What do you want me to do with Jake's fishing stuff? You want me to pack that, too?"

Another sigh. Now I had it. The pictures were gone from the shop walls. The artwork was gone. Ingrid's touch had been stripped away. She was selling. She was leaving Black Earth. She was tying western flies. She was going home.

"Inkie? You hear me? What do you want to do with Jake's stuff? His vest, rods, his waders, all these reels, this big box from the taxidermist..."

"Toss it," she called back.

"It's good stuff, Inkie."

"I don't want to see it around."

"But you must have somebody here you know…could use this stuff…"

She shrugged weakly. Like she didn't care. Like she didn't have the energy to think about it. Like she really wanted Jake's stuff tossed.

The Dog…he laid a paw on her shoulder. "Like me," I said. "I could use it."

Evidence of what exactly?

Inside the Cruise Master, I tore open the long box from the taxidermist. Not that I hadn't guessed, but Jake Jacobs had caught himself a monster brown trout. The dimensions were engraved on the mounting plate: twenty-seven inches, nine-and-a-half pounds. He had caught it on Black Earth Creek, April 15 of that year. If my guess was right, though, he had mounted it not for the boast. He had kept it for evidence.

But evidence of what exactly?

I flopped Jacobs' waders over the back of my galley bench. As could be expected, they were top of the line, nearly brand new. I spread them out to see if he used a belt to protect against drowning from filled waders. He had. But I saw, in the back, where a man sat down, a small, precisely circular hole, about a centimeter in diameter. The margins of the hole looked melted—like he had sat on a cigar—which I could believe. I'd done it. Twice, to be honest. But if Jacobs had waded in to his waist, I mused, he would have gotten wet. He would have waded back out, cursed himself, stayed in shallower water thereafter, until he could put a patch on. It didn't seem to mean much. Frustrated, I let go of the waders.

I mixed up a vodka-Tang and resolved myself to go through Jacobs' little notebook again, looking for anything that might now connect. Again I was confronted with the notations of a fish counter—but now I wondered if the Friends of Black Earth Creek founder had another purpose in keeping meticulous track of every fish he caught. I knew only one thing for sure. The guy caught a lot of fish. If the stream was fading, as Milkerson's study indicated, I guess I should have been here back when it was good. I guess we all should have.

Grasping, I decided to inspect the vest again. I had done it once, in Jacobs' office, but maybe I had missed something. I laid every item out on the galley table. Jacobs' fly boxes displayed the energy and zeal of the man. He had ten of everything. His tippets were tightly organized in a linked stack. He had his floatant bottle in a nifty little harness, and his nippers and hemostats were connected to the vest by retractable cords. Then I found something that made me think. From an inner pocket, after the flashlight, the license, and package of gum, I lifted out a nail knot tier. It was still in its package, unopened. As if Jacobs was planning to learn the nail knot but hadn't tried yet.

Now, with rising interest, I rifled through the rest of the inner pockets, finding a pack of matches and the kind of braided loops used by a fisherman who can't, or won't, attach his leader butt to his fly line by using a nail knot. It was a question of convenience, dexterity, experience. The braided loops picked up water and threw spray onto the water. That was fine on big, fast, snow-melt water, but I hated them on small, spring-fed streams like Black Earth Creek. But I had used them, too, when I had first started fishing. They were easier—if you knew what to do with them. You had to carefully shrink-melt them on, if I remembered right.

And when I laid out all of Jacobs' spare reels—all five of them—I found that one after the other had the fly line and the leader butt connected the easy way, with a store-bought braided loop. I felt my chest tighten. I knew I had it suddenly.

Someone had killed Jacobs before the sally hatch, earlier than eight p.m. But they hadn't just retied his fly. Jacobs' killer had caught him without a fly on his leader—in fact, Jacobs' killer had caught him *without any leader on at all.* Jacobs had just bought a new fly line, hadn't he? Hadn't I found the box atop his filing cabinet? So, after Jacobs was dead and shorn of his ponytail and floating discarded where I had found him, his killer, in order to attach a Jake's Yellow Sally, had been forced to *tie on a whole new leader.*

That meant, in the heat of the crime, the killer had used whatever knot came naturally. Forget the yellow sally for a moment, I told myself. This meant the killer's knot-tying skills would be on display in the connection between the leader and the fly line—and the whole braided loop thing hadn't rung a bell.

I clearly recalled the killer's choice in the glow of my LCD key chain light, through the mesh of Bud Lite's evidence locker: a nail knot.

And now I remembered my inspection of the place where Jake Jacobs had died. THE RESPECT LANDOWNER'S RIGHTS sign had been freshly hammered off its fence post. It had flopped around upside down, its top nail missing.

The killer had needed a nail, in a hurry, to put a leader on Jacobs' line. I was sure of it. Few people could tie an old-fashioned nail knot.

But Jacobs' killer was one of them.

The Dog had put two and two together

As the sun rose on another eighty-degree Black Earth dawn, I was hiding in a tool shed on the Sundvig farm across the highway from the campground. My first morning in Black Earth, three days ago now, I had been up stirring Tang, watching a milk truck pull in. I had wondered, that morning, at the voices, unintelligible over the distance and the rumble of the truck, but clearly agitated.

Now, up close, Junior's neighbor Elmer Sundvig was in a squeaky rage: "Christ all Friday, Lumen! Do you gotta cut the corner like that? Every dang time? Those are Vera's tiger lilies—no, hey, dangit, get your wheels off of there!"

The milk truck engine shut down and the door slammed. Lumen Bostock, the poacher, hit the ground in his tight little boots and said, "Whassat?"

"Those are Vera's tigers, dang it all!"

"Kiss my keester, Sundvig."

Bostock was getting right down to work, hauling his hose out toward the milk house. I rose for a look through the dust-grimed window. Bostock was followed by a limping old man in coveralls and a red cap. The milk house door shut with a bang. I slunk from the shed and into the cab of the truck.

The Dog imagined he had put two-and-two together. The best motive for killing Jacobs belonged to the village president, Bud Bjorgstad. Jacobs meant to drain his lake and spoil his property. Yet what had been discouraging me all along was the image of a Bud with his bad back negotiating the rough and swampy terrain around the creek and then wrestling a specimen like Jake Jacobs underwater long enough to drown him. That picture just wouldn't play. Now, to that difficulty, I had to add President Bud's almost certain inability to tie a nail knot. This of course pointed to the obvious possibility that Bud Heavy had hired someone else to do the deed—a killer who, when faced with the blank end of Jacobs' line, had passed on the braided loops, perhaps not even recognized them, and instinctively tied a nail knot.

Keeping low, I slid across Lumen Bostock's seat into the passenger's spot. Jacobs had cost Bostock a few hundred bucks in fines. Jacobs had challenged Bostock's notion that the stream belonged to the few who had fished it first and longest. Jacobs, I felt sure, was Bostock's primal enemy.

The cab floor on the passenger side was so cluttered that opening the door on that side would have sent a cascade of fast-food junk, newspapers, magazines, and assorted poaching supplies out onto the farmer's driveway. I pawed through this mess for the jug line set-up I had chased down the stream a day ago. On Bostock's poaching rig, I recalled, were assorted line-to-line connections of the type that would take a nail knot.

I heard Bostock exit the milk house. He crunched alongside the truck and started the pump. My sense of what would happen next stopped right there. How long would it take to pump out the milk? How big was the farm? What did Bostock do while he waited? Maybe he climbed back in the cab and read…and right there I glanced at the stuff in my hands and felt sick. Low-grade porno in one hand, real meaty stuff, a neo-Nazi rag in the other hand, announcing recent developments in the world of hatred, all of this stuff floating around in a smelly soup of A&W bags and Dew bottles and Copenhagen tins.

I hauled up the milk jug with the line wrapped around it. I could feel the hum and chug of the pump. Over that, Bostock was twanging some crap about the lilies to the farmer's wife, Mrs. Sundvig, who had come out to fuss over them. An old dog had come out with her, and was yapping and snarling hoarsely at Bostock.

I thought I had the bastard. I really did. But the moment my fingers touched the knots I knew I was wrong. I didn't even have to look. Big lumpy things, overtied, asymmetrical, ignorant. Granny knots in paranoid profusion. The big brown trout with the earring inside its gut had pulled out some dumbass knot. That's why it was swimming around under the jug. There was no way, and I knew it. There was no way Lumen Bostock had coolly tied a nail knot over the body of a dead man.

Then the pump stopped. I heard the slam of Bostock going back through the milk house door to unhook his hose. I slid across the driver's seat and jumped from the cab—straight into the business end of a cattle prod.

Mrs. Sundvig squinted up at me.

"I thought I seen you sneak in there."

"Shhhh," I told her. "Shhhhh. Remember me?"

Like the tail on a dog

By the time I had slipped Mrs. Sundvig and reached the *Pêche Tôt,* Ingrid Jacobs had a U-Haul trailer packed and hitched to a black Mercedes SUV parked out front. The vehicle had Wyoming plates, a little cowboy riding a bronco through a thousand miles of bug-spat. Ingrid's brother leaned on the hood with a foam cup of coffee. He looked vaguely amused by the sight of me coasting up in Junior's pickup.

"Ingrid's on the phone," he told me, nodding toward the shop. "She'll be out in a minute."

Not if she saw me out here, I guessed. As someone well-schooled in blowing town, I thought I knew how she was feeling. Her anxiety would be high, her senses sharp. She would know why I'd come. I'd decided that Ingrid Jacobs could tie a nail knot. Not only that, she could tie a couple extra Jake's Yellow Sallies, as needed. She might even have been clever enough to tie the second one on improperly to direct suspicion away from herself.

I looked the brother over. Big guy with an easy, rich-kid's

manner. Ingrid without all the angst. Perfect teeth. Named Wyatt, I remembered, from when he'd given me Jake's stuff. Wyatt looked like he had gotten up too early.

"So after Ingrid leaves, what happens to the shop?"

He yawned and shrugged. "She listed it. Good price. We'll see."

"And the house?"

"Same." He took a long swallow of coffee. "You a friend of Inkie's?"

"Not really," I said. "We just met." I added a lie. "She was going to tie me some flies."

I watched Wyatt's manners kick in. He overcame his sluggishness of mood and said, "Oh? Maybe I can help you. What kind?"

"I was headed west," I said. "I'm kind of a trout bum. I thought I should have some big yellow stones. But I'm sure your sister didn't get a chance."

He was already opening the tail end of the Mercedes. "She's got all her stuff back here. I was planning to hit some big water on the way home. Cheer Inkie up. How many did you need?"

"Don't worry about it," I said. "I didn't come asking for flies. I just was coming by to tell your sister never mind. I mean, with her loss and all… I just didn't realize she was leaving town so soon."

Over his shoulder, he gave me a knowing grin with just the right touch of sadness. "Not soon enough for Inkie."

Right, I thought. Not soon enough for *Jake*. I was feeling a little raw suddenly. I mean, here's a young couple, Jake and Ingrid, married without kids—couldn't they get along? Did they think their lives were tough? So Ingrid was a little uncomfortable, things were a little inconvenient for her, maybe her husband had a little juice for another woman—so…what?…kill the guy? Frame up an innocent bystander? Run home to Daddy?

I had to know if Ingrid could tie the nail knot. I could see her and Bostock suddenly—filthy little Lumen Bostock and his airs of supremacy—could see him working with Ingrid and her own airs—Bostock and Ingrid and Bud and his schemes—working together. B.L. getting wagged along like the tail on a dog.

I could see where Ingrid's reels were. "Inkie" was the psycho-organized type. Her teeth had to be straight, for one thing—braces at age thirty—even though she was already beautiful, not to mention rich and married. Her reels were packed in one of those fancy reel cases that cost a few hundred bucks in the fishing catalogs.

"You fish, too?" I asked Wyatt.

"Only the good stuff."

I felt annoyed. "And which is the good stuff?"

"We've got a stretch of the Bison River that's as pretty as you could hope for, I'll tell you that," he said as he rummaged around. "No damn trees in the backcast. No mud. Wide as a football field."

He turned with a box containing about a hundred yellow stone flies. "Take what you need," he said.

I took a half dozen. I thanked him. I asked him to thank Ingrid for me. Then I said, "What do you do otherwise, Wyatt? When you're not fishing?"

He shrugged. "Mining. Timber. Cattle. We have a resort in Jackson Hole. There's more than enough to do. I'm busy as hell, actually."

"It's nice that you could come out and help your sister get her stuff together."

"Oh," he said, and he heaved a weary sigh. "Actually I was kind of on standby these last few months. We all knew Inkie was going to leave Jake."

He looked up and down Main Street, Black Earth. "She

hated the place," he said. "No mountains. Tiny streams. Mom fifteen hundred miles away."

"But the day Jake died," I said, "Ingrid was at a village board meeting asking for a permit for sidewalk tables at the café. Why would she do that if she were going to sell the place and leave?"

He shrugged. "She cared about Jake. She was going to leave him the shop. She wanted it to succeed."

I stared at Ingrid's reel case. Then I glanced into the *Pêche Tôt,* where she stood wrapped in a phone cord, the big orange cat curling about her legs.

"So did Jake know Ingrid was unhappy?"

Wyatt gave a helpless snort, as only a brother could.

"When Ingrid's unhappy, the whole world knows."

I looked back at her reel case. Then the door of the *Pêche Tôt* squeaked open. Ingrid stumbled out with the cat in her arms and locked the door.

She looked at me without really seeing, and suddenly I felt my theories shift again. Her eyes were hollow and vacant, surrounded by a muddy discoloration that made me understand that the events of the last few days had finally caught up with her. I knew the look of grief. I knew the stumbling gait, the vacant eyes, the bad skin. I'd spent some time, years back, staring into a mirror. Grief was a slow-moving train wreck. If the Dog knew anything, the Dog knew that.

Her brother nodded at me, but Ingrid's eyes stayed down. "I gave your friend some yellow stones."

"Thank you, Wy."

She was all elbows, knees, and hair suddenly. Her braces were bared for all to see. She climbed into the passenger seat, hugging the cat, and sat there, waiting.

"Hon," said her brother, "what's kitty going to poop in?"

She didn't answer. She didn't hear. Her brother gently pried the keys from her hand and went to unlock the *Pêche Tôt*. I spent the minute he was gone coldly zipping open Ingrid's reel case. I had to know if I understood grief. Or if that face, that stagger, that wild impulse to escape—and my own—were the simple marks of a criminal.

I laid the case open. Six reels, the best money could buy. But on every reel, connecting line to leader, braided loops. No nail knots. Ingrid couldn't tie them either.

As I set the case back into its place, I noticed something surprising, snapped neatly through the stays of a backpack. It was the little wreath of knotted grass Shelly had tried to give Jake at the funeral home.

Ingrid Jacobs was still as a stone in the front seat, staring straight down the vacant main street of Black Earth. As her brother retrieved the litter box from the defunct *Pêche Tôt,* I reached through the window, slowly, so as not to startle her, and I touched the widow on the shoulder.

It's just a rock

Which left me with the riddle of Dickie Pee. I drove Junior's pickup back up the coulee, thinking about how a man in a wheelchair could manage the murder of Jake Jacobs—and such thoughts, of course, took me straight back to the idea of teamwork. So, Dickie Pee, Bostock, and Bud? It was an odd and unlikely mix of egos. And the nail knot didn't really make sense. If someone had carried the dead man's rod out to the road and told Dickie, "I can't tie on a sally. He doesn't even have a leader," then Dickie wouldn't have said, "Okay, walk back across the field, kick that sign off, and bring me the nail." Hell no. He had knot-tying tools, I was sure, in his van. Whoever tied the nail knot was on the stream, in the heat of the moment. And there was no way to get a wheelchair out there.

I was headed up the coulee past the campground at a pretty good clip when I saw the gate was open. A tow truck was backed up to the snout of the Cruise Master. By the time I bumped down the drive, a guy in a greasy green uniform was air-drilling the last of four new tires onto my baby.

"I told you I'd fix 'em for ya," slurred Shelly Milkerson, stepping around the rear bumper. She looked freshly ripped, a beer-and-a-joint-for-breakfast kind of glow on her. She wore cutoffs and a halter top, and the guy from Hellenbrand Tire couldn't keep his eyes on the job. There was something different about her, too, but I couldn't place it.

"Didn't I tell you?"

"You did. Thanks."

"He's got a tire changer and air and everything right on his truck, see?"

"I see."

"That's how they do tractors and stuff. Just come right out into the field."

"I see. How much do I owe you?"

She frowned a little. Through the fingers of her left hand she had twisted the top of a plastic bagel bag, and she swung this around as if she were in deep thought, trying to calculate. But if I had harbored any doubts about the kind of business woman Shelly was, I was quickly relieved of my uncertainty. She knew exactly how much cash I had in my safe box.

"How about eight hundred?" Shelly said.

That was the number. Exactly. I mumbled something, suddenly wondering how many fishermen on Black Earth Creek had needed their tires fixed.

"And you said I could drive it sometime. Remember?"

I mumbled something again. The tire guy threw his tools in the back of the tow truck and took a long last look at Shelly. "Ronnie's gonna bill me," she told him. He snorted and rolled his eyes. He ripped up a long patch of campground turf as he drove out.

"You got the keys?" Shelly asked me. "Can I drive?"

I looked away from her at my ruptured door, peeled open

like a sardine can. Junior leaped to mind. Where, how, was Junior? And Dad? Out on Lake Bud, the buoys for the Jet Sky Jam bobbed peacefully. Such was the disgraceful appearance of the old mill pond that a few dozen neon orange bobbers actually decorated the thing, made it look like a place where something more exciting than pollution could happen. And *was* happening—but what?

I looked back at Shelly. I was bad at knowing what had changed on a woman. But something had.

"You got bungee cords?" she asked me. "That will hold your door shut." I hesitated. "Look," she said. "I can drive. I've been driving since I was ten. I used to drive my dad home from the Dew Drop. When he was too drunk. Which was every night."

"You seem a little intoxicated yourself," I told her.

"You should talk," she huffed defiantly back. But she looked away from me, out at the orange buoys on the lake. Then she turned to me, brightly. "You let me drive," she said, "and I'll show you something."

WE WERE A HALF-MILE UP the coulee when we passed her dad, working out on the stream. She said nothing. Then, another mile up, she stopped near the point where Jacobs was killed.

"You see that rock out there, in the pasture?"

I saw it: a jagged chunk of limestone, surrounded by thistles, about a hundred yards beyond the barbed wire. The stream was another hundred yards beyond. The corner where I had found Jacobs' body was a bit north. Junior's black-and-white Holsteins were conspicuously missing from the pasture. No one had been around to milk them and let them out of the barn.

"Yeah," I said. "I see it."

Shelly had a necklace on. That was the difference in her.

She had a cheap chain around her neck, the silver, beaded kind that dangles from a light fixture, and she was fingering some ornament that hung between her breasts at the center of it.

"Take a closer look," Shelly urged me.

"It's just a rock. I've walked past it before."

"Come on," she urged me. "Take a look. You'll be surprised."

I crawled beneath the barbed wire, wetting myself in the dew-soaked grass. I was a few yards toward the stone when I got my surprise. Shelly was pulling away in the Cruise Master. Her gaze was aimed forward, up the coulee, both hands on the wheel, and the Cruise Master had been floored. My baby was straining to get some speed. I knew by the knock in the engine. And I knew suddenly what was on the chain around Shelly's neck, gripped in her left hand as she drove.

It was the big, tarnished, faux-pearl earring I had found in the belly of the trout. The earring I was guessing belonged to her mother.

I watched my Cruise Master disappear up the coulee. Where Shelly thought she was going, I couldn't imagine. But suddenly I knew where the nail knot had come from.

A step beyond

Outside the pop-up camper, I lifted up the two support ropes that had snapped in the thunderstorm. Since they were ropes, not fishing line, Shelly had repaired them using a stick—a larger and handier version of a nail—to shape the knots. And sure enough, those two ropes were rejoined with nail knots.

Sleek, tight, shapely—perfect nail knots.

Shelly Milkerson? The thought wouldn't settle with me. Sure, she had the ability to get close to Jacobs, perhaps to surprise him, and she had the ability to tie the nail knot. I could believe she had busted the fisherman's sign and used the nail. She was that resourceful and more. But why would she be interested in drowning Jake Jacobs? And how would she do it?

The sun was high now. From the outside, the pop-up camper smelled musty and hot. I circled it once, more as a nervous diversion than anything. I found Shelly's potty spot around back. I had noticed a few days before that at one end, under the camper, she had kept a plastic bucket with a few things inside—a scrub brush, a screwdriver, a pump bottle of liquid soap, a steak knife, a pair of pliers. Now that was gone.

I returned to the front of the camper and twisted the door knob. The door stuck. I tugged and the camper shook. But another tug overcame the chalky aluminum friction and the door came open. The heat hit me first, carrying upon it the pine scent of a car air freshener that spun from the ceiling. In the dim light below I made out Shelly's bed. But the Scooby Doo sleeping bag was gone. So was the little suitcase. So was the shrine to the mother that had abandoned her.

I scrambled to process a new sequence of events. Didn't Shelly understand she would be pursued? Didn't she understand it was clear now that she had killed Jake Jacobs and robbed the Cruise Master to set up Melvin O'Malley a second time—after her first attempt fell through? Didn't she comprehend that a drunk girl in a halter top driving a thirty-foot RV with Massachusetts plates was going to get exactly nowhere?

I couldn't imagine she was that drunk, or that stupid. I knew she wasn't. Nor could I explain how the second yellow sally on Jacobs' line had been tied with a granny knot, when Shelly clearly knew better. And how, after all, had Shelly's mother's earring ended up in the belly of a brown trout?

And there was another problem, too. Shelly hadn't taken everything with her. She had left behind a brand new tool box under her sleeping platform—and inside that tool box were wire cutters and wire strippers, gloves, and cable. Beneath the box was a file folder, recognizable as belonging to Jacobs by the neat left-handed lettering on the tab. The tab said *Dam— Structural Analysis*. Beneath the folder, covered with muddy fingerprints, lay three pages printed off the internet. The pages were from *The Anarchist's Cookbook*. They were instructions for laying dynamite.

The murder of Jake Jacobs wasn't the end of it, I realized. Shelly Milkerson and her partner, Dickie Pee, were taking things a step beyond.

Turning back to the pack

While I can understand now how wrong my instincts were at that moment—almost fatally wrong—I remain rather proud of them. Maybe I've picked up a little wisdom along the trout road after all, because my hunch now is that we all die with a searing flash of awareness that we have been utterly wrong on any number of big assumptions. But if you are going to die (and you are—you can quote the Dog on that), I guess you would be lucky, at that moment, to find yourself having erred on the side of faith and hope. At least that's the way my friend Junior O'Malley would see things.

Shelly Milkerson was a kid. That's what I was telling myself as I looked around the Lake Bud campground that hot August morning. True, she was a kid who had cleaned me out, who had left me with nothing to my name but a frayed aluminum lawn chair, a set of wheel chocks, and my waders slung over a burr oak limb. But she was a kid who needed sympathy and guidance. Her life had taken an awful twist, and she had adapted in self-destructive and violent ways.

She was a kid with a father, I was telling myself. A father who ought to know what she was doing. Who ought to crawl out of his own pain and do something to help her. That was my thinking. That was my fatherly instinct. Another sign of the Dog, unconscious, turning back to the pack.

I SLIPPED INTO MY WADERS and hiked back up the road. Across from Junior's, I rolled under the barbed wire.

When I found Manfred "White" Milkerson, he was nipping from his flask in mid-stream and whistling to a bird—an eastern kingbird, I thought. He wore his hard-plastic yellow backpack, and his shocking probe dangled downstream.

"Hey, White. How's it going?"

He turned unsteadily. I could see he was trying to recognize me. He was smashed.

"The trout bum," I reminded him. "The guy who found the body."

He nodded, preened back his sloppy moustache, gave me a little smile.

"Drink?"

"Sure."

He tossed me the flask.

"Thought you'd moved on."

"Not quite."

"Saw your rig heading up the road."

"Wasn't me."

He busied himself with a cigarette. A bird warbled nearby. I said, "That a kingbird?"

"Nope."

"Waxwing?"

"Nope."

"You got me then. I'm an easterner."

"Dickcissel." White Milkerson squinted at me. "Little seedeater. Big voice. Hard as hell to see." He took his flask back. He stuck it under his moustache. When the burn had cleared, he said, "You're not fishing."

"Nope. I came out to talk to you."

He moaned, "Aww crap," and propped the cigarette in his lips. When he had it lit, he said, "So my daughter cut your tires, right? That's what the last guy who camped there said. And I suppose that was her driving off with your rig. What am I supposed to do about it?"

"She needs help."

"Hell, we all need help."

"So let's help each other."

"I can't pay for everything she does. She stole something of yours, you gotta call the cops."

"She's in a lot more trouble than that."

Milkerson turned away like he didn't want to hear any more. He sloshed to the bank. "I got work to do," he grunted as he slung his shocker motor into the grass and pulled the starter cord. The little engine kicked and spat, then settled into a steady snarl on his back. He waded up the stream away from me, sweeping his probe through the current.

I went with him. "She's mixed up in the death of Jake Jacobs," I hollered into his ear. "She and this Dickie Pee character. I think she may have helped him kill Jacobs. She's been tampering with evidence to cover it up. And now she's playing around with explosives."

Milkerson wallowed forward without replying. Stunned fish began to ghost up around him. He had left his long-handled net on the bank. I followed him with it, scooping up eight-inch brown trout until the net was full. But he didn't seem to have any plan for them. Suddenly I wondered what work he was doing, and I intended to ask him.

But when I caught up with him, White Milkerson was weeping. Fat tears squeezed from his creased eyes and were quickly subsumed in his great, sloppy moustache. He pushed forward, sweeping the electric probe, seeing nothing.

"White," I said, turning the net over, watching the paralyzed trout drift away, "what are you doing? What's going on? Look, I'm trying to help your daughter."

His shoulders caved. His tears streamed. Trout sailed numbly into him, spun away. He looked helpless and pathetic. "God bless you," he said. "Somebody has to. I'm a horrible father. I've made horrible, horrible mistakes. She's on her own now. I can't help her."

I turned off his shocker.

"So what's going on, White? What are you really doing out here?"

I helped him to the bank.

"You're out here every day, probing this creek. Are you really doing studies?"

He stared at the water. He took a big breath and snorted it out. "The studies are faked," he said. "Hell—it takes more than one guy to do a decent stream survey. You gotta have a damn sled, a tub, a couple guys to haul and chart."

"The stream is not dying?"

"Hell no. It's worse than dying. It's living dead." He laughed roughly and looked at me like we both knew it. Like there was so much pain in what he had just said that he had to spread it around. But I wasn't sure what he meant. He kept his sad eyes on me. "Studies don't matter for shit, partner. Twenty years from now, thirty years from now, whatever, the guys in the suits will have their way. What we're sitting on right here is gonna be a parking lot, or somebody's goddamn backyard. We just don't know it yet."

"It can't be that bad, White."

Abruptly, his sorrow shut down. He looked at me cagily. "No. It's going to make some people happy, that's for sure. It's going to be great habitat for junk fish, too."

He kept his eyes on me.

He said, "Ice fishing's going to be good down on Lake Bud in a couple more years."

He still looked at me.

"And I've seen towns like Black Earth take a stream like this one here and get it channeled real nice so it never floods anymore. Then they put railings around it so kids can't fall in anymore." He dipped his cigarette butt in the stream and dropped it in his shirt pocket. "Shit, I used to fall in this crick all the time."

"What are you doing out here, White?"

He lit a fresh one. "It's too late for cute shit like ponytails," he said, exhaling. "You know? Every man for himself at this point. That's what I figure. But then I'm a certified bad person. Not like Jake. He was good. He was really good. It's just that this world... Hell, I don't know..."

"You don't want that dam out, do you?"

"No, I do not."

"You disagreed with Jacobs."

"No. I agreed with him. The dam is a problem. Jake was a good man."

I paused to think a minute. We seemed to be going somewhere. The studies were faked, Milkerson had said, which made their results even more telling.

"You said in your study this was going to be smallmouth bass water in another few years. Not junk fish water. You knew Bud Bjorgstad would jump on that and use it to fight for the dam. He'd use it to fight Jacobs."

He shrugged.

"What is it, White? You're looking for the first small-mouth out here?"

Milkerson laughed smoke. "Fuck smallmouth."

"Bud's feeding fish out on the lake," I said. "Those aren't smallmouth?"

He looked at me. He looked up and down the stream. Above us was one of Junior's cattle fences, stretching across the stream. Above that was a deep hole. A fisherman's ladder straddled the fence on the far bank, making it easy for a man in waders to get over Junior's barbed wire. White Milkerson looked back at me. Now he had a sad little grin. He looked more than a little like Shelly.

"Okay," he said. "Look. There's a little business going on in here. A little bit of put-and-take. I tell you what it's about, partner, and you can get into it for free, as long as you just take your trophy and drive away, don't blab it around."

"Drive away in what?"

I waited. The dickcissel chirped from a nearby dogwood, but White Milkerson didn't seem to hear it.

"See," he said, "President Bud and I go way back. Old turkey hunting buddies. Him and me and Mel O'Malley. Then Mel had all them strokes and Bud got rich on the Cox Hollow development and then he got in with this safari crowd. You know, big-game hunters. Guys that go down to a fenced farm in Arkansas or Texas and shoot some kind of African goat with fancy horns, put it up on the wall. Shit—pay five, ten grand for it."

I nodded and let him continue. I'd seen the exotic trophies in Bud Bjorgstad's Village President office. I'd found the number in Jake Jacobs' stream log. *Hanson's Safari*.

"Some of those same guys," said Milkerson, "like to think of themselves as fly fishermen. But nothing's a fish to them until it's three feet long. So Bud had this idea of raising some big brownies in the lake down there, then letting them go for his pals to catch in the creek. They pay him five hundred bucks for every inch over twenty. Five-fifty an inch, and Bud takes care of the taxidermy."

"And you?"

"I get a little cut. Retired state worker, you know, I gotta make a living."

"A little cut for what?"

He squinted through smoke at me. He aimed the flask under his moustache and took a long pull.

"You know. Big trout like those find a home real quick and just hunker down. They hunt at night, but then they go right back to home base. I find where they live. I mark the spot."

I remembered Jacobs' little notebook—maps and checkmarks, measurements and fish counts. Milkerson was marking big fish. Jacobs was figuring it out.

Milkerson said, "If one of Bud's clowns still can't catch one, I come out, turn this sucker up," he patted his yellow shocker, "and I pull that big old hog up to the surface." He laughed. "Shit. Some guys, they'll just grab it and take it home right there. Never even put a fly on the water. Other guys, they stick their fly in the jaw and wait for the fish to wake up. Then they have a fight. Shit. One guy hands me his goddamn camera. Kicks the fish downstream until it's bending his rod. Gets himself all lined up, his hat just right, and says, 'Okay, shoot!' Hell—that's probably the same guy who'll be building a golf course under our asses in about ten years."

"And you're helping them out."

He shrugged again. "I'm scum. I'm a moral waste product. Just ask my daughter."

We sat there a while. He finished another cigarette, did the dip and tuck into his ashtray-pocket.

"Now I guess you want your trophy," he said.

"No. I don't."

"But I guess you've got sense enough just to leave us all alone."

"Well…" I felt my face curl into an odd little smile. "I guess you kind of caught me at the wrong life moment."

"Nobody gets hurt in this."

"Like hell."

"You're going to make some noise."

I nodded. "A man died over this, White. Your daughter is involved. I don't think it's just about a big-fish scheme. What happened is I suppose Bud paid Shelly and Dickie Pee to remove Jacobs and place the blame on Junior's dad. Bud wanted to keep that dam at all cost."

Milkerson shook his head sadly. "No," he said. "That's not quite it."

"But close," I said. "I guess I left out Lumen Bostock. He knows about it. He's out here trying to catch those big ones for himself, and you can't exactly say anything about it. But Jake did. He got Bostock in trouble for it. So Bostock helped kill Jacobs. He was the one who snuck into the *Pêche Tôt* and slop-knotted another yellow sally onto Jake's tippet."

"No," said White Milkerson quietly. He was shaking out yet another cigarette. "You still don't have it."

"Then there's something else out there in Lake Bud, out there where those cones for the Jet Ski thing take a detour. Something that's worth killing to protect. Maybe I ought to dive down and take a look."

He looked at me.

"I've been learning to dive," I said. "Down in New Mexico. That big reservoir above the San Juan River tailwater. Gives me something to do when the dam flow is too high to fish."

Milkerson lit the cigarette and aimed it upstream, past the

fence to the next big hole. There seemed to be surrender in his movements.

"Can I show you something?" he asked me.

And I said he could—he could show me something.

It was perfect

"After you," said White Milkerson at the fisherman's ladder, and I led him up and over Junior's slumping barbed wire. At the top rung—the ladder was wobbly aluminum—I heard a faint hiss and smelled what I thought was burning rubber. I jumped down. Milkerson was just plugging his cigarette into his mouth and using both hands on the ladder rails. I figured he had just burned his shirt sleeve, or his moustache, or something.

"You take the net," he instructed me, and he pointed into the deep pool ahead.

"Go on," he said, "farther."

He started his shocker motor and I waded in. I was about crotch deep and sinking into mud when I started to feel the water coming in—a cold spot in my waders first, then a trickle absorbed in my trousers—but within seconds my entire leg was filling up.

I looked back at Milkerson. He was still at the bank, adjusting something on his shocker. A moment more and I was standing in a bag of frigid water. In the instant before

Milkerson's shock probe touched the water, I understood. He had lured Jacobs out here. He had burned that perfect round hole in Jacobs' waders with a cigarette. Three days ago, Jake Jacobs, too, had found himself suddenly standing in a bag of cold water up to his waist, uninsulated from electricity.

Milkerson had used the maximum power on his shocker—the big fish setting. The rest, the murder itself, I couldn't quite picture. But I was about to experience first hand.

"You killed Ja—"

My voice stopped as the probe hit the water, and in that same millisecond, I belonged to White Milkerson. I belonged to him utterly. I wasn't shocked hard. I don't think I was even injured. But I was tingling, stunned and jellied, unable to move. A yell for help stopped cold in my throat.

Milkerson wasn't even looking at me. He was poking around in the streamside brush. I felt oddly hot, and at the same time freezing cold, and for a long moment my heart did not beat. I had been looking at my attacker when the current hit, and I could not so much as redirect my eyeballs as Milkerson found a stick on the bank and waded deliberately toward me. My heart began to skitter and thrash. I knew suddenly where Shelly Milkerson had learned to tie a nail knot. Her dad had taught her. He had taught her well. But all she had done with the skill was to repair her camper ropes. It was Milkerson, stalking toward me, who had kicked off the RESPECT LANDOWNER'S RIGHTS sign in order to tie on Jake Jacobs' leader. That was his nail knot. Milkerson was the killer. The snapping turtles I'd seen feeding on small, dead trout—those trout had died when Milkerson turned up his shocker to the highest setting. I knew all that—but like Jake Jacobs, Founder and President, Friends of Black Earth Creek, I could not raise my hands. I could not cry out. I could not fall over. Nothing.

Knowing he shouldn't touch me, Milkerson worked the stick under my shirt collar and used that leverage to shove my head under. What might have been panic was electrically mixed up into something like relief. Movement was relief. Cold was relief. My face touched water and my body followed, until I was face down in the creek with my assassin gently holding me under, finishing his cigarette, I imagined, waiting for me to breathe.

I could not struggle. I would have no marks. It was perfect. I was drowning. I was gobbling water…gobbling knowledge at last…the heart of my little boy, Eamon, racing again beside mine…the two of us seared together in icy panic.

Except the feeling was calm. It was calm—drowning, dying. As a bubble of bizarre pain rose through my aorta, I felt myself drift free and scrape the limestone rubble of the bottom. I heard gunshots. And I was calm enough to wonder: *why?*

Better than okay

Junior helped me figure out the rest. Shelly Milkerson had tricked me out of the Cruise Master as her way of getting her hands on my Glock again. She had held the weapon once before, when she had broken in to steal the ponytail and the earring, but she must have hoped for something better and put the pistol down. But when Melvin O'Malley was arrested for the murder of Jake Jacobs, she had wanted the Glock back. She had wanted to kill her father.

"I had no idea anything was happening," Junior told me. She was jittery and smelled of burnt hair. "I had just gotten home, walked into the barn, ready to milk some very unhappy cows, when I look up and here comes your RV, up the drive, then off the drive, through that fence, through the chicken house, then right into the side of my propane tank."

I stared numbly at the wreckage. Shelly had driven clear to the top of the coulee, ten miles, before she could find a spot wide enough to turn the Cruise Master around. Then, coming back, she had seen her father trying to drown me. She had jumped out with the Cruise Master still in gear and rolling downhill. Struck with a four-ton blow, Junior's propane tank had spouted gas like a blow torch. The blast had tossed the Cruise Master on her side and melted her brand new tires. She was beat-up good. Junior was damaged, too. The back side of her ponytail was singed short, and her elbows were red.

At first, she told me, she had thought I was in the Cruise Master. Then, finding me about fifty yards downstream of where I'd been shocked, she thought the blood that pinked the creek was mine. She had hauled me to the bank. She had gone up and down me, looking for an injury. Nothing. And after a minute or two I was breathing fine. Then she had fanned out her perspective a little. She had spotted Shelly Milkerson huddled upstream under a box elder, curled up in a ball, sobbing. My Glock was on the ground before her. Her father, Manfred Milkerson, was washed up and moaning across the creek, shot through the gut, both arms, one leg, and a hip. Shelly had emptied the Glock. But she had failed to kill him. Moments later, B.L.'s siren was screaming up the road. The Black Earth Volunteer Fire Department was about five minutes behind him.

"But, why?" Junior was saying at my side. She slung a towel around my neck and left her arm there. "Why would White kill Jake? Why would he frame Daddy? Why does Shelly hate him so much?"

I didn't know yet. "Hey, wait a minute," I said. I shifted on the porch steps to look at her. "Where did you come from?"

"Bailed out." She nodded toward the road, where Dickie Pee's blue van had arrived among the squad cars—two more from the county sheriff now—plus an ambulance. "Dickie bailed me out this morning. Friends of Black Earth Creek money." She aimed a thin, worried smile across the coulee.

"He said if anybody was a friend of the Black Earth Creek, it was me and Dad, sitting on this land all this time when we could easily sell it."

"So," I said. "I guess you might forgive Dickie now?"

"I guess I might."

"I guess that could kind of move you ahead on the Darrald thing."

"I guess it might," she said. She stared at me.

"Okay then," I said.

WE WATCHED QUIETLY out at the road, our legs brushing sometimes. Junior went inside and made coffee. She called her lawyer and he said her dad would be out soon. After a while, Milkerson left in an ambulance. He was still alive enough to warrant more sirens, along with a county escort, and long after the vehicles were gone, we watched Junior's spooked cattle gallop in fits and starts across the pasture, tongues lolling, udders flapping. Then, voluntarily it seemed—nobody led her—Shelly stumbled into the back seat of a sheriff's squad car and sat numbly.

"She could have stopped," Junior said. "She didn't have to shoot him all those times."

I didn't know. Maybe she did have to. She understood things we didn't.

"There's more to it," I said. "Milkerson didn't have to drown me either. Not based on the little I know." I sipped hot Folgers, the kind from the red can. It tasted better than my instant, better than Ingrid Jacob's Brazilian shade-grown, better than any coffee I had ever tasted before. "All I know is that he was helping President Bud run a trophy trout operation."

"Oh," said Junior beside me. *"That."*

I looked at her in surprise. "You knew?"

I felt her fingers at the base of my neck, kneading in a worried fashion, like she was feeling for injuries. But I was okay. Better than okay. Nothing like nine hundred volts and a lung wash, I guess.

"I knew," said Junior.

"Everybody knew?"

She shrugged and gave me her wrinkle-nosed little smile. "Well, kind of."

"What about Jake Jacobs?"

"Jake found out," she said, "but he couldn't really prove anything. He never saw anybody walking on whatever out there on Lake Bud, feeding those fish, I guess, and he needed Milkerson for the study. So I guess he never felt like ratting on White. Nobody really cared anyway. Those guys who came up here for trophies, they spent a lot of money. And for poachers like Bostock, it was kind of a game for them to catch one of Bud's big fish. It's old news. Jake finally figured that out and kept his focus on getting the dam removed."

"Then why would White kill him?"

Junior shrugged and sighed. She didn't know either.

I sipped my coffee and watched Bud Lite heel-toe up Junior's drive toward us. "How many years ago did Shelly's mother run off?" I asked Junior.

"Twelve or so. I think she was five."

"And those big trout," I said, "have been in here only a couple years."

Junior gave me a puzzled look.

"Which makes it hard to understand how an earring belonging to Shelly's mother could end up in the belly of one of Bud's trout."

B.L. had entered earshot and I stopped. He aimed a

pudgy finger at me. "You stick around here," he said. "We're gonna talk."

I nodded. He tugged his belt a bit and worked his chew at Junior. She waited until he turned to walk back. He got halfway down the drive. Then she said, "Hey, B.L."

"What?"

She made him wait. His dad was coasting up in his red Suburban. B.L. was pulled in both directions.

"What?"

I watched her nose wrinkle. "Sorry I gave you a nosebleed." He glared at her.

"Sure was easy, though," Junior added.

The Black Earth police chief turned and spat and stalked back toward the road. President Bud flopped out of the red Suburban.

"Tell me again," I said to Junior, "about that flood. The one that washed your farm buildings down into Lake Bud."

She repeated her story. She was a girl in grade school. The creek had come all the way to County K, picked up a corn crib, a hog house, and a half-mile of fence and carried them down into Lake Bud, where they sank somewhere and were never seen again. "That's why we moved the summer kitchen and we don't build over there anymore," she concluded, nodding at the other side of the road. "Pasture only."

But I had stopped listening. The walking on water—I'd figured it out.

"Come on," I told her. "Get your tractor. And some cable." She looked at me.

"The stuff you haul out stumps with. Get it." She was waiting for an explanation. "I'm going diving," I told her. "In Lake Bud."

A grim convoy

We made a grim convoy down County K that afternoon. Junior took the lead in her big Case tractor, rumbling down the center stripe so that nobody could pass. I followed in Junior's blue pickup. Getting enough diving gear from the Cruise Master was easy: the windows were busted, and stuff was spilled all over. I had loaded a reduced version—a waterproof flashlight, a mask, and a pair of flippers—into the bed of Junior's pickup. It was okay, I told myself. I could hold my breath. I didn't figure Lake Bud to be more than ten or fifteen feet deep.

Behind me on the highway, restless and irate and trying to get around, followed President Bud in his red Suburban and B.L. in his cruiser. Junior and I had gotten out on the road before they could find out what was going on. Dickie Pee brought up the rear.

As we came down County K past Lake Bud and the campground, Dickie Pee peeled off down the campground drive. I watched him go, and I wondered, but I had other things on my mind.

We progressed at Junior's heavy-cleated pace down Main Street to the left turn between the Lunch Box and the Hardware Hank. Soon enough, we were moving up the far side of Lake Bud, past the cheese factory road and into the dirt lane that led through oak and birch forest down into President Bud's lakeside lots for sale.

Junior stopped about a foot from a brand-new, three-pipe gate. I could tell by the way she flared the big Case engine that I had her full cooperation. Her *faith*, I guess it was, since I hadn't told her what I hoped to find. I wasn't exactly sure myself. From the truck bed, arranging my meager gear, I watched the village president humpty-dumpty out of his Suburban and storm up. He braced a hand on Junior's side mirror.

"Now what in hell is going on? This is my property here."

"We can open that gate with a key," I said, "or we can open it with a tractor."

"I haven't done anything wrong." His face wobbled with rage and panic. "There's nothing out there. Fish. There's fish out there. What's wrong with that?"

When I jumped out in flippers he seemed so startled he nearly fell over. B.L., meanwhile, had made his way to the front of the tractor, where he and Junior appeared to be reenacting a scene from fifth grade.

"No!" he hollered. His voice was whiny. "Damn it, Junior! Stop!"

Junior grinned back at him. She gunned the big Case engine until it made a noise like an avalanche in a junkyard. Then she opened the gate with the tractor.

FINNING OUT into Lake Bud, I used the orange buoys for the Jet Ski Jam as my guide. President Bud had laid them out, and they swung unnaturally wide around a point about one hundred yards north and west of the cheese factory. That was where the big brown trout were farmed—in Melvin O'Malley's old corn crib, I figured, which had been washed down by the flood.

I dove there. Five feet down, I felt the heavy wire walls of the corn crib, slimy now and stuck with flotsam. I came up for air and dove again. This time I felt the thrumming energy of big trout darting inside as I ran my hands across the top. The crib was on its side. I found the place where Milkerson must have cut an opening and then wired it back shut.

I came up for air a third time. Across at the campground, Dickie Pee had managed to get Shelly's little pop-up camper onto his ball hitch. His wheels spun grass as he hauled it up and out. The sight put an odd little panic into me that ballooned when I got underwater on a shallow breath. I popped back up. Dickie Pee and the camper were gone. Shit, I told myself, use the light.

I used the light. I drove myself deep along the slimy wire arc of the corn crib, watching big browns spook and dart through the dark water. There must have been twenty of them, not one under two-and-a-half feet long. Smaller fish, blue gills and perch, darted out through the crib into the wilderness of water beyond.

I was running out of breath. Fighting it, I hooked my fingers in the crib and pulled down. My light sprayed wildly around as I wrestled buoyancy and bursting lungs. Twice in one day I was on the verge of drowning, only this time I was courting it, clawing my way to the murky bottom of Lake Bud. I was at the dim fire of surrender when my knees grazed the bottom. I held tight to the crib's slimy mesh with my left hand and aimed the light inside. What I saw there tore the last bit of breath out of me. I saw a mud-crusted suitcase, and then... I let go of the crib and thrashed for the top.

"AHHHGGGG!" I TREADED WATER, gasping and choking in the soft slap of waves. Junior said later that she had waded in as if to help me, I was down so long. I didn't notice. I wasn't seeing anything but the spotlight image burned into my oxygen-starved mind. I had been looking for it all along, I guess. The return to elements, the whole gruesome surrender of the human body to water. And I had finally seen it. I still see it.

I swam to shore. I heard voices. But I wasn't answering questions. Maybe at that moment language itself had dissolved to elements. Junior said I was weeping. Okay, so the Dog was weeping. Weeping for little Eamon. Weeping for Mary Jane. Weeping for myself. Weeping for Shelly Milkerson. Weeping for Shelly Milkerson's mother. I didn't even remember her name.

I'll say this for Bud Heavy and Bud Lite. They were silent. They stood there like two bad boys in church. They really hadn't known jack about White Milkerson's orchestrations. After all, they were flat-out stump-ignorant. White Milkerson had played them. Preserving the dam meant even more to him than to the Bjorgstad real-estate fantasy.

I asked Junior for the winch hook and swam it back out. Her dad's old corn crib had steel ribs that connected the wire base to the tin-cone roof that was sunk at an angle into the bottom mud. I slung the hook around the lowest rib and back onto the cable. Junior would have to pull from the bottom, I figured, or the rusty crib might split and spill its horrid cargo across the muddy lake bed.

Junior gunned the big Case engine and her six-foot wheels dug into the bank. She eased twenty feet forward and then, with a watery gasp, the crib broke the surface, shedding muddy froth as Junior drew it slowly toward the shore.

At shallow water, the crib stuck. The tractor strained and

rumbled. Junior got down and looked things over, mumbling and cursing to herself, lost in a farmer's calculations. Then she jumped back into the tractor's big snow-shovel seat. She backed up ten feet, creating slack. I watched the crib relax against the weedy shallows. Then Junior surged the tractor forward. Her gambit worked—at least for a stunning moment as the crib breached and skidded nearly to shore, huge trout slapping and wiggling in the mud and air. But then the crib snagged again, rolled until the winch hook was on top. Then it rose, the entire thing, like it was being re-erected, then listed, fell, and split, spilling mud and weeds and trout and finally a sloppy clatter of human bones.

The forensics people would later tell us they were the bones of an adult female, shot once through the head. Around those bones, vomiting out of the split corn crib—rotted, spilling—came the remains of clothing, shoes, jewelry, toiletries—all of the woman's suitcases.

I know her name now. Junior's been saying it, over and over in disbelief. Her name was Nanette. Nanette Margolis Milkerson.

She had been running away from her husband all right, fifteen years ago. Maybe she had even been running away with a farm equipment salesman, as the story went.

But Nanette Margolis Milkerson had never made it out of Black Earth.

Isn't it stupid to go backwards?

It took the better part of a week for B.L. and the county sheriff to sort things out, and by the end of that time, Melvin O'Malley was cleared of all charges and released to Junior. That was on a Monday morning. By Wednesday afternoon, Manfred John "White" Milkerson, guilty of two murders fifteen years apart and draining away in Madison Saint Mary's Hospital, had laid himself bare to anyone who would listen, apologized to all, and passed on.

I stayed in the old summer kitchen at the edge of Junior's barnyard, and I have to say those seven days were about the best week of my life since—well, isn't it stupid to go backwards? Love, life, joy—those are forward-looking things.

On each of those seven days, I had breakfast and supper with Junior and her dad. On each of those seven days, I made love to Junior. On each of those seven days, we laughed and cried in each other's arms.

Funny thing, though. Junior never invited me to sleep in the house. She worked like a dervish all day. She milked and fenced and cut hay like there was no tomorrow—because I guess when you farm, there isn't any tomorrow. Go fishing, she kept telling me. Go fishing. She gave me that cute squinchy-nosed grin every time. No more bodies out there, she kept telling me. Nothing you can do around here. Try Teal Creek, Flynn Creek, Frye Feeder. After supper, after the *Mary Poppins* video, she bathed her dad and put him to bed. Then, if I was outside on my lawn chair in the barnyard, smoking one of my so-called cigars, sipping a lemonade and watching bats catch moths in the yard light, I could count on hearing the shower start up, seeing the light-infused sweet steam start to drift out of the little window in the back of the house. She showered for an entire hour, until the whole night smelled like Melvina "Junior" O'Malley.

Then, between ten and midnight, at the precise moment when I would give up on her—at the exact inner instant when I would start to backslide, thinking my luck had run out, thinking it was time to fix the Cruise Master and roll, Junior would come to me. She would tickle the summer kitchen's screen door with her finger tips and whisper, "Ned?"

That's my name. Not Dog. Ned. Ned Oglivie. Stodgy goddamn name, I know. But what can I do? And I hope every other man out there gets a chance to hear his name sound as right as mine did on those Black Earth summer nights, drifting on the sweet barnyard air from the lips of a woman who saw me right to the core, and seemed to love me anyway.

"Yeah? Who's there?" I would respond as if groggy and surprised, as if I hadn't been thinking about Junior's every move in that long and fragrant shower.

Beside me on my narrow bunk she told me about her own real name. Melvina. She hated it. The only name she hated more was Junior. Or Mel. But she loved her dad. So whatever could she say? "I just thank God they didn't name me after Mom, anyway," she said.

"Oh yeah?"

"Racheletta."

"Come on."

"I'm serious. It's my middle name."

Then she told me about Darrald—Darrald with the "d" on the end—and how for a long time that "d" just made her giggle every time she thought of it. Until the time Darrald blushed and then got mad at her, stormed off and wouldn't talk to her for a month. "I did some serious falling in love after that," she said.

But that kind of talk came later. What with both of us having so much stored up, and what with both of us feeling the need to correct the ineptitude of our initial grapple in the cheese factory, we always started with a fast and hot one, the kind of lovemaking where the old kitchen rocked on its cinderblocks and stuff fell off the shelves and the cattle lowed back from the barn. The challenge in those first few heats was to keep Junior from hurting me. Then, later, in the wee hours, we would make love again, this time so long and slow and lazy and complete that the release for me was always directly into a sleep like I hadn't felt in—well, there I go again. It was just good.

And in between all the lovemaking was the talk.

We talked about everything, and I guess most of us know what that means. Beautiful, beautiful *everything*. Junior was always gone when I awoke in the morning. Sometimes, if I stirred in the pre-dawn, I could hear her clanking in around in the barn, milking, the radio going, Junior talking to her cows. Teal Creek, a place she had told me about, had so damn many fish in it that I started killing a couple, bringing them home for our eight o'clock breakfasts of frozen waffles, bacon, coffee...and trout.

In our long talks upon the summer kitchen bunk, Junior and I wrapped up the Jake Jacobs murder into a pretty tight package. White Milkerson had killed Jake in the hope of keeping his secret safe beneath the water held back by the Lake Bud dam. He had set up Junior's father because he could, because the opportunity presented itself, and because he had convinced himself that both Junior and her dad would be better off with the old man in a mental facility. Then Junior could get on with her life. Milkerson had told an investigator this, who in turn told Junior, who told me, with a snort of rage. "Imagine White Milkerson," she said, "trying to improve *my* life."

Milkerson had been clever to change Jacobs' fly, putting on the Jake's Yellow Sally—which he had seen from Jake and tied up himself—so that everybody would assume Jake died around eight at night, giving Milkerson the alibi of the village board meeting. What Milkerson hadn't counted on was that Jacobs would have a brand new line on his reel, with no leader connected. And so after he had shocked and drowned his victim, after he had sawed off Jacobs' ponytail and stuffed it in his mouth, he had climbed out of the creek and kicked down the RESPECT LANDOWNER'S RIGHTS sign, and he had used the nail to tie on a leader. He never guessed that Jacobs couldn't tie a nail knot, or that a guy like me would be around to notice.

Junior and I wrapped it all up except the Shelly-Dickie Pee connection. What was she doing with explosive cable and instructions in her pop-up camper? What was Dickie Pee doing in Junior's barn? What had he stolen? And why had he been so intent on hauling Shelly's camper up out of the Lake Bud campground?

"What have you heard about Shelly?" I wondered at breakfast near the end of the week.

"Missus Sundvig has a daughter working at the county

hospital," Junior told me over waffles and trout. "She says Shelly's mostly just sleeping. They've got social workers coming in, shrinks, cops, everybody trying to figure out what to do next, but Missus Sundvig's daughter says Shelly sleeps about twenty hours a day, eats like a horse and watches TV in between. She won't talk to anybody."

"God. I'm sorry for her."

"She's tough," Junior said. "She's got some answers now."

"She killed her dad," I pointed out.

"Her dad killed himself," Junior replied. I looked at her. She looked away. She wasn't going to cry. She never cried with sun up or the lights on. But we both knew we had just summed things up for Shelly. The daughter of White and Nanette Milkerson would see her way through life now... or not. For my part, sad as I felt, I had hope. People could recover. I knew that finally. And Junior had hope, too, of course. Junior always had hope. She didn't know any other way.

"I dropped her off some vitamins," she said. "Big-ass horse vitamins, I mean. The kind that burn your stress up. And this really cool book." She glanced at me. "Crop circles. Puzzles we can't explain. Kind of lets you know there's something out there, maybe, setting things up. Things happen for a reason. Even bad things."

We sat quietly on that one a while.

"And where did Dickie disappear to?"

"Dickie," Junior said, sighing and shaking her head at another chapter in the life of Darrald's old buddy. "Dickie's AWOL. Shelly's camper is missing, too. Nobody knows."

"And your dad." I nodded at the old man. Melvin O'Malley sat across from me, working on about his tenth slice of bacon, wiping his fingers on his coveralls. "He's doing okay?"

Junior squinched her nose at me, giving me the grin. "Never better."

AND SO WE PASSED a period of waiting during which most of the big questions around Black Earth were answered, and it finally became clear to Junior and me that what we were waiting for was something else entirely. We weren't waiting on the fate of Shelly. That one was long-term, and life went on. And Dickie Pee was going to come back or not. So it wasn't that, either. We had figured out who had gotten into the *Pêche Tôt* and tied on the second yellow sally. It was President Bud, so eager was he to see Melvin O'Malley go down. Where he got the sally wasn't clear—but our guess was that Jake had tied one himself, based on Dickie's gift, and left it around the vise in the *Pêche Tôt*. And President Bud had planted Jacobs' ponytail in Junior's barn, too, after Shelly showed up to turn it in, wanting to talk about her father. So President Bud Bjorgstad was in a bit of trouble with the law, which was just fine with everybody, especially B.L., who had the unique privilege of busting his father for what must have been a lifetime of harassment and meddling. So it wasn't that, either.

No, it was something else, building inside the both of us, and it flared up at supper on the seventh day.

"You're leaving, aren't you?" Junior said abruptly.

We were having meatloaf, creamed corn, and some sugared beefsteak tomatoes that Mrs. Sundvig had dropped off. I had brought in a fistful of watercress from the creek. Junior's old man puffed like a brick mason, spreading ketchup over a slab of meatloaf.

"Am I leaving?"

"I asked you."

"You haven't asked me to stay."

"Well," said Junior, looking down at her plate, "you got your insurance money on the Cruise Master."

"I don't have it yet. Harvey said I'd get it tomorrow."

"Right. So basically you have it."

"I don't yet. But that doesn't seem related exactly."

"How could you leave without the money? To fix your RV?"

"True. There is a connection. So I guess maybe I'm leaving."

"Well…" Junior looked at me darkly. "Thanks for telling me."

"I'm not telling you. All I did was ask Harvey to settle my insurance, and you decide I must be leaving. I don't know. Am I?"

We went around like that for a while until I had an idea. I rose to the old yellow telephone on the wall between the kitchen cupboard and the door to Junior's bedroom. I lifted off the receiver and dialed my tax guy. Of course I was interrupting something—this time Harvey was getting rolfed on his living room floor by the ex-girlfriend of his nephew—but I persisted in explaining our dilemma.

Harvey released a long draught of inter-fascial tension and asked a clarifying question.

"You mean you want to be with each other, but neither one of you has the guts to say it?"

I repeated his impression aloud. Junior seemed to confirm it by looking down at her plate.

Then my tax guy started to laugh. He laughed so loudly I had to move the receiver away from my ear. Then, because I guess that laugh was the entire reason I had called, I stretched the grimy yellow cord out and laid the receiver upside down on the middle of the kitchen table, where it spun like a turtle on its back, belting out the laughter of Harvey Digman.

Junior looked at me like I was nuts. But that didn't last long. Because the bug caught old Mel O'Malley and soon enough he was laughing, too—big, sloppy, meatloaf guffaws that got Junior and me going until we were all pitching and snorting over our plates. We never even noticed that Harvey himself had stopped. When we finally caught up with Harvey's silence, the voice in the middle of the table was saying, "Hey Dog? Dog? You there, pal?"

"Yeah, Harv."

"Good to hear you laugh. But just an FYI, partner. Dog?"

"Yeah?"

"On that vehicle, I had to keep your premiums low. You knew that, right?"

"Sure, Harv. I knew that."

"So that vehicle of yours. As far as collision, it wasn't insured for a whole lot."

Junior was looking at me.

"Um. Okay. How much, Harv?"

"Two fifty," said my tax guy. "Two *hundred* fifty. Sorry, pal. I know it's just lunch money. Not enough to fix the thing. Not right away."

I sat down. I was mute for a while.

"Uh, Harv?"

"Yellow!"

I didn't know what I was asking. I couldn't even remember why we had been laughing, a long, long time ago. I was lost as hell for a good long moment—lost with the sudden realization that the Dog...the Dog wanted to stay...but the Dog wanted to go, too.

"Yellow!" barked my tax guy again. "We talking or walking, pal? What's it going to be? There's a young lady here with her knee bone in my...what is it darling?...ahhhh... yes...in my goddamn scapula."

I let him go. I carried the phone back to its hook. When I returned to the table, Junior was bussing the dishes. She leaned over me from behind, her strong hands crossing my chest, locking, and holding me tight.

"Bad news?"

"Maybe."

She squeezed me.

"Need an idea?" she asked.

"Okay," I said.

"How about I take you and Dad up to the bluff—watch the Jet Ski show?"

Go, Dog, go!

The bluff Junior meant was the one I had often gazed at from the creek. Rivers pouring from the tongues of glaciers had converged around Black Earth an epoch ago, carving the ancient limestone seabed into a great snakehead of rock that rose above Lake Bud and the coulee to the west, down past the Sundvig farm.

We had to drive halfway across the county to get at the bluff along a dirt road that ran up the ridge from the back. Junior parked her pickup on a flat spot littered with beer cans and old campfires.

We set up lawn chairs and looked down on the meandering creek dressed in the sunset's pinkish golds. Even Lake Bud looked okay from up here. For about a half-hour more, Jet Skis ripped around the wide, flat surface, sounding like angry hornets that had been bottled up by the week's postponement. Then thankfully the event ended, and everybody went home. Soon enough, Einar Johnsrud was closing down the cheese factory. Sundvig's cows were wandering back to the barn for milking. In town, the street lights were just coming on, and the softball diamond had already staked its gemlike claim amidst the gathering darkness. *Ting!* went bat on ball, and someone screamed, *"I got it!"*

"So anyway," Junior said, "I really can't go on like this."

I nodded falsely. I had no idea what she meant. I wasn't sure I wanted to know.

"About three hours of sleep a night," she said, "by the time I leave you and then get up for milking." She took my hand. "Don't get me wrong."

"I'm not getting you wrong," I said.

"It's only going to get harder. I've got another round of hay to put up in a week or so. Then I cut corn. Then Jake convinced me to put in winter rye to keep the soil down until spring planting, so I'm going to be sure to do that, in his memory."

It was one of those evenings when the dust over Kansas, or somewhere, filters the sun down to a precise red ball and that ball sinks at a shocking rate. I worried that Junior was asking me to help out on the farm. And I worried that she wasn't.

"Anyway," said Junior, squeezing my hand, "it's boring in Black Earth. And you wouldn't believe the winter. Not a damn thing to do here in winter except milk and feed twice a day and gossip at the Lunch Bucket." She added, "Oh yeah, and get drunk playing euchre at night."

"Snows a lot, I guess?"

"Snows a lot. And cold. Twenty below down at the bottom of the coulee."

"Well, gee," I said. "Thanks for the invite."

The sun slipped, slipped, half gone, then three-quarters.

"You, too," said Junior finally.

She had startled me. "What do you mean?" I said. "You

mean you wanted to go with me?" She didn't answer. She stared off over Lake Bud. *Ting!* went bat on ball.

"I can't go anywhere," she told me finally.

We were silent a while.

"Well," I said. "My goddamn tax guy—he skimped on insurance. He kind of trapped me here until I can get the Cruise Master fixed."

No more words for another good long time. The sky got orange, then high-pink, then blue-dark. I thought I'd have to call Harvey for inspiration again. Junior's dad had brought his fishing pole, and he was soaking it real good in the thin air over the side of the bluff but not getting anything.

"Well," said Junior at last, "there's always the summer kitchen."

"I'd be in your way."

"It's on blocks," Junior said. "I was going to move it."

"I'd need land to put it on."

She laughed. "I've got land. I mean, that's *all* I've got. You want land? Take some, please."

Her father made a loud rumble. We both looked at him. It was *his* land, properly. Melvin O'Malley looked back at us. He reeled up and hitched his hook to the cork on his rod butt. For a bizarre moment it looked like he was going to scold us, going to turn and speak in coherent paragraphs, tell us not to be stupid, tell us we had no business trying to work all this out. But it turns out he was simply responding to the fact that the sun had now officially gone down. It was now nighttime.

"Ice cream," said the old man. "Poppins."

Junior sighed. She leaned out to stroke his big sprawling leg. "Okay, Daddy. Okay."

She took his rod away, freed the hook, and cast again. The

red-and-white bobber tumbled out over the view of Black Earth and crashed into the brush somewhere below.

"One more time, okay Daddy? A little night fishing, like you and White used to do."

We sat another while.

"I am going to fix the Cruise Master," I said finally.

"And I am going to cut hay and corn and plant rye and look after Daddy," Junior said back.

"So," I said, "I really can't be sure…"

"Nobody asked you to be sure."

I thought a minute. When, I asked myself, had the Dog ever been sure of anything? I mean, really sure? And how far could sureness ever be trusted?

"I was hoping to fish the Big Two-Hearted before fall."

"Sounds nice."

Junior took my hand.

"Move that summer kitchen where you want it. Use it when you want it."

"Or—" I said.

"Or not," Junior said.

I let out a huge breath out. "You know," I said, "about your idea…that everything happens for a reason…"

"Yeah?"

"It's nice to believe. It seems true once in a while. I guess. But I just don't know."

She was silent, still as a rock.

"But about getting over things…about letting go…"

"Yeah?"

"I guess you could say I'm started on that. Finally."

"Yeah," she said. She sighed. "Me, too."

Then Junior stood and pulled my hand and led me around behind her pickup. My posture must have been stiff, my following uncertain, because she tugged at me and gave me one last squinchy grin. "Come on," she whispered. "I think we just got through something. Something just broke down. I think we need to celebrate."

We moved surely on the tailgate of the pickup—not slow or fast, but just like lovers who knew how to touch each other and still felt the thrill. Junior had shaved her armpits. She wore new underpants with little blue forget-me-nots on them. When I was inside her, she whispered hotly, "Go, Dog, go!"

I was laughing. I was going. And then, a moment later, I heard a boom that sounded like heavy fireworks. Softball party, I figured. Junior, squirming and shoving under me, gasped, "The earth moved!"

I murmured, "Already?"

"No! I'm telling you! I heard an explosion, and then I felt the earth move!"

She pushed me over, jumped into her pants, and led the way back to the bluff edge. Her dad was standing, howling, pointing and shaking like he was speaking in tongues. Below us, Lake Bud had belched upstream in a giant wave that peaked and then washed forward over the campground, sweeping up the twisted tables, scattering the neon Jet Ski buoys. Then the dam collapsed. The whole lake heaved out over crumbling concrete and dike mud and spilled out over Sundvig's pasture, filling it like a mud puddle and spreading onto the county highway. The roof and frame of Shelly Milkerson's blasted pop-up floated toward separate corners of the pasture, as though tossed from the epicenter of the explosion. As we watched, Dickie Pee's blue van raced down County K toward the Village of Black Earth, spraying a triumphal plume of water behind like a giant Jet Ski.

I don't know how long Junior and I and her dad stood

there swapping our various grunts of astonishment. But it wasn't all that long before the stream itself calmed us. The stream knew what to do. The stream knew right where to go. And in no time at all, Lake Bud was history, and Black Earth Creek was slipping back toward its banks, carving, seeking, finding its groove again, flowing.